PART ONE

"I believe an independent country run by a government not much richer than the People has more hope than one governed by a big rich neighbour."

Alasdair Gray

Chapter 1

The Rock (1985)

It was dark and raining. Glasgow rain – slightly sooty, slightly acidic, and wetter than water. She could taste it on her lips, feel it already soaking through the seams of her anorak. It had not been far from the student residence hall to the pub, and she had wanted to look her best so had resisted the urge to put the hood up. She had left it just a little too long and now she was going to look half drowned.

The warmth and the bright lights of the pub welcomed her. She took off her coat and shook it out, freed some wayward strands of hair that were stuck to her cheeks, and hoped they would dry out quickly. She ordered a Coke from the bar and joined a small group of students who had naturally coalesced together around a pair of tables. She was surprised that they were so early but pleased that she no longer needed to worry about no-one turning up except her and a couple of friends. She introduced herself and told the others that they would wait to see if anyone else arrived before getting started. She felt her nervousness slip away – it was going to be how she imagined, a group of like-minded people and sensible discussion.

Isobel had been at school at the time of the 1979 devolution referendum. One of her teachers had made the class study the proposal in detail and then discuss it. She and her classmates had been enraged at the result and the unfairness of the conditions that were imposed on it. They had formed a protest group, but it did not stretch beyond the school gates.

Several years later when she had moved on to university, she realised that, just like her schoolmates, a high proportion of all the new people she met were for a separation from

3

England. This emboldened her to try again with a much wider audience. One of her friends had suggested The Rock – a pub not far from the university campus. And although known to everyone, it was not solely a meeting place for students, so she hoped to also attract other members of the public. Her friends helped her make up the posters that invited anyone interested in seeing a self-governed Scotland to attend at the pub on a weekday evening. Only one thing had changed during those intervening years; she no longer thought devolution was a good idea – full independence was the only way to go.

People continued to arrive in small groups, and some were noisy as though they had already had a drink or two. Isobel began to feel nervous again and she was glad that she had prepared some notes to start off the discussion. She was not expecting the forty or so people who turned up. They were mostly students from many different faculties at the university, along with some members of the public who had seen the posters and were easily spotted by being somewhat older than the students.

It was a tribute to her still developing force of character that she managed to quiet the hubbub and bring the meeting to some sort of order. She managed to get at least an introduction to the subject and some of her points from her notes across, but it soon developed into a shouting match as people started speaking over each other as though taking the opportunity to vent their anger and frustration.

The bar manager ushered her aside, and she noted wryly that her exit from the front had no effect on the meeting whatsoever. He explained that usually a group this big would have given some advance warning, and that his place, being a little outside the normal beat of the university, was not normally a 'student bar'. He intimated that it was OK for now as the bar was doing good trade. 'But,' he had said, 'they are annoying the other customers. Can you quiet them down a bit?'

She looked around the pub. There were several old guys playing dominoes, and a couple had paused in their game to light cigarettes and were watching the proceedings with a little more interest than the others. Several other regulars were sipping pints and reading newspapers at the bar. None of them seemed particularly annoyed, so she was about to object when a tall, sandy-haired student came up and offered to help her.

'Hello, I'm Richard,' he said, and she noted his posh accent. 'Perhaps I can help you with the meeting.'

'Isobel.' She managed a smile. 'And yes, please do, though I don't see how.' The manager left them to it.

Richard walked back to the front of the crowd, which had largely fragmented into small groups. Some were standing, while others had remained in their seats, and some with more than one person talking; others were just chatting to their friends. He pulled up a chair from one of the tables and stood on it. The noise died down substantially as people turned to watch, and gradually more and more followed their lead until the meeting was quiet except for one person talking animatedly to a group that surrounded him and were listening intently.

Richard called out in a loud voice. 'Excuse me, yes, you there!'

The man stopped speaking and turned in his direction.

'What you are saying seems interesting, so please now address the whole meeting. If you would stand and give your name first, that would be good. And listen, everyone, if you want to speak, hold up your hand and you will get your turn. We will get a lot more done if we all do this. Thank you. The floor is now yours.' He gestured to the man, who stood up.

'I'm James Sinclair, and I study Civil Engineering. I guess that may help explain what I was trying to say to this group here, which was basically that moaning about the unfairness of the referendum and how it was already set up to favour a no vote etc., etc., will not get us anywhere. We should be considering building something, and I don't mean bridges.' This raised a small murmur of laughter in the audience. 'Whether that is a political movement or a campaign for another referendum – this time on independence, not devolution – does not really matter. What does matter is that whatever the next step is we should be intent on building something better than what we have now.'

'Taking control by force is the only way,' someone shouted.

A number of arms were raised, and several more shouted out trying to draw attention to themselves. A female student with long, dark hair caught Richard's eye. She stood quiet and still with her hand raised to shoulder height. Richard stood back up on the chair and pointed at her. 'You, make your point,' and he raised his arms to quieten the others.

'If we are going to talk full independence, then it has to be worthwhile. I agree that huge changes are needed to reform the present system. And I mean socially, as well as ditching the union, but I'm not sure we should be talking revolution just yet.'

'Oh aye, yes! The third Jacobite!' someone shouted.

A few others started a chant of 'Scotland, Scotland,' until Richard quietened them down and asked James to respond to the question.

'Ah, OK, it wasn't me who mentioned revolution,' said James, 'but it is a valid point and should be included in the list of possible ways to gain self-government. History and, for that matter, more recent times are full of examples where the only way to overthrow a government, especially one of a foreign power, was by armed insurrection. So it is perfectly possible that the only way to attain full independence may well require the use of force.'

There were a few cheers but not whole-hearted support for that idea.

'Just to add that the possibility of that happening in the UK is extremely remote. There is no identifiable disadvantaged ethnic group that would support an insurgency or, for example, an exiled political party building up a rebellion outside the border. More importantly, there is no underlying loss of freedom or oppression to such a degree that would bring the mass of people out to support the venture. There is also no source of arms that could make that possible, as the UK has some of the strictest gun laws in the world, left over I believe from the fear of a general uprising in the 1930s.'

'Except for the shotguns and hunting rifles of the landed gentry, and whose side would they be on?' someone shouted.

'There is one thing we do have,' said Isobel, 'and that is a deep sense of national identity. That has never diminished since the union, and that is what will power the drive to independence.'

'Ok, we are getting sidetracked. Let's move on. Next question.' Richard selected another raised hand.

'Don't we already have a political party in the SNP, with exactly these aims?'

Isobel motioned to Richard, and he took it that she would like to respond.

'Our chairwoman Isobel will take that question.'

'Perhaps I can answer that,' she said. 'The SNP has been around in some form or other since the 1930s, so that basically answers your question. I'm sure there are SNP supporters here and, whether they agree or not, it is clear to me that their time is running out and it is doubtful that they can ever take Scotland to independence. They have never had more than a handful of MPs at Westminster, so they are not going to change anything. We should not just want to separate from England for the sake of it.'

The student with the long, black hair added her voice. 'And it has to be a better system of government; a better social structure, and an end to inequality of wealth. A Socialist Scotland, if you like.'

A small section of the crowd jeered at that, and one of their number shouted out, 'You do know communism is dead, don't you?'

Richard quieted them down with raised voice and outstretched hands.

'I don't think she meant that at all,' said Isobel, 'Socialism is not the same thing as communism. For socialist, think fairer.

7

What I think they both meant was improvement over what we have. A superior system like, uh, James has already said. What would be the point of an independent Scotland with a British-style parliament and political system? We deserve something better.'

There was a sense of approval from the crowd, a scattering of applause, and a few shouted comments in support of the SNP. But with no clear questions, Richard decided to move on and picked an upraised arm that he had noticed before, and the discussion took another turn. As the evening grew later, the debate had begun to turn back to moaning about the unfairness of it all and a general anti-English sentiment, so Isobel decided to wind things up. She called a halt to the discussions, improvised a brief summary, and thanked everyone for coming.

The crowd started to drift away, some to the bar and some putting coats on and heading out. Isobel was chatting with Richard when the female student who had spoken several times approached them.

'Hi, where do I sign up?'

Isobel was non-plussed for a moment, but Richard understood immediately. 'Yes, good idea to get names and addresses.' He tore off a sheet of paper from Isobel's notepad and hurried over to the door, where he began asking people as they left.

'Thanks, I should have thought of that,' said Isobel, noting with a small twinge of jealousy that the girl had long, straight, lustrous dark hair and bright blue eyes that made an unusual but attractive combination. In stark contrast, she thought, to her own rather curly and mousy brown hair.

'I've joined too many clubs!' she said. 'It seemed logical, and I'm really interested in being part of this. I'm Karen, by the way. Karen Black.'

'Pleased to meet you, and I'm Isobel Anderson,' she answered, turning over a page of her notes and starting a list on the back of it. 'Add your address under your name, and a phone number if you have one.'

Several more people, seeing what was happening, had started to line up behind Karen, who finished writing then headed over to the bar. Isobel carried on taking names and addresses, and by the time closing time was approaching and the pub was emptying out, she had a list of twenty or so. Richard had gathered up some more at the door before retiring to the bar for a pint, where she spotted him.

She was heading over to him, hoping to get a drink as the barman had already called 'Last orders', when she was halted by a call from behind her. She turned to confront a man aged around fifty – he could have been older, as he had a worn and craggy face, was dressed in a rumpled brown suit with a broad pale pinstripe, no tie, and had a hard look about him. His right-hand fingers were stained with nicotine, and a half-smoked cigarette hung between them as though it belonged there. This was an older version of the sort of guy one avoided on a night out in the town.

She recognised him from the domino players earlier, and she thought at first that he was going to berate her for ruining his evening in 'his' pub.

'Aye, hen,' he said, 'add me to yer list.' His voice was gravelly hard and with a deep Glasgow accent to it that she found hard to decipher. It did not feel like a request.

'Of course,' she answered, and rummaged around in her bag until she found her notepad and a pen. She poised expectantly, but he reached out and took the pad from her. He scribbled his name and a phone number.

He handed it back. 'Keep in touch, aye.' He turned and left.

She saw he had written Jake and a phone number, which was unusual – there were not many phone numbers among the students.

The bar was almost deserted now but Richard was still there, so she leant on the bar beside him and ordered a half pint of cider. The barman nodded, and when he came back with it, he leant over towards her and said, 'Be careful of that guy. He's not someone to mess with.'

'Oh,' she said, 'in what way?'

'Just dodgy, you know. Runs a couple of hamburger vans round the West End, like "Wimpy-on-wheels" type thing, only he sells more than food if you get my meaning. He also supplies bouncers to some of the pubs,' he laughed, 'so if you need help with your next meeting, he may even be useful.' The barman moved away, shouting, 'That's it, folks. Drink up. Closing in five.'

She turned to Richard and thanked him for his help in bringing the meeting to order and helping to keep the discussion as a debate and not a riot.

'Oh, I don't think it would have turned that bad,' he said. 'Was it what you hoped for?'

'Good grief, no. I'm not sure what I expected, but definitely not that. A wee group having a drink and a discussion is what was in my mind! Sorry, I was totally unprepared for so many people, and I had no idea how to control the talkers.'

'Shows strength of feeling about the issue, though, and right across the spectrum, from far right to socialist. What are we going to do with all these names?' He took a carefully folded sheet of paper out of his pocket and handed it to her.

The lights went out in the main part of the room, and the barman was standing pointedly at the door. Isobel had a last swig of her cider but had to leave some in the glass. The barman gestured for them to hurry, but all the same wished them a cheery goodnight as they left. They hesitated outside the pub; it was a drizzly, gloomy night, but the rain at least had eased off. The streetlights added a faint yellow haze to everything.

Isobel pulled up her collar against the cold and pointed to the right. 'I'm in the halls, not far.'

'I'll walk you back. I'm in a flat a bit further on. We should decide what to do next.'

She wasn't sure if that was a come on or not. She was a bit nervous, as there seemed to be a trend at the university for everyone to sleep with everyone else – a leftover from the 60s and 70s – but it was not something she felt a part of or wanted to be. She eyed him from the side; he seemed fine, and he walked with a respectful distance between them, although that should not necessarily make her feel any better.

She hated that feeling after a date where she had really got on well with a guy and then it all changed as he walked her home, and he expected the night to end in bed. She hated that conversation, which to be fair, was usually taken well, but often it resulted in some awkwardness and even occasionally in some nasty insults. It was as well to find out early, she always thought.

What almost always guaranteed a second date, she smiled to herself, was the boy taking charge, no awkward conversation, just a kiss on the cheek and a 'hope we can see each other again'. She stopped herself; this was never a date. He was good looking in a tall, posh sort of way, and boy! did he have a posh accent. There was a certain self-assurance about him as well, especially in the way he had stood up on that chair. She was attracted to him, no doubt, but no, let's not go there.

'That's a posh accent, almost English – don't mean to be insulting – where are you from?'

'Edinburgh, well originally. My father was in the Army, so we moved around a lot and I went to an English boarding school. Where I got my accent, I suppose.'

'Wow! I've never met a public schoolboy before. I can't imagine what it was like. Did you have to dress in tails?'

'What? Oh no, that's Eton; it was a much lesser-known school. Two actually, both not well known.'

'Why two?'

'The first is prep school for eight- to thirteen-year-olds, and then the next one takes them from thirteen up to A levels.'

'You went to boarding school at eight? Like, home at weekends or... I don't understand how that works.'

'I was eight. My father had a posting abroad, so they left me there. It's not unusual.'

'Left you?'

'I saw them once a year in the summer holidays. The Army flew us out. I stayed with my gran in Edinburgh for the other holidays.'

'Jeez – the other half, eh!' They were by this time at the entrance to the Halls. 'Thanks for walking me.'

'No problem. Will we meet for a drink next week, say same time and place, and go through the names and decide what the next step is? Keep it to a small group if you can, or ones you have telephone numbers for. We can hold a wider general meeting again when we are a bit more organised. The guy who first spoke, James, was it? Get him if you can?'

'Yes, good idea. See you then. Night.'

The night warden nodded at her from behind his table as she entered the foyer and made her way up to her room. Now was that a come-on or not? She was not sure. No, he definitely said a small group, not just them. She smiled. She was actually strangely attracted to him, English accent and all. She would go early next week, and perhaps he would too, meaning they would have some time alone before the others arrived. She wanted to know a little more about him.

She pushed aside thoughts of Richard and reflected on the meeting. It had gone well, no doubt, and better than she had expected. There was such strength of feeling, such anger, and it was interesting how some people stood out from the crowd. Richard, of course, but there was also James. He had some strong ideas. If only all that national pride, frustration, and anger could be harnessed, perhaps something could be achieved.

Chapter 2
James (2020)

He had waited many years for this; too many. James Sinclair sat at one end of the large dining room table that took up too much space in the living room of the West End tenement flat and waited for the others. The streetlights outside cast pale, blurry reflections on the polished wood. Normally it had both ends folded in and was pushed up against one wall, but tonight it had been moved out and extended to its full length in preparation for the meeting. The curtains were still open, and he could see himself reflected in the glass of the window. The image of a silver-haired, bespectacled older man sitting alone at an empty table, was not one he relished, but it was at least hazily more flattering than the one given by the cold heart of a mirror. He ran his hand over his beard, smoothing it down, more salt than pepper these days. He kept it as short as he could without appearing to be unshaven, as it helped hide the wrinkles and craggy parts of his face – strange days, when you looked younger with a beard than without.

Too many years, perhaps, but he knew that without Richard and the slow progress of his Army career they would have achieved nothing but endless talk and pointless protest. All of the senior members of the organisation would be at the meeting tonight, and of all the meetings they had held over the years, this one was crucial. Finally, they had the means to do it, but to instigate outright rebellion required more than just the means; more than just talk, it required courage. Tonight, they would decide to overthrow the government of the United Kingdom or, more accurately, to throw it out of their homeland. They had avoided using the word that really described what they intended. They had used 'take power' or 'the change' or 'the takeover', because these lesser words did not alarm them so much. It was time to accept the risk and start calling it a revolution. Even if they were determined to make it bloodless, it was still a revolution.

It had all started with Isobel, who had gathered a group of people together in a Glasgow pub over thirty years ago. The meeting had been pretty much disorganized, he remembered, until Richard had stepped in to help and brought some sort of order to the proceedings. It was Richard also who had singled him out and had him speak to the crowd. He remembered Karen being there and even then speaking out strongly for a more socialist country. And then there was Jake. Jake, who had been at the pub playing dominoes with some very dubious looking cronies, but who had listened in and approached Isobel after the meeting wound up. He had later offered to fund them, and that was how they ended up indebted to a minor Glasgow gang lord.

In the early days it had always surprised him that Jake more often than not attended their meetings, since he was much older and also from a world very alien to theirs. He seemed comfortable in their company, and although he did not say much, he had a sharp, enquiring mind, so that when he did speak it was worth the listening. He remained part of the group right up until he died of lung cancer in his sixties, and James knew that without his initial financial support, which ironically added some legitimacy to their campaign, they might not have lasted so long.

Until recently it would have been hard to label anything they had done as illegal or subversive, but the many years of discussion had invariably led to only one conclusion, namely that for Scotland to gain its independence positive action from within would be needed. They considered themselves more hard line than the many other pro-independence groups that were distinct from the SNP but nevertheless were aligned with their main aim.

As a group, they did not regard themselves as either right or left on the political spectrum but accepted that both strands were present within their structure, and that it was the thirst for independence that was the driving force that held the disparate views of the group together. When the press had started identifying them and sometimes confused them with other Scottish socialist or republican organisations, they had adopted the old Roman name and called themselves the Campaign for Caledonia.

It was the failure of the 2014 referendum to deliver independence that had shifted them further towards direct action. The Caledonia group had put aside their distrust for the SNP and campaigned hard for the YES vote. The end result only served to heighten their poor regard for the Scottish government, who may have been adept at dealing with the press and of course had the luxury of laying the blame for any failure on the UK government, but did not instil any confidence that they could actually run and develop a new country in any other way than as a shadow of how the UK itself was run. There had been the chance, for a while, that another referendum with a positive result or a major shift in the political landscape could make the cause redundant, but as the years passed, this seemed increasingly unlikely, and the group had pivoted ever more strongly to positive action.

It was also the NO result which reignited Isobel's long-held wish to start a political party not only with an agenda for independence but with a viable government brave enough to embrace change. She had gained the support of the others, who had agreed to finance it, as she argued that even though the chance of getting an MSP elected was very small, they would have a much more visible platform to attract members and raise funds and also to broadcast their political aims. The Caledonians at best could only muster several dozen hard core supporters, and perhaps a hundred more who would only become active when there was a specific reason to campaign, such as a referendum. James had wholeheartedly supported it, because the political party gave a foundation to what he believed was the most important part of their activities, which was the think tank that strived to envisage a more inclusive and responsible system of government.

So, within weeks of the result, she had signed the papers and paid the deposit, and the Caledonian Independence Party was officially born. That was six years ago. It had certainly solidified their commitment to action, and they had all put a lot of work into setting up the Party. However, rather than raising money, it had become a drain on the financial resources, and the need for a more substantial financial backer became more pressing.

From the outside they were just another small pro-independence party and campaign group, but they harboured a deeper secret, an actual mechanism to deliver independence, without which they would be as ineffectual as all the other aspirants. This was in the form of another of the original members — Colonel Richard Ogilvy. Richard had been an Army Cadet on a graduate entry programme at the time of the first meeting. And even then, in his youth, James recalled he had a commanding presence. He was tall with sandy hair and an athletic body, and carried himself as though he was always in uniform even when casually dressed.

From his very first days in the Army, Richard had begun – on his own initiative – identifying comrades who were pro-independence and signing them up to a loose club of sorts. He started with the young officers of his own peer group. At first it was very slow, but for every man and – later, when the number of female soldiers grew – woman he recruited, they too would recruit. So, like a pyramid selling scheme, the message spread until there was a significant network of independence sympathisers of all ranks permeated into the structure of the Scottish Army units. They did nothing other than declare that they were in favour of Scottish Independence, and Richard kept it above board with a monthly newsletter, and whenever he or his fellow officers could, they facilitated discussion groups or the creation of clubs with a Scottish focus. There were some senior officers who disapproved, but there was never any hint of disloyalty. The military were allowed to vote for whatever political party they supported or sided with in the case of a referendum. If anyone had ever bothered to look, they would have found a surprisingly high number of clubs within the Army's social structure with names like the Scottish Historical Society, Scottish Regimental History Group, Scottish Battalions in Major Battles, and of course, Gaelic language clubs.

At the beginning, the others had not really given much credence to Richard's reports of how his network was growing, but they all agreed that it was a good way to spread their message through all sections of society. Privately, they shared jokes regarding images of burly soldiers step-dancing to the music of *Riverdance*, but they did not share these with the rather humourless Richard.

He was often unable to attend the meetings, but as the years passed, he had begun to refer to the Network with a capital N. They had come to realise its potential as he described the depth and complexity of the organisation that he had created within the British Army.

Colonel Richard Ogilvy had re-appeared after a posting abroad and contacted James to request a meeting of the Board, as he would like to address the group on the future, with the intention of, in his words, moving the campaign to a 'war footing'.

It was two years ago that they had finally found a financial backer who was willing to support their cause, and they had started to call themselves the Board. This was largely for his benefit, as they wished to promote an impression of authority and permanence, since the amount of money that they were asking him to commit was significant. The formation of the Board had also had the effect of instilling a more ordered approach to meetings and organisation. If Richard had not been away so much of the time, he would, James was sure, have been their natural leader.

So, James had – almost accidentally, and certainly not by intention – fulfilled that role, and they now looked to him as though he had all the answers. It was true that a large part of the proposed changes in government had come from him, but many others had added to those ideas. He thought wryly that his position probably depended more on his ability to chair a meeting and stick to an agenda than any innate ability as a leader.

The Board was made up of the four remaining original members: the financier, who had insisted on a place, and the three younger members who James thought of as the 'second generation'. It still somewhat surprised him that after all these years, the four of them who had been there at the beginning – himself; Isobel, who had started it all; Richard, now a full Colonel; and Karen, who had always been their social conscience – were still committed. Although Jake had smoked himself to death, he had given them his son Jack, Jake Junior, although no one would ever be brave enough to call him that to his face. Jack had taken his father's place and proved to be a very valuable member of the group, and he had continued the financial support until they had found the much wealthier backer.

All eight of the Board were on time, except for Karen who always arrived a little late. Once she had arrived and said her hellos to everyone, they all seated themselves around the table. James opened the meeting and then motioned for Richard to address them.

'I and my senior men, and all of you here, have believed for a long time that the only way to free Scotland is by force. My team have a provisional plan and believe it is actionable in one day with the minimum of violence and bloodshed, and without alarming the public unduly. I cannot hold the Network together indefinitely without a clear end in sight,' he paused. 'In short, the options are: talk some more, or take action. It is time to decide.'

He went on to explain that he had recently been promoted to full Colonel and had taken up a position on the General staff in Scotland. He was still several years away from achieving

General rank, but the experience in his new posting would almost certainly make him a likely candidate for the role of Commanding General in Scotland in the future.

The result of the referendum had also had an effect on the members of his Network, and the number of pro-independence supporters had grown since 2014 and was as strong as it had ever been. Furthermore, he explained that there was a growing clamour for action from the more senior members of his Network, and if nothing was done soon it may start to gradually dissolve. The Network could call on a significant number of officers and enlisted men within the Scottish battalions, and there was also a large cohort of retired personnel, many of them working in civilian roles. He finished with what was, for Richard, an emotional plea.

'The chance will come in a few years' time when I am in command of the Army in Scotland, but we have to plan now and be ready, or else it will slip away from us. The window of opportunity will be limited – postings generally last for only two or three years, and that will probably be my final position before retiring.' The Colonel sat down.

It was an indication of how much the group had become disillusioned by the passing of the years and the failure of the referendum that there was no outright objection. There were some questions, but there was an underlying feeling that this should be the way forward.

'Can you explain the plan?' said Isobel.

'Taking a country, even a small one, requires a huge commitment of resources and personnel, so it is not easy to give the whole picture. In summary, I will close the borders, control all transport and communication hubs, and isolate and contain all non-loyal military forces within the country.

'You have enough men to do that?' asked James.

'As I said, it is complex, but yes, we feel that even those troops that are not part of the Network will fall into line when they realise what the intention is. I will have core leaders for almost all units, and troops follow their leaders.'

Isobel looked unconvinced.

'And how will we avoid bloodshed?' said Karen. 'The last thing we want is Scottish troops killing Scottish people or other troops. I don't believe it can be done, not without a popular uprising.'

'No. That is something to be avoided. A general uprising will just get in the way. Very few revolutions are conducted by the people. The French Revolution was one, but the people were subjugated and needed to overthrow a powerful and corrupt system. We are not a subjugated nation where the people need to rise up against an occupying army. Most coups are carried out by the armed forces, and only if the people are totally against the takeover do they take to the streets in opposition. That won't happen here, as we know that there is already a high level of support for independence.'

'So, you can't guarantee there will not be deaths then?' said Karen.

'We should hear the plan first,' said Isobel.

'The plan involves containing all the military units not with us. I don't say it will be easy. Of course, I cannot guarantee there will be no casualties, but we have been working on a plan for several years, and my team believe it is feasible. It is complex, but I will lay out all the details for the Board at another meeting once we have decided. Tonight, we only need to make the decision. The plan will solidify as we approach the time – it cannot all be done too far in advance, as there is continual change. I will lay out the plan in precise detail at the appropriate time,' said Richard.

'You didn't answer my question,' said Karen.

'I thought I had. The difference, between all the armed coups in recent history, or for that matter ancient history, is that the majority of them were for personal gain or to the advantage of one tribe or ethnic group, or class over another. If... no, *when* we do it here, it would be for the benefit of all the people of Scotland, and I repeat one important fact. We know, from the referendum result and later polls, that around half of the population are already committed to the idea of an independent Scotland. When it happens, the support will already be there, and it is the same within the Army. That's why I think the troops will follow their leaders because the cause will be popular.'

'Not much of an answer,' said Karen, determined to continue.

Richard sighed. 'I hope we can manage it with no casualties, but there is no guarantee. Remember, we are taking a whole country; it will be an immense achievement.'

'So, the means, no matter how hard, justify the end?' said Karen.

'Yes. Don't you agree? We are aiming for something transformative, making history. There will undoubtedly be a cost.' He paused, but she did not respond. 'We all know James has been working on a superior system of government. In fact, we all know James is not as committed to independence as the rest of us; he just wants a chance to try his theories out.' Richard rarely joked, but this hit a chord around the table and raised a few laughs amongst them. It certainly eased the tension.

James good humouredly waved his acceptance of the jibe.

'We need to think of a name,' said Jack, impatient with the discussion. 'So far, we have "the revolution", "the takeover", "the day". We need a name.'

So, thought James, *we are not arguing for or against; we are thinking of what to call our revolution. A good sign, surely.*

'UDI,' said Isobel. Some members looked blank. 'Unilateral Declaration of Independence like... ah, Ireland, Rhodesia, and more recently the breakaways from Yugoslavia. I believe Catalonia announced it, even though it did them no good.'

'Rarely a good outcome,' said Karen. 'It certainly caused a lot of long drawn-out wars in Yugoslavia.'

No one liked Isobel's idea, and the table lapsed into silence.

'Independence Day,' said Jack, 'just so we can talk about it. We don't need anything else.' Everyone agreed, and Richard's military mind swiftly changed it to IDay.

'A vote then, if you will,' said James. 'Do we take Scotland? Raise your hand for a yes.'

Karen was the last to raise hers, making it unanimous. James stood up as Nancy, his wife, placed a tray of glasses in front of him, and he slopped a substantial shot of whisky into each one before handing them round.

'Ladies and gentlemen, a toast!' They all stood and raised their glasses.

'To Scotland – Independence Day!'

Chapter 3

Simon (2018)

It was Maggie, Isobel's daughter, who had suggested approaching the billionaire gambling mogul Simon O'Sullivan. As the need for more funding had grown, the group had considered approaching wealthy Scottish people, but that raised problems about security. Many well-known personalities, who may have been highly visible to the public, were actually hard to contact. Some famous celebrities who were supportive and outspoken about the desire for Scottish independence actually lived in the United States, so were not much help.

Simon O'Sullivan was immensely rich and very vocal about his support for the SNP and Scottish independence. He had been a key figure and had very publicly contributed money to the YES campaign of the 2014 referendum. Compared to some other well-known figures, it had been relatively easy to find his address. He had been involved in a highly public dispute with the local council over a plan for other properties to be built in 'his' valley. The dispute with the other landowner had appeared in the press, and from that, his location was easily determined on the map. The planned houses were not in the immediate vicinity of his home, but he had complained that it would impact on his wider view of the countryside and be the thin edge of the wedge for further building. He had argued that this would seriously impinge on his amenity, and as he was a contributor to many local events and charities, he somehow deserved more respect. The arguments were so laughable that the local press were only too keen to publicise the story.

Maggie and her long-term partner Stevie, who were both what James thought of as 'second generation' members of the group, had driven down to the billionaire's estate in Ayrshire on the off-chance of getting a meeting. They had found the house with no difficulty, or to be more exact, the high fence and heavily gated entrance that hid the house from view.

'Some garden fence. You think that's it?' said Stevie, dipping his head a bit to look through her side window as he slowed the car.

Maggie had been looking at the fence for the last several hundred metres. It consisted of a low, stone built, solid looking wall about a metre-and-a-half high, into which were set steel railings about three metres high. Each bar was topped with a curve that looped into the next bar. Two horizontal bars braced the vertical railings: one set very low, and the other just below the top loop. These horizontal support bars were positioned at these points to ensure no assistance would be given to anyone trying to climb the railings. All the steel work was a pleasant shade of green and appeared freshly painted. At regular intervals a vertical steel pillar was inset into the wall to support the panels of railings.

The house could not be seen behind the railings, as the ground rose gradually upwards from the boundary, and was well hidden from the view of prying eyes. The ground was neatly kept with scattered specimen trees and bushes. In the centre of each panel was – well, Maggie could not quite decide what to call it – a logo, a coat of arms, or an insignia perhaps, which was detailed in white paint, making it stand out against the green bars.

'It's a fucking fortress,' said Stevie, as he drove into what was apparently the entrance to the drive and came to a halt facing a pair of massive gates. The gates replicated the fencing, both being made of green steel railings. They rose to the full height of the fence, but the upper half was curved so that the apex was reached at the join. A white circle of the insignia was positioned at head height in the centre of each gate. Each gate was mounted on robust looking stone pillars at either side.

'It must be a real bad neighbourhood,' he said, as they both got out of the car. 'I see cameras but no intercom or opener.' Stevie walked over to the nearest pillar.

Maggie stood in the centre of the gates, examining the coat of arms. A double entwined S shape, with one being the mirror image of the other, occupied the centre and was surrounded by a complicated ring of small heraldic devices. She picked out an elephant, a lion, a shield, oak leaves – they all merged into one another in a rather unpleasing way. Someone's idea of a heraldic device, she thought. The whole was enclosed in a circle of white steel bar.

Stevie sauntered over, having given up searching for an intercom at the pillars, and joined Maggie at the gates.

'Should have just stuck to the two letters rather than all that gunk,' he said after a moment. 'Why the reverse one, do you think?'

'Avoiding the SS reference, I guess.'

'No, look, there's a small O in between them.'

Even from here the house was not visible. The gravelled driveway curved away between two high banks only a short distance from the gates. They both heard the sound of a motor approaching, and soon a red quad bike appeared around the curve. It came to an abrupt halt, sending a small spray of stones skittering from the wheels. It was driven by a fair-haired man of about fifty, wearing a small-checked country gentleman's shirt, and over it a tweed waistcoat sporting a dull tartan pattern stretched tightly across his stomach. A double-barrel shotgun was slung diagonally across his back by a leather strap, and round his waist he sported a fat leather cartridge belt with only a few spaces.

They instinctively backed away from the gate as he dismounted and switched the engine off. He was a short man, heavily built – the sort of build that would inevitably get fatter later in life.

'Simon O' Sullivan, I presume with a big SMS,' whispered Stevie.

'Huh?' But Maggie's response was cut off by the newcomer. 'Why are you hanging around my property? Get lost!'

Maggie put on her brightest smile. 'Hello, Mr O'Sullivan, we were hoping to speak to you. I'm Maggie, and this is my partner, Stephen.'

He did not approach the gate or respond, but just waited.

'Uhh... we would like a few moments of your time, if that's possible. It is important.'

'Let me guess... you've a sick child that needs specialist treatment, and you need x thousand pounds. No, no wait! You've a killer business idea that will make us all rich. Bugger off now, I've heard it all before.'

'None of that shit,' said Stevie. 'We need ten million.'

O'Sullivan, on his way back to the quad, shook his head and started to mount it. He paused, 'Oh, big fucking spenders! For what?'

They had his attention, at least. 'Scottish independence,' said Maggie.

'Bollocks! I'm sick to death of that as well.' Disappointed, he turned back to the machine. 'Just endless talk.'

'NO!' shouted Stevie. 'We're *not* talking about campaigns or political time wasting. We have an action plan for a Unilateral Declaration of Independence, and the means to take Scotland by force. We are talking about a Free Scotland with or without you – it's your choice if you want to be in or not.'

O'Sullivan froze with a leg suspended in mid-air half across the machine. He slowly returned it to the ground and turned back to face them, then stood for a while longer. He smiled as though enjoying the joke. He was not one hundred per cent convinced, but it seemed worth a little more information, just out of interest, and the pair of them did look in deadly earnest. He had not reached where he was today without some feeling for people.

'OK, you've got a meeting. Follow me up to the house.' He pressed a remote in his pocket and the gates started to open slowly.

'I thought you'd gone too far,' said Maggie. 'Should we have told him so much?'

'Seemed like the only way.'

'SMS?'

'Oh that – Small Man Syndrome – makes everything else big to make up for it.'

Maggie just laughed.

They motored after the quad, and although somehow they had expected a much longer drive, the first bend almost immediately curved into a second, and once they emerged from the resulting double bend they could see the house not too far ahead. It was a substantial L-shaped sandstone mansion built with a nod to Scottish baronial by incorporating a full height turret with appropriately small windows nestled into the apex of the corner. Only a hundred years old or so, it was pleasant enough to look at.

It was surrounded by well-kept gardens dotted with more specimen trees and shrubs and extensive lawns that had been too well manicured and looked almost plastic. There was a group of mature trees to the left of the house, and a few others scattered around which had survived the obviously heavy landscaping. It had been designed so that the house sat in a hollow surrounded by gently sloping banks that also hid the house from view from the road and hid the fence from the house.

The drive opened up into a large circular area in front of the house, and they parked beside a big SUV. A couple of sports cars and a much older grubby looking hatchback were also lined up in front of the house.

Stevie was surprised how tasteful the house appeared. He knew that Simon's father had come over from Ireland and opened a betting shop in the East End of Glasgow. Simon had taken over the business and expanded it into a handful of premises through the central belt. The physical expansion stopped when Simon had launched one of the first, and arguably the most successful, online betting apps that had turned him into a billionaire, with an annual income in the tens of millions, much faster than the shops ever could have.

'Too many pigeons,' he said, gesturing to the shotgun. 'They roost in those trees right outside the bedroom and start cooing at each other too damn early in the morning.' He led the way into the house. In the hall, a smartly dressed woman was berating a younger woman about cleaning bathrooms. She looked up and gave Simon a quizzical look, as though it was strange to see people she did not know.

'My wife, Louise.' The woman nodded and ghosted a smile at them that showed the briefest flash of overly-white, even teeth. Her perfectly styled richly blonde hair, her make-up, her designer clothes, all shouted expensive but in a tasteful understated way. Maggie was slightly envious.

'Maggie and... uh...'

'Stevie, pleased to meet you,' interjected Stevie, and stretched forward to shake Louise's hand. Maggie did the same.

'They're here to talk about the independence movement.'

Louise seemed completely uninterested. 'Sorry. Can't stop; off to Glasgow. Rena here will look after you. Rena the cleaner.' Louise laughed and waved in the general direction of the woman.

Maggie was impressed that the young woman's facial expression did not alter in any perceptible way, but she somehow conveyed her distaste for her boss. She had extremely short, bleached blonde hair which was cut spiky. Maggie noted the contrast and winked at her.

'See you later.' This last comment was directed at her husband, who waved her away in response. Moments later, they heard a powerful engine start up.

They sat in a huge sitting room at the back of the house with glass walls on all sides, except where the extension joined onto the back of the original house. To one side a swimming pool with its own glass walls, complete with hot tub and sun loungers, lay behind another glass partition, while on the other side sliding doors opened onto a terrace overlooking the garden. Stevie was slightly disappointed that his first pleasant impression of the mansion was marred by the glass structure tacked on the back, but he had to admit it was impressive.

'So, convince me. How big is the group? I assume it's not just the two of you? What is the money needed for?'

He was not in any case going to give these two chancers any money, but he was interested enough to pass a little time hearing their story. He was sick of the whole independence thing, campaigns, rallies, endless meetings, politicians and ex politicians, all pointless. He was going to enjoy tearing them to shreds. Besides, he liked the look of the girl; she was well rounded, just like he liked them – perhaps there was even some Irish in her. Maybe it was time he looked for another mistress. And where did *she* think she was heading off to, again? There's only so much shopping you can do. He had started to notice that Louise never left her phone unattended, and he was becoming suspicious; perhaps he should have her followed.

He checked for a wedding ring on Maggie's finger, but there did not seem to be one.

Rena came in with a tray of cups and a cafetière. She served them all deftly, shared a smile with Maggie, and slipped away. Maggie made a mental note to recruit her for the Party if she could. Once Rena had left, Stevie stood up and interrupted Simon's thoughts.

'There is one thing before we carry on. We need your word – your oath, if you like – on your silence, as anything we tell you may affect the security of the organisation.'

Simon managed to stop himself bursting into laughter and succeeded in holding it to a chuckle and a wave of his hand. 'Of course; consider it done.'

Maggie stood as well. 'We may not look much, but we are more than you think, and that includes a means of enforcement. Think carefully before you give your word, and understand that it fully commits you to silence.'

Was that a threat? Means to enforce? Oath? What the fuck are they talking about? He was tempted to throw them out, but there was something, some feeling in his gut, some vibe that they both projected, that made him hesitate. They waited. He suddenly realised that they were waiting for him to stand. *Fuck, stand! Surely not to kneel?* He stood.

Stevie, having made up the idea of the oath on the spot, was grateful for the pause as he collected his thoughts. 'Repeat after me.' *Oh God*, he thought, *it's going to sound corny.*

'I, Simon O'Sullivan, swear on my life to protect with my silence any privileged information that I may receive, and I swear my loyalty to an Independent Scotland.'

Maggie had almost intervened when Stevie stood up, but as he spoke it seemed to make sense. She regretted not having discussed what they should and should not say before coming here, but she had not really expected to make so much progress straight away. All in all, not bad; it had sounded OK. Stevie had always been a quick thinker – one of the many reasons she loved him – and the oath could be a lot of use as they started to expand more quickly.

Steve led Simon to repeat the oath, and if there were a few minor differences in the second repetition, they were not noticed.

'We have the Army,' she said, and even though Maggie was exaggerating wildly, she held his gaze, and these were the words that captured Simon. From then on, he started to really listen.

'One of our number has been in the British Army for his whole career and will be promoted to General very soon. He expects to be the senior office in command of the Scottish regiment in a year or two. You can imagine what sort of control that would give him over units based in Scotland.'

'I can't possibly see how that would be of any use,' said Simon.

'Scotland is unique in having our own army subsumed into the British Army; the Scottish regiment. There are six battalions based at various barracks in the country. These battalions are almost exclusively made up of Scottish nationals.'

'I have heard of the Royal Regiment of Scotland, is that what you mean?'

'We tend to drop the "royal" part,' said Stevie. 'It has taken decades, but our man has built up a significant network of supporters within the officers and men of these battalions. There are different layers of awareness within that, of course. Some of the upper echelons of the network are fully aware of the long-term intention, while others have merely indicated their support for independence.'

'You intend to use them to take the country by force?' said Simon. 'Won't that just be carnage between your network and the rest of the Army?'

'There are two important facts,' said Maggie. 'You have to remember that these battalions are made up almost totally of Scots. We believe that even those as yet uncommitted will follow their leaders, under the right circumstances. Two, the soldiers are proud of their Scottish heritage.'

'It's true that there is a very strong national identity in our people,' said Simon. 'I would need to talk to your Army man before I make any commitment.'

They did not give names, but they assured him that they were speaking on behalf of the leaders. They told him about the group and how long it had been in existence, how deeply committed and for how long they had been planning the takeover. They explained about the political party that they had formed and which would be the basis for a provisional government. The money was needed to fund and expand the political wing of the movement, as well as to fund the operations of the group.

He was definitely interested, and they had made a substantial case, but he reminded himself of one of his own maxims that had helped make him rich: namely, that punters often bet on who they wanted to win rather than any educated assessment. But he also sensed that there was a lot in it for him, and he would need time to think about that. He rarely took a bet unless the odds were stacked to win, and if that were the case, why not bet big? His instinct told him it was worth the gamble, and it was trusting his instinct that had made him the success he was today. One thing was for sure, these days, he could afford to lose.

'Ok,' he told them, as he led them out, 'you have got my attention, but I need to meet with all your people, especially the Army man, before I go any further. You have my number now, so get back to me when you can arrange that.'

Maggie slipped Rena a party leaflet as she opened the door for them.

Chapter 4

Isobel (2018)

They were at James and Nancy's flat for a meeting to appoint Simon O'Sullivan to the Board. Isobel did not care to guess how many times she had been here over the years. The couple had been in the flat since they first married and had never shown any sign of leaving. She guessed that because they did not have children, they had never sought anything larger. It was convenient for the West End and for the centre of Glasgow.

She remembered the first meeting of the Board; it was not called that then, it was just a collection of people with a common interest, but it coalesced into a group quickly in those early days. And even though many came and went over the years, the core remained the same. Their first meeting occurred sometime in the autumn of 1985, although none of the present members who had been there were exactly sure of the date. They had all been changed to some extent by that first meeting.

She had always thought it logical that those with the strongest held beliefs and passion had attended the meeting, provided, of course, that they had seen her poster. It had been encouraging to meet other like-minded people that were all, perhaps in different ways, committed to and believed that Scotland should be independent. And for herself, she knew, it had cemented and strengthened her resolve. Not only that but she had made lifelong friends that day.

She had become close friends with Karen, and between them they had largely been responsible for organising the meetings, rallies, and marches in the early years. It soon became apparent that the general public would lose interest very quickly when independence dropped out of the news cycle. It was only possible to gather the troops when a specific event occurred that they could latch onto. As Karen had remarked, nothing denotes failure more than a protest attended by only a handful of people.

The Caledonians had seen a resurgence of interest during the second Devolution referendum and campaigned hard for it, and they were pleased at the positive result, although they worried that the creation of a successful devolved Scottish Parliament would detract from the ultimate aim of independence.

Even when there was no on-going campaign, the five of them continued to meet on a relatively regular basis, when they would discuss politics and political history and explore new ideas. James was the main advocate of what he called the think tank and liked to push the group to explore theories of government. She had always found James a little strange, and he had some very unconventional and even bizarre views about politics. His pet theory was seeking to extract the best parts of various ideologies, government systems, and economic theory, and combine them in such a way that the perfect system would be created. He had spent many hours inventing alternate ideologies that would correct some of the failures of capitalism. No one could argue that capitalism and democracy hadn't helped make the world a better place for a significant number of people, but it had become ever more efficient at funnelling wealth up from the workers to be hoarded by the wealthy.

Isobel suspected that the problems of politics, government, economics, culture and society, were too many, too varied, and too interconnected to hope to solve them all with one overarching theory, but she wholly agreed with James that there had to be substantial change. James's father, a staunch union man, had been a casualty of the collapse of the shipbuilding industry on the Clyde. He had been made redundant, become an alcoholic, and eventually abandoned his family. He left his young son with a fractured mixture of not well understood or explained socialist thought, and a smattering of Marx. Isobel suspected that his father's influence was the main reason for James's obsession.

She was finally beginning to feel that her life was going in the direction that she had always wanted. The political party was important to her and she had committed a lot of her time to it in the last few years. The future was uncertain, but even if the takeover did not happen, she would still run for parliament even if the chances of getting elected were slight. For now, the party fulfilled another function, and this was to prepare in part for a future government. The manifesto would lay out some of their intentions, and although membership was still low, it was growing. And as every new member was carefully assessed for suitable skills that may help them govern, she had already identified several that fitted that bill.

She had been highly politically motivated at university, but the everyday life of teacher training, learning her profession, then marriage, always claimed preference. Then of course her beautiful baby Maggie came along. It was only when Maggie was old enough to attend secondary school that Isobel had joined the Labour Party, on the advice of Karen, who had been a member and activist as long as she could remember. Isobel had then run in two local council elections, being beaten on both occasions by the SNP candidate.

Her marriage may have ended badly, but it was more than made up for by Maggie. A bright and happy child from a very early age, she was the sort of child who would set herself arithmetic sums of many lines of addition and subtraction and spend hours solving them with the greatest of pleasure. Isobel remembered taking her along to a meeting while she was still a toddler, and how she had charmed everyone. She was not a whiny child, or one given to demanding constant attention; she was interested in everything and everyone. She could not be prouder of her, especially now that she was also a Board member.

Maggie and her long-time boyfriend Stevie had only recently been brought in as full members of the Board, and they were both keen to make their mark. Maggie, as Isobel's daughter, had grown up with the group and she was fully involved with the campaign as an adult so it had always been assumed that one day she would join. Stevie had been her partner for several years, and there was nothing that she knew that he did not. But even so, Isobel knew that Maggie had been surprised and pleased when the Board selected him as well. The original first-generation members were all of an age, and even Jack was in his early forties, so the others had all agreed that some new blood and fresh thinking would be beneficial.

The addition of a financial backer, with what appeared to be almost unlimited resources, had been a big step forward. The amount of money that Jack could provide was limited, and although his family business was now largely legitimate, it still retained links with and was not wholly removed from the criminal activities that had been more prevalent under his father, Jake. It was not a good look to finance the party from the proceeds of low-level drug sales and a bouncer operation, though she knew Jack would amend that immediately to 'security staff".

The party still operated mostly from Isobel's kitchen, and they were in dire need of paid clerical and admin support. Furthermore, Richard was seeking funds to pay a retainer to members of the Network who were leaving the Army or were already in civilian roles, to hold them as reserve support for the Army when the time came. So far, the Board had not agreed to this, and there was no way they could have funded it anyway.

Maggie had been the driving force behind finding the billionaire, and her unexpected success at recruiting him quickly had come as a bit of a surprise to them all. Simon O'Sullivan seemed to be prepared to fully commit to the cause. He brought with him not only a major amount of financial power, but also a desire to take control that the group found difficulty in holding in check.

This was not the only downside. Since becoming involved, he had made them jump through hoops. Although, they had used the term 'board' for their group in the past, they had now formalised it for Simon's benefit, and he had demanded a seat on it. Now they all referred to it as the Board. He had insisted on meeting with them all individually to question them intensely not only about their future intentions but also their history. He had made it clear that before he would risk committing any resources, he intended to completely understand what they intended. He had spent a significant amount of time with herself and Karen discussing the party and how he could use it to push funds their way if he agreed to finance them. He seemed to have taken a special liking for Karen, and for all his reading of people, he had not figured her out at all. Isobel had been long enough in his company to nurse a growing dislike for Simon, but she could surely live with that. She had already started looking around for office space.

Simon had appeared this evening with a large, sturdy and sealed cardboard box that he had deposited by the door, and she could not guess what its purpose was. Isobel could see across the room that he was chatting to Karen and had captured her in conversation as soon as she had arrived. He gave off an air of absolute confidence, and being in the presence of a group of would-be terrorists did not seem to bother him in the slightest. He was a short man with a paunch. Somehow, you'd expect a billionaire to be tall and imposing. She wondered how much that fine wool jumper cost that stretched over his portly middle, or those shoes – handmade surely?

James called for the meeting to start, and they all took their seats. He welcomed Simon to the group. Simon remained seated and leaned back, relaxed in his chair, arms resting on the table.

'Good to meet you all,' said Simon.

He then continued with a reassuring talk laying out his absolute commitment to the cause and assuring them of his loyalty. He made positive comments about the Caledonian Independence Party and how it could be used to funnel large sums of money to the cause. It would still require some creative book-keeping from them, but he told them it should be doable with the minimum of risk. They would also need to sort out how they would move money to the rest of the organisation, but these were details that could be worked out.

'I must say that I agree Scotland will never be independent unless it is forced into it, and I think you may have hit on a way to do it. I believe from what I have heard that it has a good chance of success. One thing for sure, on the day it will require overwhelming and unstoppable commitment. I agree that there is no need for a public uprising; secure the country, and the people will have no choice but to accept it. The national pride of being Scottish is deeply rooted, and even if a person did not support independence in the past, it should be enough to carry the people with you after the event.' He paused. 'If you accept my conditions, I will agree to finance the party. Isobel is already looking for a suitable office premises. I have discussed with Richard his needs and will finance that as well.'

'The conditions?' said James.

'Not much really. All the money must pass through the party so that I can be seen only as the funder of the political party, nothing more. If it all goes haywire, you keep me out of the fallout.'

'Ah, the well-used "plausible deniability",' said Isobel.

'Secondly, I am given a role in the new government, if you succeed. Something prestigious but not too arduous.'

'Right, like minister for gambling?' said Karen, with barely concealed hostility. 'And I notice you are not taking any risk of being totally committed yourself then?'

'Not too onerous,' said James, 'but remember Simon's financial risk is large.'

Simon ignored them. 'One more thing. Your security is crap, and I suggest from now on you start taking it very seriously. Richard has protocols for his network, and you should adopt them as well. No message apps or texting, and preferably restrict all communication between yourselves to voice only. Who knows when the security services may decide to take a peep at political parties with an agenda?'

'As a gesture of goodwill and a token of my commitment,' he nodded in Karen's direction, 'I have brought along ten ultra-secure satellite phones. You will find them in the box there, all set up and ready to go, and I suggest you start using them immediately. I already have one, and my number is in each one.'

Isobel thought that perhaps he was more interested in protecting himself than the group, but James took a vote and they unanimously voted Simon onto the Board. Karen was the last to raise her hand. So now they had a lot more financial power, and Isobel knew that would really kick-start the Party. It was a huge step forward, and together with Richard's growing network in the Army, it seemed as though at last they were making headway.

Isobel really felt, for the first time, that the Board was worthy of its name. The vote for the billionaire to join them had made it more official somehow, and given it authority.

Chapter 5

Kenny (IDay minus 8)

The van hit another pothole in the poorly maintained minor road, and the impact jostled Kenny against the lad next to him, doing little to improve his state of mind. The back of the Transit was jammed with young men, and the air was stuffy with overuse. They were an hour out of Glasgow, and Kenny was having second thoughts about what he had let himself in for.

Before they had set off, the driver, who they had never seen before, had taken all their phones and searched their backpacks to check for any other electronic equipment. Some of his fellows had been reluctant to give up their mobiles but complied with some grumbling. It made Kenny think that it was getting serious. They had been told to expect to be away for two weeks, and so to family and friends he was going abroad on holiday.

He rubbed absently at the stubble on his chin, which had already grown even though he had shaved that morning. His Italian ancestry had given him skin that always looked nicely tanned, and his beard grew quickly so that his chin and cheeks were almost always in dark shadow. He had black hair and he liked it to cover his ears, so he always looked a little untidy. Kenny was almost twenty-eight and was conscious of the fact that he had not done much with his life so far. He had never bothered much at school, and he had resisted all the efforts of his parents to get him to study harder and go for a university place. Now that he was older, he wished he had listened to them, although he was never going to tell them that.

He had worked in the family café for several years, learning the business, and he knew his parents would like him to take it over. But as a means of broadening his experience, he had started working in the city centre pubs, which seemed to him a step up. It was at one of these that he met Malcolm, who had urged him to join in the pro-independence rallies that were going on at the time.

An ex-soldier who had served in most of the recent war zones, Malcolm swore a lot; almost every other word was adjectivised by 'fucking'. He was built like a weight lifter, small and broad, and walked like one, with his legs wide apart. He was always neatly dressed in a toned-down kind of way. No bright colours, no combats, nothing that would make him stand out. Kenny reckoned he was old, at least over fifty anyway. He recalled when he had first seen him, being impressed by the sheer size of the man's forearms as he had leant on the bar and ordered a drink.

Kenny knew all the other occupants of the van. He had hiked and camped with them, trained and paintballed with them, and apart from his present misgivings it had been a lot of fun. The training consisted of unarmed combat, fitness training, hiking and outdoor skills, and a surprising amount of paintball. Malcolm was always there, and he had access to a unit in an industrial estate where he had set up a gym with rudimentary weights, benches, and padded mats. The martial arts training did not follow any particular formal system but was more akin to street fighting. It was good and mostly fun, but there was always a hard edge to it. When they went hiking, they went extreme, almost to the limits of exhaustion, and then had to camp out with only the bare essentials. Kenny was smart enough to recognise that a lot of the training was to build a bond between them, and he had enjoyed that feeling of being part of an all-male group.

All of them were younger than him, and some he knew were barely over eighteen. Sometimes he had the feeling that a few of them had started to look up to him as the 'older', more responsible member of the group. It was true he had often been the one to lend a hand with the less capable members, or to encourage those struggling on the intensive hikes, or to repeat over and over some of the unarmed combat techniques that some found really hard to master. But the role of father figure was not one that he encouraged.

He had especially enjoyed the paintball exercises. These were good days out. They would all cram into the van, and Malcolm would drive them to various paintball sites around Scotland or northern England, but never to the same one twice running. Malcolm supplied the paintball guns, but they were not the usual ones that the gamers used which carried hundreds of paintballs and had gas tanks that lasted all day, so that the participants could splatter their opponents without stopping to reload.

Malcolm had an arsenal of what he called T4E guns; these were weapons that mimicked the real thing and were exact reproductions designed to replicate the action and capacity of real guns. They were used by police and Army trainers to 'Train for Engagement'. They were cheaper and much safer for training new recruits. The revolvers held only six paintballs, and the pistols and assault rifles used magazines with realistic and limited capacities.

He taught them that the capacity of a gun is its main weakness – an empty gun is useless and becomes nothing but a club as soon as the last bullet leaves the barrel. He showed them speed loaders for revolvers and taught them quick magazine changes for the semi-automatic guns. He insisted that they learn to count the rounds out and leave one in the chamber so that the gun was still loaded during a magazine change. If you lost count, which they almost always did, you had to trust your subconscious and reload as soon as you could, and hopefully before the gun was empty. For a pistol this was relatively easy, but for the rifles very hard, and usually they would lose count.

Malcolm knew it was difficult even for experienced soldiers, but he had an ulterior motive in that it meant they tended to limit their urge to just keep pressing the trigger without thinking about each shot. He taught them the difference between reactive shooting, assaulting or protecting a position and sniping.

Kenny most enjoyed the sites that had buildings. Clearing a room with a pistol was best. Malcolm had taught them that with a pistol in close combat like a room, they should just point and shoot on instinct. Don't aim, just let your arm and eye do it, he instructed. It worked surprisingly well, even on the move. Splatting every target in a room was extremely satisfying, especially if Malcolm gave an approving nod at the finish.

He allowed them no other protection apart from safety goggles to protect the eyes. If you got hit, you knew it, and you carried the bruise for a few days afterwards. They trained against each other in woods and ditches and ruined buildings. They learnt how to move, how to stay still, how to use cover, how to scan their surroundings quickly and in more depth, how to set up defensive positions and fields of fire. He forced them to learn to shoot with their weak hand and left eye, if cover was positioned inconveniently on the wrong side. He pointed out that in the movies the cover was inevitably suitable for a right-handed shooter, while in real life that was likely to be only half of the time.

When Malcolm had judged they were ready, he started to put them in to play against gamer teams. The object of the game was to seize the flag of the defending team. On the first occasion, Malcolm had put a guy called Craig – a natural marksman who had really taken to the paintball training – in charge of a six-man team, and told him to get on with it. The rest of the group watched from outside the fire zone. The gamer team defended first and holed up in a series of dugouts and trenches. With their superior firepower. they assumed it would be an easy task to hold off their opponents, who only carried the limited capability replicas.

Craig had thought for a while and then set up six firing positions in front of the enemy dugouts, and let the team fire away for a short time. He left two men behind, moving between the six positions and firing at random, while he led the other three in a long detour behind the enemy. The gamers had long since stopped watching their rear or their flanks, and they concentrated their fire to the front, expecting a frontal assault at any moment. Craig and his three team mates jumped down among them and double-tapped them all before they knew they were there. The gamers, a little unsportingly, returned a barrage of post mortem paintballs, giving Craig and his men some bruises, but it was clear who the victors were. Kenny could see Malcolm was pleased, although Craig and his attack team were spattered with paint. The gamers only sported two or three marks each, but they had obviously been well killed.

The return match was just as easy. The team set up the flag in the dugout system and manned their positions. Craig placed two men hidden in the undergrowth forward of the dugout, one on each flank. Their opponents' simple frontal attack was immediately hit by paintballs from the dugout and both sides. This time, the gamers gave in with more grace and acknowledged their defeat to superior tactics. As they rode back in the van, they had all been in high spirits, and Malcolm had given Craig a pat on the back.

'Fucking A, I'm almost fucking proud of you,' Malcolm told him. 'Now tell me what the deliberate fucking mistake was?'

Craig looked bemused, and the chatter and banter of the others quietened down as they listened in.

'Anyone?'

No one answered. 'Guarding the two flanks was good,' said Malcolm, 'but that created a parallel ambush.' Craig still looked blank. 'Ok, it's simple really. With live rounds, which will shoot fuckin' miles, remember, rather than fucking yards, you start shooting at your pals on the other side of the ambush. Get it now? Parallel ambushes only work if you have terrain like a valley so both teams are shooting down. If you have very well-trained troops, you can work it with diagonal fields of fire, but 'L' or 'T' ambushes are much better in lots of ways.' His voice tapered off, realising that he had lost most of them. 'Good fucking day anyway, lads. First round on me.'

One of the team, emboldened by a couple of pints, had once asked Malcolm if he knew any other swear words other than 'fuck'. Malcolm had deposited his pint glass gently on the beer-sodden table top, waited for a bit of quiet, and said, 'Fuck is the most useful word in the language. What else do you need? Listen, it can be a noun – "I don't give a fuck." An adjective – "You're a fucking idiot." A verb – obvious that one, but also it can be a verb for what you do or what is done to you, like "He was fucked up by the police." It can mean hello – 'How the fuck are you, mate?' or even goodbye – "Fuck off." Depending on how you stress the word, it can be a term of endearment – "I'm gonna fuck you." Or of absolute hate – "I'm gonna *fuck* you." Not only that, it works in almost any language.' Malcolm took a long pull at his pint, enjoying the laughter of his squad.

'One more thing,' he said. 'What do you think the most frequent last words are? Do you think yer granny shouts, "Oh dear" as the ten-ton truck hurtles down on her wee Mini? Does the squaddie cry for his mummy when he's bleeding out? Do all those airplane passengers shout "Help!" when they're falling out of the fucking sky? No! What do they shout?'

'OH FUUUUCK!' they all shouted, some banging the table with their fists.

The van took a bend a little too fast and pushed him against the metal wall, breaking his train of thought. He looked up and caught Craig's eye. Sitting opposite him on the other side of the van, Craig smiled and nodded back, and Kenny would have started a chat to reminisce about the paintball, but thought better of it as the noise in the van made it hard to hold any sort of conversation. Craig had his sleeves rolled up almost to the shoulder, revealing muscular arms with matching stylised eagle wing tattoos on each arm that he proudly showed off whenever he could. Kenny had his own tattoo of a girl riding a dragon. He remembered he had been proud of it as well for a few years, but now it was more of an embarrassment.

The training had been hard, but that's what had made it worthwhile and enjoyable for the most part. He was pleased to have made friends and to be part of a team. The team, yes, but there was also the reason behind all of this and that was now coming to pass. By the air of expectation in the van, he knew the others felt it as well. Of course, they all knew it was to do with the independence movement, but what would be required of them was hard to guess. He was not at all sure that he would be willing to carry out, for example, terrorist attacks in England such as those carried out by the IRA. Some of his colleagues thought this the most likely, or why else were they being trained as a fighting unit. And Kenny was smart enough to know that a considerable amount of money had been spent on their training, so payback time was now due.

He had been surprised to be contacted about a year ago by Malcolm who he had not heard from since the rallies organised by the 'YES' campaign during the 2014 referendum. They had had a good chat on the phone, reliving some of the wilder moments of the campaigning, and had agreed to meet up. They had met several times; at first, just him and Malcolm, and then later with small groups which had eventually settled to the team in the van with him now.

Malcolm had told them he was recruiting a small group of like-minded people to prepare for the next referendum. The talk was always on independence and was somewhat anti-English, and sometimes it took on the form of a lecture more than a chat. Kenny had always been an ardent supporter of an independent country, which was one of the few things he and his parents agreed on. His father watched the *Braveheart* film with tears in his eyes at least once a year.

After a few months, it was always the same lads that turned up, and the tempo and content of the meetings changed. There were less pub meetings and more training sessions at the unit in the industrial estate.

Around this time, Malcolm started talking about the Militia that was being formed and how they could be a part of. It was implied that should they complete the training to his satisfaction, they would have the opportunity to become full time members and be paid a wage rather than the small retainer they received each month to cover expenses. As the meetings went on, Kenny became a little concerned about the way it was heading, as rather than protecting protestors or resisting police intervention – all of which he was perfectly willing to do – the talks and lectures, and indeed the training, took on a warlike tone. But he went with it because he was thoroughly enjoying the comradeship and the games, warlike or not.

The van slowed down, and Kenny could see green railings unwinding behind them through the small square windows of the rear doors. *Big fence*, he thought, dipping his head to try and see the top. *Very tall.* The van came to a stop, and there was a brief conversation outside before they moved on again. The view through the windows was of well-maintained garden grounds, and Kenny caught a glimpse of a big manor-type house between the trees, but before reaching it the van turned off the gravelled drive, through an opening in the trees and onto a rutted track. The van bounced along the track for another uncomfortable half mile or so until eventually they drove into an area that looked like a disused farm yard. There was a wide, open area, part grass and part dirt, and some rickety looking buildings. Further away was a dilapidated house, with part of the roof missing and open wounds where the windows should be. The land rose behind it, cloaked with spindly silver birches.

They pulled up next to several other similar vans and a black Range Rover. There were a large number of young men sitting on the grass in groups, chatting and seemingly in a buoyant mood. Several others leaned against one of the vans vaping. Two others dressed in combat gear stood off to one side talking.

The rear doors of the van opened, and Malcolm was there. He was wearing Army-issue camouflage shirt and trousers with a web belt. Kenny had never seen him in anything other than plain and unassuming civilian clothes. But what really surprised him was the sight of the pistol mounted in a holster attached to the belt and strapped to his upper thigh. It was definitely not a paintball gun. The welcome speech was loud and not what Kenny had expected.

'EVERYONE OUT! FORM A FUCKING LINE FACING ME. NOW!'

The group formed a rough line facing Malcolm surprisingly quickly. Kenny thought their faces were expectant and excited rather than pissed off.

'This is us, men. You are my team. You're the ones that made the grade. Some others did not believe me.' Malcolm walked up and down in front of them as he spoke. 'Listen to this carefully – this is your last fucking chance to back out – no hard feelings, I will understand. Speak now and you can travel back with the fucking van.' He paused, looking around at them. 'If you choose to stay, there is no going back after you take the oath. You will use the skills you have learned, and now you are going to fight for the cause. You know what the cause is? Anyone want to go fucking home?'

Kenny thought that perhaps he did. No one moved.

'Fucking A. You will make history, and you'll be fucking well rewarded. Now to business.

'You are Team G3. That is our call sign: G3, Glasgow 3, to avoid any doubt. Over there are Teams G4, G5, and A2. A is for Ayrshire. A3 is on the way. There are fifty or so of these platoon-size teams across Scotland, most in the central belt and the borders, and the rest further north. There are nineteen of you, two sections, eight men in each, with a section leader and a runner for me. Kenny and you, Craig, get out here. You are now the section leaders.'

Kenny was not expecting that at all but stepped out to the front and stood behind Malcolm with Craig. They exchanged glances. Kenny could tell from the look that Craig had had no idea either.

'OK,' Malcolm continued, 'when the Ayrshire 3 get here, if ever, you will be inducted into the Militia. The Militia Commander,' he nodded at the Range Rover, 'will oversee that and your oath of loyalty to the Militia and to Scotland.

'We call him General Jack – not a real fuckin' general, so don't call him that to his face... Jack will do. After that, we get armed up and equipped. There's a container-load of rifles, all courtesy of Afghanistan. Combat gear as well. Over the next few days, we will live fire with assault rifles and pistols. Pistol ammunition is limited, so only team leaders will have them in addition to a rifle. They are mostly US weapons – the Yanks left a lot of stuff behind – but there are AKs if you prefer. Not much between them, so try them both. But, and this is a big fucking *but*, all members of a section should use the same rifle, same ammo, for obvious reasons. Section leaders have the final say.' He indicated Kenny and Craig. 'If you've any sense, you'll both agree on the same.

'No firing on the range without permission,' he went on. 'We will have lookouts on the surrounding roads to check it is clear to shoot. We don't want any nosy fuckers complaining about the noise. If ordered to stop firing, you stop instantly. Get it?

'Ok, next item. Communications. You won't get your fucking mobiles back until after kick-off day. But don't worry, if we can't get the job done in a day or two, it will all be fucked. So only another few days.

'All the team leaders, that's me, have a sat phone. Secure. Some of the section leaders will get one as well, depending on the job. The supply is limited. Our orders will come through them. Right, I need a runner. Fast on their feet, good with phone, good fucking ears. Any volunteers?' Without waiting for a response, he singled out the youngest member of the team – a tall, gangly, red-haired youth. 'You, Ryan, or whatever yer fucking name is, get out here.'

Ryan scampered out of the ranks looking a little sheepish and took up a position behind Malcolm.

'There's a barn, behind the ruined farmhouse, for sleeping and eating. May be crowded, so you can sleep outside if you like. Latrines in the woods behind the barn. Food will be delivered from the main house. The main house and the gardens around it are totally off limits. Any questions?' He paused. 'Ok, Kenny, Craig, choose eight lads each for your section. Relax when you've done that. It won't be long.'

Malcolm left them to it and went to talk to the other team leaders who were also dressed in Army gear.

Choosing the sections was so reminiscent of playground football teams that the two section leaders shared a laugh halfway through. Afterwards, they stood a little apart from the others. Kenny scratched at the stubble on his chin and reflected on how quickly space had appeared between him and what was now his section. Although he was proud at having been chosen, he also felt uneasy at the way he was being swept along without time to fully consider what the implications would be. Craig was also silent and rubbed nervously at his eagle wing tattoos. Neither of them had much to say as they pondered what was coming next. Kenny was amazed that some of the lads seemed completely unfazed and were already talking football.

A fifth van turned up soon enough and disgorged another group of men who formed up and were given roughly the same talk by their leader. When that was finished, Malcolm returned to his team and got them back into a line while the other teams did the same. One of the leaders carried over a wooden crate that he dropped in front of them and kicked into alignment with the centre of the line. The men were arranged until there were almost a hundred men lined up in two ranks, with the five leaders standing in front of their own group.

A man appeared from the Range Rover wearing the same combat clothes but with the addition of a black baseball cap. He also had a sidearm in a belt holster. He approached the group and stood on the box, surveying them all for a while.

'My name is Jack. I am in overall command of the Militia.' He had a strong Glaswegian accent but spoke clearly and slowly. 'Your team leaders will have already given you the choice to leave, so if you are not fully committed, step out of line now. Once you have taken the oath, I will explain what is expected of you, and there will be no going back then.'

He stepped down from the crate and, accompanied by the five team leaders, he stood in turn in front of each unit while the leader recited the words, and the oath was repeated in unison by the team.

'I swear my allegiance to the Militia and my commitment to the fight for a free Scotland. I renounce my British citizenship and swear my loyalty to an Independent Scotland.'

The Militia leader then walked along the lines and shook hands with every single man. Alongside him, the respective team leader handed out the Free Scotland armbands to each man. When his turn came, Kenny shook hands and was impressed by the firm handshake and the eye contact. It gave him the impression that Jack knew what he was doing and was determined to see it through. He hoped that was true.

The Militia leader returned to his makeshift podium.

'You are now all members of the Militia. I appreciate that you have trained hard for months with little reward and were not fully aware of what you were training for. I'm sure that most of you have guessed. So, I can tell you now that on successful completion of our mission, you will all be awarded five thousand pounds as a bounty, with the option to stay as a permanent paid member of the organisation.' There was a thin cheer from the ranks.

The Commander held up his hand for silence.

'What the SNP has failed to do in twenty years, we are going to do in one day.' He paused. 'In eight days' time, we are going to take Scotland.

'NO! There will be no REFERENDUM!' he roared.

'NO! There will be no VOTE!

'And NO! We will not be asking permission from FUCKING England!'

At this, a cheer rang out from them all, and some waved their arms and punched the air with their fists.

'ARE YOU WITH ME?'

'YES!' the men shouted and stamped their feet.

Kenny shouted with them; it was an emotional moment that swelled inside him.

The Commander let them cheer for a little while before raising his arms to quieten them down. He continued, 'On Independence Day, IDay, we will announce our independence and we will take Scotland by force. You will already know of the Caledonian Independence Party, and most of you are members. The Party is our political arm, and this will form the new government of Free Scotland. Ok. So where does the Militia fit in? There are three main parts to this movement. The CIP that I just mentioned is the political wing; the regular army; and us, the Militia.'

'We going to have to fight the regular Army?' someone shouted, totally confused.

'No, of course not. The loyal Scots of the regular Army are with us and will be led by General Ogilvy, who is the Commander in Chief in Scotland and has been working towards this for decades. The Militia will assist them in taking strategic sites throughout the country. You, the five teams here, are the best of the Militia, and your job will be to take and hold Faslane, the submarine base, and to secure the major fuel depot up in the hills above it and the nuclear weapons storage facility at Coulport. You will start planning and training for that tomorrow.'

The Commander dismissed them with the promise of food in the barn, and the men made their way there, accompanied by the noise of excited chatter. Kenny fell in beside Craig, and again they felt slightly removed from the body of men that surged around them talking excitedly as they all headed to the barn. Most of them had already slipped on their armbands.

Kenny examined his more closely. It had Free Scotland embroidered across the top of a coat of arms in the shape of a shield, with a unicorn and crossed weapons inside. It was well made and hinted at the deeper level of organisation behind the Militia, which made him feel more confident. It had a broad elasticated sleeve that was designed to hold it securely to the upper arm. He slipped it on over the arm of his shirt and Craig did the same.

'Fuck,' said Craig. 'Know what I mean?'

Chapter 6

Isobel (2022)

The Board meeting had been intense with some heated debate around Richard's new proposal, but in the end they had accepted the need, and she could tell Richard was pleased with the outcome. On the way out she had offered him a lift to the station for the Edinburgh train, and he had suggested they go for a drink first.

Isobel regarded him across the heavily starched pink tablecloth. Pink seemed to be a signature of this Chinese restaurant, and the décor was a weird mixture of Mackintosh and Chinese art. Elongated Mackintosh roses – pink, of course – competed with colourful Chinese landscapes and paintings of exotic birds on the walls. As they had passed the restaurant on the way to her car, Richard had indicated that he was hungry and asked if she'd mind. So, she found herself seated in a corner booth of a near-empty restaurant, surrounded by a sea of pink.

He had changed, lost most of his hair – or so she assumed – as his head was shaved to the bone with only the finest down remaining. It was a ghost of the sandy hair she remembered, although the freckles in his weathered and tanned face were still there.

During the time he had been assigned to the Army's Scottish headquarters and was living in Edinburgh, she had seen him regularly at the Board meetings, but they had not been alone together since their relationship ended. The posting was due to end soon, and he would be posted to England for the next few years. After that, he was very sure, he would be back to command the Scottish regiment. He had called the meeting that evening so that he could tell the Board what he had already told her and James.

As always, she was unsure of his intentions. She knew he was still with Samantha, and she had in recent years resisted the inclination to renew their physical relationship that had endured off and on for many years including, much to her shame, during the time that she was married. They had become lovers at university, but they had never really taken the step into a full-time relationship. Obviously, his career was not conducive to long term relationships, unless becoming an Army wife was in your nature. She was not sure that she could have actually managed to be that sort of wife but was positive that she did not want to try it.

Richard was a dominant lover and knew no other way, and yes, occasionally she enjoyed being sexually submissive; giving herself up to someone else's control in a safe way could be fun. But occasionally was the operative word – mostly she did not want to be dictated to in or out of the bedroom. In the end, she felt that there was something to be said for a less intense lover, where both parties were actually deeply involved rather than one person being intent on striving for perfection. She had known instinctively, even at university, that anything permanent with Richard was not a real possibility for her. He was, she thought, wholly unknowable, and even in the closeness of sex – she would never have described it as lovemaking with Richard – he gave little of himself away. Soon after he had taken up with Samantha, Isobel had decided that there should be no more clandestine meetings with Richard, and for his part he hardly seemed to care.

She thought back over the meeting and how this man sitting beside her, whom she had known most of her adult life, held a power that few other men did. But she was not exactly sure what it was. Whatever resided in him, it was subtle, but men respected him, deferred to him, listened when he spoke, and presumably followed him into battle. She thought some of it was Army training, but it had been in him well before the Army.

He had the capacity to think big, to make decisions that carried weight and consequence, and to believe that he could do it without permission and with utter confidence. Only accidents of history and politics separate the heroes from the tyrants. This evening, he had persuaded the Board to adopt his proposal to form an armed militia, and unlike the last time, he had addressed them with his call to take the decisive step in committing to the revolution. This new proposal had shocked the group. She and James had discussed, over the satellite phones, the reason Richard wanted the meeting, and they had decided not to pre-warn the others so that they would give their initial reactions.

At the start of the meeting, Simon had wanted to discuss the monetary arrangements with the Caledonian Independence Party, but James had interrupted and said that before they discussed financial details, they should hear Richard's proposal because it would substantially alter the need for money, and it was not something that could be left to the future.

Richard had stood up as he often did when making a major point. 'There is another problem that we need to address, and it will add considerably to the financial load. I have already discussed this with Jack, and we are in broad agreement.'

Jack acknowledged this with a brief nod in Richard's direction. James and Isobel exchanged a quick glance; they did not know Jack had been meeting with the Colonel.

'And that is?' asked James.

'The Network is limited by the necessity I have to maintain security, so the ultimate aim has to remain known by only the most committed followers of the cause. It has therefore limited me in recruiting large numbers, and although I believe that when the actual event takes place, whole units in the Scottish regiment will follow their leaders, I cannot guarantee that all will. So, we need another force.'

It was clear to Isobel and James that the others were not sure what he meant, but they stayed silent, letting them digest it.

'You don't mean the Police, do you?' said Maggie.

'No. The Police are a closed group, and we have no influence there at all. Does the CIP have any police members?'

'No, none at all,' said Isobel, 'as far as we know.'

'We need something new, something we have complete control over. An armed force, a militia.'

James and Isobel watched the others, interested to know how they would react. Stevie and Maggie were taken aback, and Karen looked horrified, while Simon seemed surprised but not unduly worried.

'Jack and I and some of my senior men have put together a proposal of how this would work. Recruitment, training, security, organisation, that sort of thing. Jack has a handout with the details.'

'No! Surely that's a recipe for disaster,' said Karen. 'You'll likely create a monster that you cannot control. An armed force? What will they do after the takeover?'

'We have thought of that. We will have a significant number of trained men that can be assimilated into a border force, new police force, coastguard, navy, or absorbed into the new Army once independence is complete. Remember, we will need to rebuild all these institutions.'

Karen shook her head in denial.

'But before that, we think it should remain independent from the Army, and administered and led by Jack here. Does that ease your concern?'

Karen did not answer.

'We need them. We cannot take a country half-heartedly. You only need to look at the number of failed coups, people who thought they only needed a handful of men to storm the parliament building and take the radio station, to see that. We need to be over prepared, not skimping on this. Remember, I will not have the whole Army in Scotland; I will only have a proportion of it.'

'You've been telling us for years that the Army is what we need to take Scotland, and now you're saying it can't do it.

There are just as many failed army coups as there are successful ones,' said Karen. 'I have always had doubts about relying completely on the Army.'

'The thing to remember with armies is that generally soldiers are conditioned to obey orders, and their loyalty lies with the unit. It's why so many military uprisings are successful, and those that are not are usually the ones where another part of the armed forces remain loyal to the government and intervenes. That won't happen here. We know that there are already a large proportion of people who want a free Scotland. I believe that proportion is just as high, if not higher, among Scottish troops.

'Before IDay it cannot be general knowledge, but when it becomes clear what the aim is, it will make a big difference, and I am convinced that almost all Scottish soldiers will follow their officers when they know the purpose of the takeover. The Militia will be most needed on IDay to take and hold objectives and to support the Army. As I said before, we are not just rolling into Holyrood and the BBC. We are going to take every port, every airport, every major government building, the media centres, the police HQ, military installations – need I go on? The list is long.'

Karen still looked unconvinced. 'It should be the people that we are mustering support with to make sure it is successful.'

'And how do you propose we do that?' said Richard.

'Look at Sudan a couple of years ago. It was the people who overthrew the government, without any help from the army,' said Karen.

'Yes,' James cut in, 'but creating chaos and leaving a total vacuum in government that the army filled. They ended up with a military government.'

'Doesn't anyone worry we may have that problem here?' said Karen.

Richard laughed. 'Let's not get carried away. Taking over the country will be my part, and it will be easy compared to what you as the new government have to do afterwards.

That will be much harder. Surely, the creation of a civilian militia, directly under the control of the Board, puts your mind at rest?'

Karen tossed back her long hair but said nothing.

'What sort of finance are we looking at?' asked Simon.

'I can't give you an exact figure yet. We have been working on recruiting around a thousand, split into teams of fifteen to twenty men each, so between fifty and sixty teams spread around the whole country. We will recruit young, part time, volunteers and committed Bravehearts; most will have jobs, we think, but we will pay everyone a retainer, probably around a thousand each, whether they have jobs or not. We will pay platoon commanders – we are calling them team leaders – we will pay these leaders a full-time salary. Also, there will be equipment and training costs, but these will be minimal in comparison to the retainer for a thousand men.'

'Ballpark?' said Simon.

'Two million plus, a year. That includes equipment.'

It amazed the others that the billionaire did not blink an eyelid; they supposed that if your income was over a hundred million a year, you'd need something to spend it on.

He merely nodded and said, 'Five years max, and I expect some position in government as well as recognition, and if all goes well some recovery of funds when we have control of the coffers, so to speak.'

'Aye, King Simon!' said Karen. 'And no way. We have to fund a far better society, not make mega-rich people richer.'

James held up a hand to calm her. 'We can't expect this sort of finance for no return. We should leave it open to discussion.'

'These will be mercenaries who can be bought by the highest bidder,' said Karen. 'We will have no control, just a bunch of trained neds. And why are you only talking about men? Are women excluded from this?'

'No, of course not,' said James, 'no reason why they cannot be female as well – we will not restrict that. And not mercenaries, not neds, but Bravehearts; Scottish lads with a cause. Oh, I mean all young people with a cause.'

'Bravehearts?' Karen laughed.

'After the film about William Wallace,' said James. 'These will be young men, and women of course, wholeheartedly committed to a free Scotland. Just like history before us, we can use the enthusiasm and bravery of the young to commit to a cause. Wars are mostly fought by them. I can see the advantage in that and, like Richard says, we cannot go into this unprepared. It has to be overwhelming, unstoppable. I think it's not only a good idea but a necessary one.'

Isobel was nodding. She was already mentally adding a thousand new members to the CIP. 'We can throw in reduced party membership and pay the retainer through the party office. Some may even be useful for campaigning if they can be persuaded to. I'm for it.'

'How can we arm this militia, then?' said Stevie. 'Can the Army really supply that many extra rifles? Or do you mean just armed with batons, like the Police?'

'No,' said the Colonel, 'they will be armed. We will have to arm them. I have some useful contacts that I made in Afghanistan, and the place is awash with small arms but lacking in cash. I can get a container load of weapons for about two hundred thousand, which will include the transport by truck across Europe.'

'That's not possible. I don't believe you can just transport a container of weapons into the UK without someone checking,' said Stevie.

'Good point,' replied Richard. 'It has never been done before with weapons, only for people smuggling and contraband. There is a risk, but less risky than if you transport it in many small loads. As I understand it, the first part of the journey of the truck is easy enough, as it can pass through well-established border crossings where money buys safe passage. It will then reach a depot somewhere in Eastern Europe, where it will be stored overnight. Another container arrives at the same depot on the same night. This container is entirely legitimate; it will be one that circulates between European ports like Rotterdam and Hamburg and the big container port at Felixstowe in the UK. It delivers goods from Europe to the UK and the reverse. It moves between these ports on a near weekly basis.

'In the depot this container swaps identities with the one carrying the guns. Let's call it container A, from Afghanistan, for short, as it gets complicated. Container B is the legit one. Container A becomes container B. All its ID numbers, electronic tracking, and logistics tags are swapped. Container A is made up to exactly match B. Container B has a distinctive and very visible paint splodge on it, so is easily identifiable. Container A now looks like B even down to dents and rust patches. It crosses the Channel as though it was B. Border guards and customs agents are so used to seeing it, helped by the paint splodge, that they are very unlikely to check it among the thousands that arrive every day. They know it will contain consumer goods, kettles or fridges, just like it says on the manifest.'

'But they don't have to look inside nowadays – they have sensors and stuff,' said Stevie.

'If discovered, could it be traced back to us?' asked Simon.

'True, there are sensors that detect heat or carbon dioxide from breathing and chemical emissions from drugs, but they would have to open the container to find inanimate objects like weapons. Only a tiny percentage of the thousands of containers that pass through each day are physically checked. There is a high probability of success. Yes, Simon, there is a risk, of course, but even if discovered it would not necessarily lead back to us, although we would lose the money. These people have a lot of built-in "circuit breakers" to protect them and their wealthy clients.'

'Sounds possible then,' said Stevie.

'Once in the UK, Container A is taken to another convenient depot to await the arrival of Container B, which will arrive empty. The paperwork says it is empty and sold to a new owner. The electronic swap again occurs overnight, and to be safe the identifiable splodge is painted over on A. Container B then returns to Europe to pick up its original cargo. There will be a few disgruntled customers who complain about their vacuum cleaners or suchlike being delivered a week late, but nothing that flags up a warning. This is to keep the paperwork all in order, as the system presumably needs to operate long term. Container A is then released to us on the second half of the payment, and I will select careful drivers for the trip to Scotland.'

He paused and looked at Simon.

'The payment is to be in US dollars, Simon, so it's a little less than it sounds in pounds!'

'Remember, with my financial contribution, I expect to be at least an honorary president,' said Simon. Isobel was not so sure that he was joking.

'I'll need to make some changes to my government plan then,' said James, continuing the good humour.

'In order to take the country and then implement the sort of major systemic change that you envisage,' said Richard, 'requires not only decisive action but the acceptance of some risk.'

*

The warm spicy smell of the food returned her to the present, as the waiter placed their main courses in front of them.

'You're very quiet,' said Richard. He pushed the chopsticks to one side and signalled to the waiter that he wanted a knife and fork.

'Just thinking. The militia was a surprise, but everyone agreed eventually. You must be pleased.'

'Yes, I am. Karen abstained, remember, so not a unanimous decision.'

'Yes, it's hard for her.'

They ate for a while in silence.

'Do you want me to come back to your place tonight?' he said, as though it was only yesterday and not several years since they had been together.

She looked him in the eyes – there was no expectation, no excitement, just a simple request. She shook her head. 'No.'

The fact that he did not show any disappointment did not surprise her.

*

She remembered the night she first met him; that very first meeting. He was so tall, so athletic, so handsome looking, *and* he had come to rescue her when the meeting was getting out of control. She never did understand what he saw in her. She was ordinary to look at and she knew it – mousey brown hair, a little on the plump side, curvy if you were being generous. Homely, her mother called her, even though she knew her daughter hated the term and hoping perhaps to encourage her to adopt some changes. Her mother mostly overlooked her intellect and her drive and commitment to any challenge she took up.

She recalled the first time they had got together. There were far fewer people at the subsequent meeting a week after the first. She had gone early, but several people had showed up before Richard, so she did not get a chance to speak to him privately before the meeting. He had smiled at her when he arrived, sat near to her, and she caught him looking at her several times when he thought she would not notice. It made the evening much more exciting. James, the civil engineer, and Karen, the dark-haired student who she remembered from the first meeting, had also attended.

Isobel opened the meeting and the group had discussed how to move forward. The prevailing mood seemed to be for a series of rallies in George Square or outside the Scottish Office in Edinburgh, to draw attention to the issue and to have it once again on the political agenda. Support for the SNP was also raised, and the need to raise funds for more Scottish Nationalist MPs. It was obvious Isobel did not support this latter suggestion and pointed out their right-wing tendencies.

Someone raised the issue of the recent activity of the Scottish National Liberation Army, and Richard had snorted and told them that was probably best avoided. Sending fake or impotent bombs to royalty or blowing up the odd electricity pylon would not achieve much except raise police awareness, and they did not want that. And they should be thinking along bigger lines.

Jake – the gangster, as she thought of him – had turned up even though she had not phoned him. He was dressed in the same suit, only this time it had darker patches where the rain had soaked into the shoulders. She was not sure if that was the same open shirt as well. He smelled of smoke. He pulled up a chair and joined the group. He rebuked her for not contacting him, but after that he said little but listened politely, and by the end of the evening she was a little less frightened of him.

By the close of the meeting, they had agreed to organise the first rally in George Square and had formed a committee consisting of Isobel, Richard, Karen, and James. James had been against being on the committee at first, but there were so few offers from within the group that he accepted when Richard asked him. They agreed to produce a newsletter and make up posters and flyers for the first rally.

Jake had hung back until only Isobel and Richard were left. He approached them, handed her a wad of grubby banknotes, and told her that he was happy to finance the rally – for printing, postage etc. Isobel had immediately refused, remembering that the barman had previously hinted he was on the dodgy side, and she was worried about the legitimacy of the money. Jake insisted that it was a gift not a loan, and in his longest sentence yet he had added that he did not want his kids growing up in anything other than a free Scotland. Richard stepped in and took the cash, thanked him for it, and told him it would all be used in the cause and accounted for.

There was five hundred pounds, mostly in single pound notes and fivers, with a rare tenner. More money than a student sees in a year or two, come to that.

When the meeting had wound up, she and Richard stayed on for a drink. She was pleased that he seemed interested in her, and she told him that she had grown up in a middle-class family living out in the suburbs, and that her mum had been a teacher and her dad an accountant. She was doing a degree in History and was planning on going into teaching, but she had a deep interest in politics and wasn't sure whether the two could be combined. She felt relaxed in his company, although she did not learn any more about him than she knew from their first meeting. He seemed to prefer to ask questions rather than answer them.

She had already decided, and all he had to do was make a move; she was thrilled by the wait to see if he would. On the walk back to her halls, they chatted easily, and after a while she had taken his arm and moved closer, and it seemed natural enough. When they reached the entrance, he had without preamble turned her towards him and kissed her. It was a good kiss, a sensual kiss, and one that spoke of experience as well as desire. When she came up for air, she had invited him up to her room without hesitation. She ignored the smirk of the warden seated at his table as they passed.

In her room, he pressed her back against the closed door, captured a hand in his and held it by the thumb above her, and then did the same with her other hand, capturing both her thumbs in his one hand. His grip held both her arms above her head, while with his free hand in the small of her back he arched her body against his. He kissed her again deep and hard. She had never known a man so confident, so sure of what he was going to do and so in control, which was far removed from her previous experience of nervous, fumbling students. Her willingness to submit surprised her, as did the pleasure that came with it. That first time with Richard had forever claimed a place in her memory.

Chapter 7

James (2022)

James sat in a comfy chair, placed so that he could see the view of the street through the window. He was reading some obscure philosophy book by some long-forgotten author. He had continued to widen his search for new ideas, hoping to come up with inspiration for a better way to manage a country. Recently, he noted, there had been some well publicised critiques of capitalism that pointed out the long-term disadvantages of the system; perhaps there was hope yet. He was struggling to extract anything useful from the dense prose of this book, and taking notes in the margins with a pencil or underlining paragraphs that at first reading seemed significant, did not help. As was often the case, the philosophers were good at deep erudite theory and complex ideologies that showed off their intellect, but not so good at explaining how to put them into practice to solve real world problems.

None of the texts really allowed for human nature and the fact that self-interest seemed to be evolutionarily built into all humans, with some more endowed with it than others, and these were often the ones who rose to the top to take control and tilt the system to their own advantage. These were the people who put themselves or their families, and even their local groups, before the greater good. Unfortunately, capitalism was the only system that allowed for this and thrived on it, which was perhaps why it had been so successful.

However, something in this particular manuscript had given him an idea that he could work on. Government could have the most profound effect on the economy, society, culture and the wellbeing of people, so was arguably the most important profession, yet it was run largely by amateurs.

The Civil Service did most of the day-to-day running but were departmental silos and often commanded by misguided politicians.

Why not train people to be professional administrators? Educate them widely in all aspects that affect good governance: town planning, transport, energy, housing, economics, population, resource distribution. Further, train them to stand apart from politics and vested interests, and to be aware of their own personal bias and personalities, much like the self-awareness training that psychologists and counsellors undertake to avoid judging or putting their own slant on the problems of their clients. Call them 'Commissioners' and make them part of the parliamentary process, and position them as leaders of citizen panels, set up to monitor government at both local and national level, with the power to challenge, verify and veto new legislation or major decisions. Perhaps AIs could be developed to support unbiased decision making, and to ensure that they benefit the most people while taking into account the effect on other local and regional areas.

He had begun to think that he was looking in the wrong place, and that perhaps the best government should remove all ideology and theory and be operated on purely engineering principles. If there's a problem, fix it. Need a system, then design one. If it works, do not mess with it. If it needs improving, improve it. If it's fucked, scrap it and make a new one. Make the best decision on the best available data.

He knew that it would be hard to make significant changes to a system that for centuries had provided growth, jobs and better lives for millions of people, but which had become ever more efficient at pumping wealth upwards through the 'gaping maw of capitalism'. This last had been a favourite phrase of his father.

James was an engineer, and he recognised that it had instilled in him the need to build, fix, or improve things. His father – also James, but known as Jim – had been a hard-wired socialist and had believed that the unions and the labour party could change things. His son had shared that view for a long time before coming to realise that change required more than politics.

He came from a long line of shipyard workers; both his father and grandfather before him had built ships. His father had been a welder and his grandfather a riveter, essentially the same job just in different eras, but both were key skills in the building of the mega-structures that were ships. His father had taken him as a child to the yard to show him what it was all about. James remembered the noise, the continuous clamorous clash of metal on metal, the roar of the smoky diesel engines driving the giant cranes, the huge flanks of steel towering above him, the wet, gritty, slaggy grime that was everywhere. He recalled most vividly peering through the black visor of a welding mask, his head squeezed in with his father's, and seeing metal instantly turned to liquid under the blast of the ultra-bright light of the welding arc, and, finally, identifying the smell of burning steel which for as long as he could remember always formed a faintly exotic miasma around his father's overalls.

His father was proud of his work, proud of his skill, and proud of John Brown's, the shipyard with a grand history that built the mighty warships like *HMS Hood* and the Queens, including the last great trans-Atlantic liner, the *Queen Elizabeth 2*, better known as the QE2. He had often been heard to boast that he had welded up most of the hull plates around the Queen's arse. He had always been actively involved with the union at the yard and continued in that role when it was subsumed into the Upper Clyde Shipbuilders.

Over several years, successive Labour and Conservative governments had failed to give wholehearted support to the industry, and as the years passed more yards were closed or were lost to mergers. When another crisis developed and there were more threats of redundancies, and with the government reluctant to throw more money into supporting them, instead of calling strikes the shop stewards at UCS went against all previous labour disputes and staged a 'Work In'. They set out to prove that they could still build ships, and this caught the attention of the media, which raised huge public support for their cause. This persuaded the government of the day to back down and come up with a plan to save the Clyde yards.

James remembered that his father had been a different person during that time – so positive, so enthusiastic, and almost joyful, as though he believed that real change was coming. He believed this would be the start of something much better, with the workers part-owning and part-controlling the yards to make them more efficient and competitive. So, James senior had thrown all his energy into the 'Work In' at the shipyard and worked tirelessly with the shop stewards to make it a success.

This was how James liked to remember his father; a man full of hope and bursting with enthusiasm. It was a good time for the family, and he had never felt so close to his father as in those days. It made such a strong impression on him, because prior to that time his father had not spoken to him about anything other than mundane things like school, football, or family, and even this sparsely.

Jim explained to his young son how during both the world wars the men at the shipyards had contributed massively to the war effort, by building ships at a rate to keep pace with those sunk by Germany. The yard famously completed a destroyer from keel to launch in six months during the First World War. After the more recent war, the boom in shipbuilding to replace the losses of the conflict kept all the yards busy, but instead of modernising and developing the industry, the owners and shareholders took massive profits while other European countries and Japan were developing new and faster methods of modular fabrication. The British shipbuilders were repeatedly undercut on price, but rather than put money into modernisation, the owners expected the workers to work ever harder and with an ever-smaller workforce.

His father also explained why unions were so important, and how throughout history the upper classes had always taken advantage of the workers and kept them in their place by controlling wages, while they got rich on the fruits of their labour. The unions gave power to the workers, as only by being united could they demand better pay and conditions with the threat of withdrawing their labour as a group.

He quoted Marx to his son, and told him how the German philosopher had written that eventually the working class would rise up and take control of what they earned, that the people would own the means of production, and that the natural wealth of the world belonged to the people not the favoured few. 'The revolution is coming, son, you'll see.' James had tried hard to take it all in, but he was too young to fully understand, and for a time he had even assumed that Marx was one of the comedy brothers.

With continuing coverage by the media and strong public backing, some sort of agreement was reached between the owners, the workers, and the government. John Brown's was sacrificed and turned into an oil rig fabrication yard. Many jobs were saved, it was true, but there were still many redundancies. And although they could not touch the shop stewards who had become household names, it did not protect those second-tier union men who had worked hard to organise the workers and now stood out as easy targets. Among them was James's father, who was made redundant from a job he loved, ending a long line of Sinclairs who had worked in the Clyde shipyards.

When his father lost his job, he also lost his pride and his spirit. A man who considered anything more than two drinks with the lads on a Friday night excessive and practically ungodly, now adopted it, opened his arms and his gullet to it, and wholeheartedly embraced it. Being in the pub was preferable to being in the house and exposing his failure to the eyes of his family.

Some remnants of pride stopped him from signing on the 'brew' for unemployment for months, and when James's mother finally persuaded him, he was already too far gone to care about pride, so the money went straight into the coffers of the pub – firstly to pay off his ever-lengthening tab, and then to fund his continuing descent into alcoholism. His mother picked up as much work as she could as a cleaner and fought valiantly to bring his father back, but it was a losing battle. Although she could feed herself and her only child, she could not keep the rent up, and eventually they were evicted from their homely, well-kept tenement into inferior emergency accommodation. By that time, his father was lost to them and living on the streets.

His mother would go out looking for Jim, and if she found him try to bring him home. Sometimes she was successful at this and managed to at least get a meal into him and a scrub in the bath, but he would always be gone by the next day. She found him one night, around the back of one of the pubs he frequented, drunk and rutting like an animal with a homeless woman amongst the debris of used beer barrels, litter and crates of empty bottles. She did not go looking for him again. She told James that his father had gone to live with another woman and would not be coming back.

Not long after, his mother left as well. She died of cancer when James was thirteen; she had put off seeing a doctor until it was far too late to save her.

James senior did not turn up for the funeral, despite repeated attempts to contact him by various members of the family. It was his father's sister, Agnes, who handled most of the funeral arrangements and took James out to live with her in a neat council flat in Drumchapel. James stopped communicating with anyone and refused to go to school. Agnes was a single woman, worked as a library assistant in the local library, and was happy with her life. She had no idea how to handle a teenage boy, so she did not try. She left food outside his room and did not plague him with questions about how he was feeling. She left him alone to mourn in his own way, while she mourned the loss of her sister-in-law and her missing brother in hers. After a month or so, she knocked on his bedroom door and asked if he wanted to visit his mother's grave with her. She was going anyway, so he could come if he wanted.

On the bus back from the cemetery, he asked who Marx was. She took him to the library the next day, and although there were no books by Marx in Drumchapel Library, she looked in the catalogues and selected a few likely looking candidates and ordered them from the central library. When they arrived, they did not look like promising reading material for a thirteen-year-old boy, but she took them home to him anyway. Whether he read them or not she was never sure, but he did become a regular visitor to the library and started to read several books a week, with no seeming preference for any genre. He read voraciously, which pleased her.

The library gave him confidence to return to school. It was his aunt who recognised that James was a bright child and dissuaded him from looking for an apprenticeship, encouraging him to aim for university instead.

He had considered following a degree that would contribute to his desire to know more about politics, like Philosophy or Political History, but in the end he decided that he did not want to completely become immersed in academic subjects nor remove himself from the family legacy of engineering, so he opted for Civil Engineering. Even if he was not building ships, he would at least be building roads, or bridges, or buildings. He attended the lectures on other courses that interested him whenever he could but was glad that he had chosen a more hands-on degree. History seemed too dry and dead to be of much use in the future.

*

Nancy came in from the kitchen carrying a couple of coffees and sat down in the other chair facing the window. James looked up at her and thanked her for the coffee. They exchanged a blown kiss, so minimal it was barely noticeable; just the slightest parting and shaping of the lips they both knew so well. He felt a warm glow for her. He'd had a few short relationships in his student years, but in his final year he'd met Nancy and they had been together ever since.

'Have you noticed the way Richard is giving Maggie a lot of attention recently, almost hanging on her every word? I have never heard him praise anyone else, but he takes every opportunity with her,' she said.

'Hmm, he is just fond of her, I think. He had a thing with Isobel a long time ago, if you remember.'

'Do you think Karen and that Navy man that she's found, Cammy, have a thing?' she asked.

'I never thought about it. Bit of an age gap, though. Did I miss something?'

'It's just the way they are together, and yes, she must be at least fifteen years older than him.'

'You sound wistful; fancy a younger man yourself, perhaps? What's the name of your bridge partner again?'

She laughed. 'No, I prefer old men – much easier to control!'

His relationship with his wife ran deep on many levels. They were comfortable in each other's company, and although she shared his vision for a free Scotland, she was happy to remain in a supportive role. She had her own interests that took up much of her time. Bridge was one of them, and since she had retired from teaching she'd managed a charity shop in Byres Road, to which, he thought, she gave too much time. After she became interested in bridge, she had suggested he take up it as well so that he could partner her. Although he gave it a try, cards were not really in his blood as they were in hers. She accepted his withdrawal with equanimity and immediately found a much better partner. She was now a first-league player, and he was happy that she enjoyed it, although on occasion he did wonder about her relationship with her somewhat younger male partner.

Would he mind if she had found a little pleasure on the side? He was not sure; at his age it did not seem as important as it once would have been. Perhaps all marriages had their well-kept secrets. And he was not entirely free of guilt, he reminded himself. He had been unfaithful only once over these many years, and that for a few brief months. He regretted it. It had been foolish, and he had been led along, he knew. He had been in his late forties and overseeing the planned extension of an NHS clinic on the city's north side. He had attended the existing building to verify the layout, take some measurements, and locate the service and sewage points. On his arrival, a community nurse assistant had been allocated to show him around. He presumed that was to prevent him blundering into any rooms already occupied by patients or staff.

He would have preferred to work alone, but Marie turned out to be pleasant company and they got on well together. So much so that James had strung out the job over two days, which was totally out of character. Marie was a recently divorced fifty-year-old with a bottomless pit of banter and an amazing shock of red hair. She had blue eyes and pale skin that burned immediately on the slightest exposure to the sun, she told him, and freckles that she hated but he adored. She was fun to be around and flirted outrageously with him, even after he explained he was married. He invited her to have lunch with him, and much to his surprise she readily accepted, and they did the same on the second day.

He was smitten, and so it seemed was Marie. She had a small one-bedroom apartment in a Housing Association, and although she worked all week, he could manufacture some weekend work so they managed to meet fairly frequently. He bought her gifts and helped out with money if she was behind in the rent, and he brought groceries so that he would not appear at her door empty-handed expecting her to supply the refreshments. He always brought more than she needed. She told him she loved him after a couple of months, and he responded in kind. He felt young again, and in bed they were like two teenagers rediscovering sex. Marie had no children and her husband had left some years before, enticed away by a single mother with a ready-made family of two small children. It still angered Marie to talk about it.

James had no children either, and in the first hot flush of romance he had considered leaving his wife for the first and only time. James's careful nature had held him back, and he told himself he would not even consider it until more time had passed and they were both sure. Marie did not press him but often remarked how alone she was.

He should have guessed earlier, as there were some warning signals that all was not as it seemed. Sometimes she would call off without much notice, citing a friend in need of help or a course at work that she had to attend. Once or twice, in what should have been relaxing and loving post-sexual moments, he noticed that the pupils of her eyes were narrowed down to pinpoints, not dilated with love. It was so totally at odds with the warm moment that he at least was feeling that he could not explain it. It was as though she was high on drugs or angry with him. He dismissed it at the time, but it worried him when it happened more than once.

The fall came after about six months. James had been trying to arrange a weekend away for them, as Marie had always complained she never got taken on holidays. She seemed strangely hesitant about the weekend that he had planned, using work as an excuse. Marie had indicated that two weeks in Spain would be more what she was thinking of as a holiday, and they had had some angry words. She had got up, still angry, to use the bathroom and left her phone on the bedside table, which was unusual for her. He recalled that she put her phone away somewhere whenever he was in the flat – so it would not disturb them, she had said.

A text pinged in, and although the content was not visible, the sender was. It was Mike. She had never mentioned a Mike before, and when she returned, she had pulled no punches when he asked her. 'The man I love,' she said. 'The man I'm waiting for, my soulmate. He will leave his wife one day, and then I'll be happy.'

It turned out Marie was a consummate liar. She did not want James for anything other than financial support, sexual gratification, and a way to make Mike jealous. He had jilted her to concentrate on his marriage, but apparently had taken up with Marie again soon after James appeared on the scene. So, in that she had been successful.

James was absolutely shocked. He could not believe he had been so taken in, that words of love could be so casually abused, that he could be so easily used and discarded. As for Marie, she had already decided that it had gone on long enough, and this turned out to be a perfect opportunity to end it.

James had been miserable for days and had no-one to share the pain with. He had tried once or twice to contact Marie again, thinking she may have softened, but she resolutely refused to respond to all texts or phone calls. It did not take long for James's analytical brain to start pointing out the hypocrisy of the situation and the irony of what seemed like punishment for his own abuse of the love and trust of his wife.

It was a long time ago, and he had grown up a lot since then and had learned a lesson or two from the experience. After the affair, he had thrown himself ever more deeply into the cause, which helped to take his mind off Marie and his foolishness. It was around that time that he had become the de facto leader of the group, largely because there were no other takers. This was not only because of his tendency to chair and manage the meetings, but also his ability to express his knowledge and ideas about political theory and reform to the other members of the group.

The years of studying had had their effect, and he had matured in that regard as well. He could still wince with embarrassment at the memory of how, as a young adult, he had believed he had outgrown his father's teachings on socialism. He had even, for a time, believed completely that a benign dictatorship was the only feasible way to govern a country without becoming bogged down in endless talk;

a single brilliant mind making perfect decisions from perfect information, unencumbered by influence or favour. As he grew up, though, he realised that this was as far from possible as those paper theories with no substantive way to make them work were useless. With the added disadvantage of the inevitable corruption that always followed unlimited power, and which was often repeated as dictatorships rose and fell in the world.

It was perhaps true that he did not care as deeply as the others if Scotland continued as a vassal state to England or became independent, but he had seen that a newly independent country would be an opportunity to put in place some much-needed improvements to government. He had spent many hours superimposing various largely impractical systems onto a virginal Scotland.

Chapter 8

The Plan (IDay minus 1 year)

They were waiting on Karen and Lieutenant Cammy MacDonald. Karen had recruited him last year, but this would be his first Board meeting. Nancy had wondered whether they were romantically involved, but James had concluded that the age gap was probably too great. He had met him several times but always with Karen, and he still could not tell for sure. She trusted him, and that was good enough at the moment. Nancy's searches could find nothing in his background that would suggest he was anything other than loyal to the cause. What he brought to the table was astounding and well worth the risk. He was looking forward to the surprise of the others when the lieutenant revealed what he could deliver.

All the rest were here. Maggie and Stevie were already seated and poring over spreadsheets of something or other, while Simon stood behind them occasionally explaining some figure. Richard and Jack were in a deep conversational huddle over by the door. Isobel was chatting to Nancy. Richard broke away from Jack and approached James and the others at the table.

'Recruitment numbers for the Militia are a bit lower than I had hoped for. Does anyone have any ideas how to reach more people?' As usual, Richard delivered this question in his terse, very English voice; it was so blandly flat that it could hardly be called an accent. It had been acquired after many years' service in the British Army. Although born in Edinburgh, he had been educated at an English public school, where he claimed any trace of a Scottish accent had been beaten out of him.

'What about the prisons, the prisoners? Can we use any of them?' suggested Simon.

'In the future perhaps, but I don't see any way of getting them out of prison and into the Militia in a way quickly enough to help on the day. Would we want them anyway? They would probably be more interested in getting home than joining a revolution. Maggie and Stevie have been working on restructuring the prison system, which needs to be sorted out anyway, but it's a long-term thing,' James replied.

'You could try to recruit more women; you have female soldiers in the Army,' said Maggie.

'True, and there are a small number in the Militia, but women are less likely to want to paintball or do combat training,' said Richard, and quickly added, 'but of course we accept them if they are willing.'

'Don't we have enough manpower anyway?' said Isobel. 'We have the Militia for the mundane jobs and the Army to take the strategic sites.'

'No,' said Richard. 'It's not going to work like that. I can't expect British soldiers to go to war on home territory and fight men who were their comrades yesterday. Remember, although I have a network of officers that are fully aware of the revolution, many of the men do not know the full purpose and they won't know until IDay. The Militia will have to do the fighting and perhaps the killing. We are still short of manpower for the Militia.'

'We're recruiting and building up the number of teams, but it's a slow process,' said Jack, coming over and taking his seat at the table.

'We could be a little less strict on our screening of the Party membership applicants, if that would help. At the moment we only pass the names onto you if we are sure about their commitment, and also only those who are relatively young,' said Isobel.

'Good idea,' said Jack. 'Send their details across to me even if you are not so sure, and I'll get the relevant team leader to vet them before we take them on board. Let's up the age limit to forty. Forty is not so old, you know!'

He was interrupted by the arrival of Karen and Cammy. Nancy answered the door, and they bustled in still sharing some private joke. Karen looked as good as she always did, with her long mane of black hair. *Surely she must be dyeing it at her age*, thought James.

She had told them that Cammy had turned up at the Party office looking to join, and it was not until sometime later that she found out he was a naval officer – and not only that, but in the submarine service. He was disgruntled with the Navy because of a perceived preference to promote English officers over those from a Scottish background, which he claimed had held him back. His commitment to Scottish Independence had led him to join the Party, and although it was permissible for a member of the armed forces to be a member of a political party, he did not think it wise to advertise the fact so he had kept it quiet to avoid damaging his career.

'Ok, everyone, let's open the meeting,' said James, as he waved everyone to their seats. When everyone had settled down, he turned to Richard. 'First, let us all congratulate Richard on his promotion to General. Well deserved, I'm sure.' There was some light polite applause around the table.

'OK, the main item on the agenda today is the plan. Richard and Jack, the floor is yours.'

'Evening, everyone, good to see you all again, sorry for missing the last two meetings,' said Richard. 'As most of you are aware, last month I was promoted to Major General, and I will take up the post of Military Secretary and General Officer, Scotland – yes, I know it's a strange title, but there is a lot of admin – in a couple of months. In brief, I'll control everything to do with the Army in Scotland. So, ladies and gentlemen, the time is now or within the next three years, as after that I will be retired – unless there are exceptional circumstances. And I intend there to be just that – very exceptional circumstances.' He looked around the room, but no one spoke.

'I started with a core of fellow officers, and many of them have now attained senior ranks and they themselves have built up their own networks. So there are several layers of younger officers in junior ranks below them. Over the last few years, we have expanded those with full knowledge to include NCOs. For the last five years the senior echelon has been actively positioning these people into posts in Scotland. There are also a considerable number of Network members who are now retired from the Army, and some of these have civilian jobs that may be useful, while others have been incorporated into the Militia – some as team leaders. There are five other senior men – not necessarily in Army seniority; one, in fact, is a sergeant – who will be regional military commanders.

'You've mentioned them before.' said Isobel. 'Why do we need them?'

'Think of them as managers. They will be responsible for the local plan in each area: Highland, Argyll, Central, Glasgow and South. I will have Edinburgh and the east coast under my control. Remember, it is a whole country, we are not just storming Holyrood. There are a lot of locations that require to be controlled, and it takes a lot of planning and organisation.'

'You said we were short of men, how many regular soldiers will we have?' asked Isobel.

The General paused for a moment but continued as if he had not been interrupted. 'There are significantly more NCOs in the Army than officers, and we have been careful to recruit only those that have little connection to England and have expressed a loyalty to Scotland. NCOs and troopers are more likely to be committed to Scotland because they are more likely to have family connections and roots here, but their level of awareness of the plan has been limited, although in some cases they have been brought into full knowledge.

'In short, ladies and gentlemen, I will be able to bring almost every Army unit of the Scottish force over to the cause, with either an officer or an NCO ready to take command at platoon level. That is all the battalions based in Scotland. There are, however, some problems. There are two Royal Marine units that I have no control over – one at Faslane, and another at

Arbroath. Both of these need to be dealt with, firstly to secure the naval base and Coulport, and secondly to ensure we do not have an army of Royal Marines rampaging in our rear. There are also some smaller units scattered throughout Scotland, such as the Engineer Company at Kinross.

'Apart from the two Marine units and Lossiemouth airbase, my intention is to leave the smaller non-combat units alone, but each will have a small detachment assigned to monitor them and, if necessary, block their exit from their bases until reinforcements can be brought in if it looks like they may cause trouble.

'The 4th Battalion of Scots are based in Catterick and have a much higher proportion of English troops – although I have a small number of loyal men there, I do not have overall control of this unit, and there is no way to bring them into Scotland before IDay.'

'What about the TA?' said James.

'Good question, and these are included in my figures. The Territorial Army no longer exists. It is called the Reserve these days, and they are integrated into the Army, the Lowland Battalion. Members of the Reserve are all embedded in Scotland, so we expect a high degree of loyalty, but on the down side, because of the part-time nature of their role we have had less time to recruit and solidify units. I will plan a major exercise for the time so that all the reserve units will have already been called up and will be available on IDay.

'Now to answer your question.' Richard glanced at Isobel.

'The British Army does not distinguish between home nationalities so I don't know the exact figure, but using next of kin home addresses I estimate around 75% of the men will be of Scottish heritage. This is higher for the Reserve units. The Army recruits into the Scottish Regiment from anywhere, but of course predominantly the men come from Scotland, with a small proportion from the north of England. Counting backroom, tech, engineers, I have 10,436 men to start with, so call it 7500 of Scottish heritage, and allowing for a few to refuse to comply, my best guess is around 7000 soldiers. They will be sworn into the Scottish Army on day one. They will all have committed officers or NCOs to command them, and to administer the oath and issue insignia and armband.'

'Is that really necessary?' interrupted Isobel. 'It sounds a bit weak.'

'Soldiers fight for their unit even if they don't always realise it. So yes, badges and insignia matter, and in this case the Free Scotland armbands will help to promote solidarity and unit loyalty. Great design by the way, Maggie. I believe you did the work.'

James noted this with surprise, as Richard rarely gave praise or acknowledged any of the work that the others had put in. He must have a soft spot for her, as it was not the first time he had shown her attention.

Maggie smiled back. 'Yes, I'm rather proud of it. For anyone who has not seen the drawing yet, there is a crown at the bottom, being stood on by a unicorn rampant, representing Scotland. The crown has three prongs remaining, the fourth broken under a hoof, and to the right of the unicorn is an axe/ hammer combination to represent the workers, crossed with a sword to represent the revolution. The whole contained in the obligatory shield and the words "Free Scotland" arching over the top.'

'Why a unicorn?' asked Jack.

'The unicorn is the heraldic animal representing Scotland in the United Kingdom's Coat of Arms, but it goes back further in being representative of Scotland,' explained Maggie. 'It is normally shown with a golden chain wrapped around its neck. Obviously, we have lost the chain!'

'Thanks, Maggie. We're asking a lot of the troops,' the General continued. 'I believe most will follow their officers or NCOs, but they will be nervous and unsure so I can't send them up against British Army troops on day one. They will become more committed as a free Independent Scotland solidifies around them... so the Army will do the "take and contain" jobs while the Militia do the …ah, dirty work.' He nodded over at Jack.

Maggie started to speak, but James shushed her and said, 'Let's stick to the agenda for now. Time for more questions later. Richard, please finish laying out the plan.'

The general had, over the years, been less able to attend meetings than the others, so most of the work he had been involved in had been going on out of sight of them. The Board members had been aware of the takeover plan in a general sense, but up to this point they had not considered the practicalities or logistics that would be required to enable it. Their attention had mostly concentrated on the political party and trying to formulate systems and policies to build a better form of government. They had even considered a full written constitution, and Stevie had done some research on various European ones but come back without being enthused by any of them. Karen had not seen the need, and she had pointed out that the most famous constitution which had enshrined in law equal rights and freedom for everyone, had originally excluded all women, black people, or Native Americans.

Jack got up and pinned a large, laminated map of Scotland to the wall, while Richard handed out sheets of paper. James was pleased to see that everything was on paper and that he had adhered to the no-computer rule.

'Page one is the summary – I'll just run through it briefly. All the copies are numbered, and our usual procedure is to collect them back up at the end of the meeting. This is the same way I run my Network groups. Please bear in mind that nothing is totally final. There will be changes. Have a look at the summary page.

'First, the Civilian Objectives – just a list. Close the land border. Secure all the airports. The main ports. The two main rail lines. The BBC and STV stations. The Police HQ. Major government buildings. The two nuclear power stations, Hunterston and Torness.

'Now the Military Objectives. I will already hold all four of the major barracks. English soldiers will be confined to quarters to await repatriation or accept Scottish citizenship. There are three big problems – the Clyde Naval Base at Faslane, the air base at Lossiemouth, and the Marine unit at RM Condor in Arbroath. Coulport, Rosyth, and Leuchars are smaller objectives. Ok, I'll expand on the military targets first.

'The submarine base is home to around 500 Royal Marines and is heavily guarded with armed patrols on constant duty, including fast, armed patrol boats. The gates and perimeter are guarded by Ministry of Defence Police, but although they are armed they are not of the same calibre as the Marines. Arbroath is home to six companies of Royal Marines, but at any one time almost half of them will be on detachment to Royal Navy ships, or away somewhere in the world training or on deployment.' The members around the table were silent, taking that in. It seemed an insurmountable problem.

'I did not realise there were so many Marines,' said Stevie. 'Surely we can't fight them all.'

'Yes, it looks difficult on paper,' answered the General, 'but we have spent a long time planning this. We will use the same strategy for each base: that is, to go in early morning, capture if possible, or kill if necessary, the guards then secure the armoury, isolate the men in the barracks, and prevent any personnel who live off base from returning. Basically, if we prevent the men getting access to their weapons, then a few armed men can contain them. Remember, the guards are not expecting nor will have trained for armed insurrection. They will only be guarding against clandestine terrorist attacks and protest trespassers, and that last is mostly at Faslane. We will announce the independence cause as soon as they can listen and distribute the statement leaflets which guarantee their safety if they comply. They won't have any orders, and Scottish Independence is so well known that hopefully they will accept the fact and remain docile. There is a risk, though, if we do not secure the weapons immediately, as there is a much higher proportion of non-Scots in the Marines and the RAF regiment.

'Because of the nuclear angle, the Clyde base is better guarded than the others, and it will be the hardest target. We still have not yet identified the exact location of the armoury at Faslane, but I'm hoping the Lieutenant can help us with that.'

'Yes, no problem. I know where it is,' said Cammy. 'We all have to keep up our firearms expertise every six months or so, and the armoury is adjacent to the range. It also houses the Marines' weapons. It's a fortress, though, a bunker – impossible to break into.'

'That's good. Another piece of the puzzle. And we don't have to break in, just to contain it and prevent any access.' The General continued, 'That strategy will also apply to Lossiemouth, as it is home to the RAF regiment, which means it again has a large number of combat-trained soldiers and is well guarded. It is now the only fully operational airbase in Scotland. Hopefully, we can take it, leaving most of the Typhoons and whatever other planes are there on the ground, ready to form the future air force.'

'Any Scottish pilots can, of course, take the oath and come over to us,' said Stevie.

'Yes, but probably best not to let them fly for a while. Too easy to desert.'

'The Army has helicopters, though, so you'll have access to them?' said James.

'Unfortunately not. I don't have any influence in the Army Air Corps at all. All their bases are in England, and yes, there are always a few Apaches at Lossiemouth or elsewhere, training in the Highlands. These I will contain on the ground when we take the bases, but I will not have the pilots to fly them.'

'So, we will have no air cover. Won't that put us at a big disadvantage if the English have control of the sky?' asked James.

'What I do have is several very sophisticated anti-aircraft missile systems and a large number of shoulder-launched ground-to-air missiles. While these may not ensure a complete "no-fly" zone, if they are well placed it will make them think twice about flying into our airspace.' He paused and looked around the table. 'Any other questions so far? Ok, I'll go through the Civilian side in more detail.

'First, the roads. Closing the roads for a day or two is largely symbolic – marking our territory, if you like. There is, however, a possibility that England sends troops as an initial reaction. They will need to be stopped at the border, or the whole thing will collapse. So, a company will be designated to hold the two main routes and platoon strength for each major road, and a squad for each minor.'

Stevie raised a hand. 'Surely that's not very likely? England sending troops up the roads immediately, I mean. It would mean going to war. Civil war.'

'Definitely *not* a civil war after IDay!' said the General. 'But it has to be considered – remember the Falklands, the Irish conflict. It would be the first thing I would do in their place, send my nearest troops to the border, but with orders not to engage. This is the most likely response. I will split my strongest – by that I mean most Scottish – battalion between the two main routes East and West, and hold them a couple of miles back from the border. I'll have recon in private cars one and two hours south on all the roads, so we will have advance warning of any column coming north, and time to move the reserve to the right area.'

'I can see that that would tie up a significant number of men, but you said the troops would not be too willing to fight,' said James.

'Ah, yes, good point, but remember it will be different fighting an English invasion of Scotland rather than attacking Lossiemouth or Faslane, and I don't think it will come to a firefight at the border.'

'And if it does, would we win?' said James.

'No,' said the General, 'absolutely not. We could hold them for a few days, but Scotland does not have the armour or the fire support, and by that I mean tanks, artillery and aircraft to match what they could throw at us. That is why the "ace" that Lieutenant MacDonald holds is so important.'

'It's not guaranteed, remember,' said the Lieutenant. Some of the others looked confused.

'Cammy will explain his ace in a little while, for those who have not heard,' said James.

'The Army has enough earth-moving plant to create laybys and turning circles and space for operations at the M6, A1, and the other three major A-road crossing points. We will use media broadcasts to invite local farmers or builders to bring earth-moving plant for the lesser roads.' Richard stopped and glanced over at Maggie. 'I'm sure you've got that in hand?'

'Yes, no problem. It is written into the secondary broadcasts and social media, and it will be couched as an appeal to patriots,' she acknowledged. 'It will go out with a list of all the minor roads so that people in the area will know which road is near them.'

'We stop all traffic, but we allow goods through if they wish to continue,' Richard went on. 'We allow Scots with home addresses through, but turn back everyone else. We only allow people with English addresses to go south.'

'Why stop Scots going south?' asked Karen.

'Just a precaution really, in case anyone thinks it's a good idea to decamp. We don't want queues of cars fleeing Scotland – not a good look,' said James.

'That will be in the broadcasts as well, something along the lines of: "Stay at home and do not travel anywhere for any other reason than your normal work,"' said Maggie.

'Platoons or squads will hold and guard soft strategic objectives such as the ferry terminals, airports, mainline train stations – we won't stop trains at the border; we'll stop them at the terminus – the nuclear power stations, the main government buildings, and the Parliament in Edinburgh. The Militia will take the BBC and STV centres and support Maggie and Stevie with the broadcasts.

'My colleagues and I have completed a strategic plan for the deployment of each unit to their IDay objective. It is not final; it will change and modify as we get closer, but those are the components of the plan. I will order a nationwide emergency exercise two days before IDay, when all leave will be suspended, and this will give time for those on leave to return to their units. Live ammunition will be issued the day before, and we will deploy to the objective areas overnight to be in place for 0600 hours on IDay.'

'Thank you, General,' said James.

'Not quite finished yet,' said Richard. 'One last thing. Now is the time to set the date of IDay. Once it is set, we can then work towards it with a timeframe in mind. I'm suggesting January the first, in roughly eight months' time.' He noted the reactions of those around him ranged from shock to excitement.

'Ah, that might not work for me,' said Cammy.

'Ok. I think it's time we heard from you,' said James. 'Cammy here has an amazing proposition. Perhaps you can lay out the idea now and see what the others think.'

'Thanks, James,' said Cammy, and nervously swept his lanky dark hair back from his forehead, where it promptly returned a few seconds later. 'Firstly, I should say that the idea for this came from Karen herself, so it's all down to her really.'

'If Cammy can pull this off, it will save a huge number of lives, because it will prevent England using force against us,' said Karen. She smiled at Cammy and waved him to continue.

'I've not met all of you until now, but I'm sure Karen has filled you in. I have been a CIP party member since soon after it was formed, and that is where I met Karen. I'm an officer in the Royal Navy and have been for quite some time. Promotion can be slow in the Navy if your face doesn't fit, especially for Scottish nationals. I've spent almost my whole career in the submarine service, latterly with the bombers. The majority of officers in the subs are of English stock, and it is not hard to guess why.'

'Bombers?' said Isobel, confused.

'Sorry, yes, slang for the subs that carry the nuclear missiles. We don't have any airborne bombs anymore. The UK nuclear deterrent, if you like. There are four, and one is always at sea and ready to respond to any nuclear threat. They form the UK deterrent.'

'Why four, if only one is at sea?'

'Good question. There are four basically to make sure one is always out there armed and ready to go. One on standby, and one on downtime, which means the crew are on leave and the vessel is undergoing maintenance. I know that's only three, but one has been out of service undergoing repairs for the last five years or so.'

'Five years! They could've built a new one quicker, surely,' said Stevie.

'Radiation leak – rumour is two crew died, and some are still dying slowly,' said Cammy. 'That's classified, by the way.'

'Certainly kept it quiet. But what good is that to us? England will not see us as such a threat, surely?' said Stevie.

Cammy swept back the hair back from his forehead again. 'I think I can take one.'

When no one responded, James said, 'He means hijack.'

James and Isobel enjoyed the reaction of their fellows as the words sunk in. They had both experienced the same on hearing it and as the possibilities dawned on them.

'Yes, with a little help I can do it, and I have sounded out very carefully a few other men who are committed to independence.'

'Does a sub have control over the nuclear weapons independent of the government?' said Stevie.

'Yes, of course. It is also retribution as well as deterrent. It would be hamstrung if it depended on launch control from London.'

'How does that work?' asked the General. 'Stealing a sub is not so good if we can't use the weapons or at least make them believe that we can use them.'

'There are safeguards, of course, and to launch without government instruction is one scenario that is planned for, but it is looked on as the last resort – even though it is probably the most likely. Three officers have codes and keys, locked in separate safes, and each also has a memorised code – in their heads – pin numbers, if you like. Launch requires two of these to input the codes and turn their keys simultaneously. Obviously, if we hold these three officers prisoner, no one can ever be sure that we can't break them for the codes and therefore have control of the missiles. Especially if we have their families as well, and most families live in the residences on the base or locally in the Helensburgh area.'

'Makes sense,' said the General. 'What about targets? Can the sub set the targets?'

'Yes,' said Cammy, 'same reasoning. No point having all your missiles aimed at Russia when China has just wiped out the UK. Again, target setting requires two input personnel and careful checks. This takes a little time, as each missile carries up to twelve targetable warheads, although mostly they only carry half that number. The UK has a problem keeping its warheads up to date. That's classified as well. And there are limitations to the system. It's no good for surgical strikes, as even firing one missile means six major nuclear detonations.'

'What use is it to us then?' said Isobel.

'Think about it,' replied James. 'It is not just the immense leverage that having access to nuclear weapons would exert, but there is also its financial value. Each one is worth billions of pounds. Think also of the prestige it would carry with the Americans and the rest of the world. Scotland would be a nuclear power from day one. It would give us very useful leverage over England.'

'There is one other thing,' said Cammy. 'They are currently building the next generation of bomber, the Dreadnought Class. The first one, *HMS Ambuscade*, is nearing completion and final fitting-out, and I have been assigned to the build for the last four years. I know the systems from the bottom up, and I have already sailed with her during the extensive sea trials. She will enter service and will be fully armed for her first mission in approximately another year. That's the one I am going to hijack!'

'Fuck!' said Stevie. 'If you can do that, it guarantees our success.'

'I think even Richard is impressed,' said James. 'Is that timeframe good for you Richard?'

'Yes. That's only a small extension. Sometime in May then. Mayday perhaps?'

'Mayday it is then, one year from now! All in favour raise a hand.'

Chapter 9

James (2022)

James delayed a little longer from calling the meeting to order; he was enjoying the sun on his face and listening to the chat around him. It was refreshing to be able to get together, as the Covid pandemic had started to recede and social restrictions had eased somewhat. Richard could not be here, which was not unusual, although his lack of interest in anything other than the military aspect of the cause had begun to be obvious of late. He knew Isobel was of the same opinion and was also worried about the way Jack had seemed to be under Richard's influence.

It was the middle of summer and an unusually warm and dry day for the west of Scotland, so they had moved the meeting out of Isobel's house and into the garden. The garden was large and surrounded by a latticed wooden fence, with some mature trees and bushes providing more screening. It was large enough to prevent them being overheard by any neighbours.

The house had been the marital home, but Isobel's husband – Maggie's father – had left a number of years ago. Isobel did not talk about it much, but James knew the man had never been fully on board with the independence campaign and positively hated the political side of it. Not long after Isobel had founded the party, he had left the marriage, and part of Isobel's divorce settlement had included this 1960s detached house out in the suburbs. He knew Maggie shared the house with her mother, and he assumed Stevie spent a lot of time here as well.

Taking another look around the garden, James made a mental note to himself to make sure the others did not stray into anything that could be a security risk. This meeting was being held to talk about the Party's manifesto and to discuss better ways to govern. It was something a budding political party could surely meet to discuss in the garden of the Party's leader, but better to be careful.

The Board had been divided over whether to put a candidate up for the UK general election and had eventually decided against it. However, they were all in favour of putting up several candidates to stand at the next Scottish Parliament election, even though it was unclear whether the election would be before the takeover. Isobel would be standing and had argued that they would gain much wider recognition as a Party if they had candidates. She felt it would give them a little more credibility post-takeover if the CIP was more readily recognisable. If they had an MSP, even for only a few months, they would learn a lot about the inner workings of the parliament.

Although the chances of getting even one MSP elected were slight, the Board had all agreed, and they had come together to make up a provisional manifesto. They were conscious of the fact that should they be successful they must have some sort of meaningful political structure ready to fill the vacuum, and a manifesto at least laid some of the groundwork for that.

Isobel and Maggie were in the house arranging drinks. Simon was chatting animatedly to Karen, and James had the feeling he was trying to impress her rather than make a political point. It seemed unlikely that his sudden interest in socialist values was for real. Simon still took every opportunity to make his presence felt in the group.

He looked at Karen and noticed that her distinctive long, glossy black hair had streaks of grey in it and had lost some of its lustre, but she was still a good-looking woman. All of us are getting older, he mused.

Maggie came out of the patio doors carrying a tray of tumblers and a jug of cold drinks, the glasses already covered in a coat of condensation, and the clink of ice cubes made a pleasant summer sound. Stevie helped pass them round. Isobel soon joined them, and once they were all seated, James coughed to get everyone's attention, smoothed down his beard, and called the meeting to order.

'The agenda for today is fairly loose, but the main focus should be to discuss the manifesto and make sure we are all in broad agreement with our political programme. First, Isobel, as Party leader, will update us on the "Caledonian Independence Party",' he tipped his glass to her, 'of which we're all members.'

'So far that's about the sum total of members,' laughed Isobel. 'Seriously though, we have just under a thousand members, so it is beginning to pick up. I'm hoping that we can get a few more thousand once we start advertising a bit more widely and as we approach the next election. Most of the new members are down to Maggie and her social media skills. Some of them have become useful activists in the party, and we have identified a small number of... let's call them fervent supporters, not exactly on the same scale as Richard's Network but still a useful number. We have made these people aware of our underlying project, although in a very unspecific way. Some have also been directed to Jack's Militia, including some female members.'

Karen and Maggie added a small cheer at that. Isobel laughed and continued.

'By the way, just to note, that we're not all members, as we decided that Jack and Richard should not be connected to the political party for security reasons.'

'Sorry yes, I'd forgotten they're not members,' said James.

'No problem. The political arm, so to speak, is formally registered as the Caledonian Independence Party, CIP for short. It has made a big difference having office space, and it does make us look much more legit. Thanks to Simon, of course.' She gestured over to him, and he made a slight bow of his head in return.

'Office bearers, besides me, are Karen, Maggie, and Stevie, with them sharing duties at the moment. We also have four volunteer members, including Rena, Simon's...ah—'

'Housekeeper,' Simon finished for her.

'Yes, thanks. Rena and the other volunteers have been great, and the shop front office is mostly staffed by them, which allows for much longer opening hours. We are also on the lookout for likely candidates among the membership that could be recruited to help in government positions when the time comes.

'As for the manifesto, it has been based on what has been discussed between us at some time in the past. So, it is going to be mostly familiar, and if you recognise your particular idea, it's because we stole it.' A few murmurs were heard around the table as some of them remembered the often heated discussions that had taken place over the years. 'The main aim of the manifesto is to lay the groundwork to some of the initiatives we plan to make once in power.'

'Before Isobel talks around the manifesto,' said James, 'let me just recap where we are with our core pillars, or our principles of future government. We have discussed these thoroughly and have distilled them down to these four overarching strategic policies, otherwise known as the big four. They are: One, *Not for Profit*; two, *Fair Economy*; three, *Citizenship*; four, *Sustainability over Growth*.

'First – Not for Profit. No profits should be made from what should be considered necessities for the people and for the benefit of everyone. These are the public services, utilities, transport, health and the care system, state housing, and education. Not for profit does not prevent an income being generated, but this will stay within the system to maintain, improve, or expand.

'Second – Fair Economy. A simpler and fairer tax regime will be initiated. Where profits are made from exploiting a natural resource, such as oil, gas, minerals, or even data which could be considered public property, then taxes will reflect that. Any company that does business in Scotland will pay fair taxes and share profits with those who create the wealth. For example, dividends paid to shareholders will be matched by a proportionate amount to the workers. For smaller companies with no shareholders, half of the profit will be divided among the workers.'

'I think that stifling small companies and penalising large ones may have a somewhat negative effect on the economy,' interrupted Simon.

'We are not ending capitalism, we are just taming it,' said James. 'Remember, whatever happens, we will be flexible. If it doesn't work, we will modify it as we go along. We've always said we will make changes as needed.'

Simon shrugged.

'Third – Citizenship. Citizenship is hard to define in a modern society, but there is an acceptance that the state will look after the individual no matter what, even though the individual may not hold the state in particular high regard and may see it as interfering or demanding.

'We will redefine citizenship so that it is not an automatic birthright, but one that has to be earned and more importantly is valued; and one that can be revoked temporarily or permanently for criminal, terrorist, or destructive behaviour. It will be a two-way relationship between state and the individual, so that all feel they belong, are participating, but also contributing.

'Fourth – Sustainability over Growth. Not just in the sense of climate change or green issues, although both these will be part of the new Scotland. We would aim to be net exporters of green energy by utilising our natural resources for wind, solar, hydro, and tidal. We also include sustainable jobs, sustainable services, and sustainable businesses. Decisions about manufacturing goods should not only depend on cost, as cheaper goods manufactured elsewhere merely moves the profit to big companies and increases transport costs while reducing jobs here. Large infrastructure projects will not be tendered outside the country, and they will not be built merely for prestige but for the best use. That includes shipbuilding, offshore wind turbines, ferries, whatever. Wherever possible we will build and manufacture here with government subsidies, tax breaks, or altered regulation. We will import expertise, if necessary.'

'So much easier said than done... but you all know my feelings on this,' said Simon.

James looked around the table and saw no other signs of disagreement. 'We will make it work; we do not intend to be constrained by the old-world order. We will be the forerunners of a new system, a system adaptable and able to make fast changes, a system much better suited to deal with the problems of the 21st century.'

'Problems?' queried Simon.

'He means climate change, migration, water scarcity, and food shortages,' said Maggie.

'Oh, the doom scenario. Is that not getting a bit farfetched?' said Simon. 'The world has coped adequately so far.'

'No,' said Maggie, raising her voice. 'Glib answers are so much easier! The evidence is in front of us, getting worse every year.'

'It's a cycle: the earth warms, it cools down, ice ages come, ice ages go,' said Simon. 'The earth's orbit around the sun varies. Sometimes it's nearer the sun and the other planets, and sometimes further away. The gravity can influence... can be influenced by the gravity of—'

'And just how exactly does that affect our weather?' said Maggie. 'Fire, floods, hurricanes are not because we sailed too close to Jupiter! Migration is a trickle now. Imagine what it will become when North Africa and Southern Europe become unliveable because of the heat and the lack of water.'

'Doom! Doom! So, how is independence going to fix all that?' said Simon.

'OK, OK! We are getting sidetracked,' said James. 'The point is adaptability, and whether we like it or not, the climate is changing and countries will have to adapt sooner or later. Scotland will at least be one that is prepared for the problems that are coming. Back to business, I think. I'll hand over to you, Isobel.'

Isobel paused a moment and took a breath. 'OK, so the manifesto is largely worked around the Big Four. There are three major areas that desperately need reform. First, the networks – the natural monopolies, if you like. Second, the Health and Care sectors. And lastly to sort out the Benefits/ Employment system with the Ministry of Labour, and that includes housing.'

There was a chuckle round the table.

'What?' asked Isobel.

'Ministry of Labour sounds Orwellian,' said James.

'Ah yes, probably we do need a better name for that. It started as a joke working title – open to discussion,' she said.

'Firstly, the networks, and forgive me if I belabour what you already know. The natural monopolies are the networks that cover large geographical areas where it does not make sense to have two or more suppliers. Railways, roads, electricity, and water are good examples. Thankfully, water is still in public hands in Scotland. The latest iteration of capitalism claimed that even without competition to improve efficiency, these networks would still operate better in private hands. The present poor condition of most of our infrastructure has proved that wrong, and its failure boils down to one simple fact, that private companies generate money for shareholders and the salaries of top management at the expense of maintenance, improvement, or expansion to keep pace with need.

'All networks will be taken into public ownership, without recompense to shareholders who have reaped profits for too many years.'

'That may cause huge reactions from banks, investment companies, and pension funds,' said Stevie. 'Not to mention all the individuals who bought into the privatisation sales.'

'Mostly the well-off,' said Karen, 'and think how many billions of pounds have been paid out over the years.'

'I'll definitely be selling my holdings before the event,' laughed Simon.

'No shame,' said Karen, shaking her head.

'Should we not recompense the individual shareholders at least?' said Stevie. 'And what about foreign investors? We could piss off a lot of countries as well as financial institutions.'

'Yes,' said James, 'we will have to accept that. No normal government could contemplate doing it. We do not need to get elected, nor do we need a public mandate to stay in office. Changes like this can only be made when we hold complete power and control, without having to answer to anyone. The only way it can be done is to do it hard. Isobel, continue if you will.'

'All transport – bus, rail, and ferries will be in public ownership, and income will go back into improving services or financing green alternatives. Again, no shareholders will be compensated, as they have made enough profits already. However, there may be exceptions to this where small local bus services that have provided essential services can be funded or bought out.

'Different modes of transport should not compete with each other, so wherever possible the most suitable method for a particular route should be used so that buses do not compete with trains on short routes, or trains with planes on longer routes. We will also move long distance road freight to rail by imposing stringent tax regimes on HGVs.

'Communications and the postal service should also be considered as service networks. No argument about the landlines being a network, so broadband and traditional phone lines become public, and income should go to improving infrastructure and getting broadband to isolated areas where it has not been profitable to go in the past. Initially we will leave mobile networks in private hands.

'The postal service should not have to compete with the commercial sector or pay shareholders. We will take that back into national ownership, with no compensation to shareholders. But in addition, we will give it a legal monopoly to deliver letters and parcels.'

'Won't that cost huge numbers of jobs, though?' said Simon.

'Yes, but there is an environmental issue here. At the moment, there are literally hundreds of mostly empty vans delivering parcels by different couriers. Sometimes three or four vans complete the same run, on the same streets, every day. Think of the fuel wasted. And these are not well-paid jobs. The Scottish Postal Service will, of course, need a lot more sorters and drivers, so a lot of the manual jobs can be taken up there. One postal system covering the whole country, delivering all the parcels and the mail once a day, makes sense.'

'That will be a war with Amazon,' commented Simon.

'No doubt,' said Maggie, 'but the postal service can always give them a special rate for quantity, and anyway, it will be peanuts compared to the tax they will pay to operate here! We managed before without them, and we can again.'

'OK, so moving on to the NHS, or perhaps I should call it the Scottish Health Service. All private health initiatives will be terminated, and this includes privately-funded hospitals. Private health can continue but only using private facilities with their own personnel. SHS personnel will be banned from private work; if they work in SHS then all their commitment is to that service. Privately-owned staff agencies will be banned. They pull millions of pounds out of health funds every year. There is no reason that the SHS cannot run its own staff banks to cater for those who need flexibility. Shareholders should not profit from health care or from care homes.

'Community care and care homes will revert to council administration as soon as practical. Private care homes will become council property. In this case, homes run by private individuals or family units will be compensated, and if appropriate taken into the service and jobs offered where that is feasible. Large company care home providers with shareholders will not be compensated.

'Workers in community care, care homes, and those in any capacity where their job involves caring for or with people, will have legally enforceable wages linked to SHS pay scales. It is not right that someone working in a bar or stacking shelves in a supermarket can be paid more than a carer where the welfare of other people depends on them.' Isobel paused for a moment.

'This is a great policy,' said Karen. 'It will go a long way to help fix the staffing and bed capacity problem. A fully functioning care home system and community care with spare capacity should have a rapid effect on freeing up hospital beds and lessening the strain on hospitals.'

'But how are we going to pay for that?' Stevie seemed agitated. 'We can't make promises we can't keep before we even start. It just becomes another worthless manifesto.'

'Remember,' chipped in Simon, 'the UK Government pays £60 billion or so a year to Scotland, on top of the tax receipts. That will disappear. It's always been a problem with governments promising the earth but not being able to deliver, except by borrowing and cutting back somewhere else. Scotland won't be able to borrow on the financial markets like England does, until it is much better established.'

'And another thing,' said Stevie, 'nationalisation sounds good, but there is no record of people voting for this stuff – Corbyn did not get far.'

'It doesn't matter what people think. We don't have to get elected,' said James.

'But we will have elections soon after we take power. We still want a democracy, don't we?' said Karen.

'Yes, of course, but we will need time to get the policies up and running. We'll give ourselves two, three, or maybe even more years in power, to give people time to see the changes having an effect. Then we'll hold elections.'

'We can't delay elections for too long,' said Karen. 'We need to get the people behind us as soon as we can. The SNP's reason to exist will have disappeared, so people will surely vote for us, and Labour supporters will see the sense quicker than some of the others. We'll have a massive majority, and it will be seen to be a democratic process even if born out of revolution.'

'Throwing a bit of a spanner into this discussion, but as we are talking about money, there is also the big question of currency,' said Simon. 'Are we just going to depend on the Bank of England, like the SNP suggested? It may not fly so well after we abscond.'

'I already have the solution to that,' said James. 'It is not a problem. We already have our own currency in the Scottish bank notes. Almost all notes in Scotland are issued by the three banks. All we need do is to make it the primary legal tender.'

'Will the banks support that?' said Simon.

'No, unfortunately all three of the "Scottish" banks are not really Scottish; they are owned by English or, in the case of the Clydesdale, by Australian banks. I'll let Maggie tell us more. Maggie, maybe you should start by reading out the Financial Statement.'

'OK, it's here somewhere.' She shuffled through her papers. 'Yes, here, this goes out in the second round of announcements.'

This morning at eight o'clock, Scotland became independent from England. If you have not heard the previous announcements, please check your social media or tune into the TV or radio. Please note that although there will be changes in the future, all law, legal frameworks, and taxes remain as they were.

This statement concerns all of you and is about the financial arrangements your new government has put in place.

Today, Scotland has a new currency. The Scottish Pound. Yes, all those notes you already have are the new currency. English notes are now no longer legal tender in Scotland. They can, however, be exchanged for Scottish pounds at any bank or building society.

Please listen carefully, this is important. All businesses and the self-employed should cease all payments of tax,

VAT, or National Insurance to the English government. For the moment, all rates will remain unchanged, so you should retain the sums as you will be required to pay the same amount to the Scottish Government. From today, any payment you make to the English government may not be recoverable, and you may have to pay twice as you will be liable to the Scottish treasury.

International companies should start separating their tax responsibilities for Scotland from the UK from today's date, without delay, so that tax can be paid direct to the Scottish Treasury.

Individuals should also cease all payments to the English Government. Fees for passports or licences will not be recoverable.

Later today, your new government will announce the Scottish Treasury accounts that the money should be paid into. For the time being, all laws and financial and tax regimes remain unchanged.

'I'll admit it probably needs a bit of tidying up, but that will be the gist of it,' said Maggie.

'Surprised no-one suggested this before,' said Simon. 'What arrangements will we make to receive tax, fees, etc.?'

'Yes, that has been a problem. It will take a while to get control of the SNP government accounts, so we need an interim. We wanted a purely Scottish bank, but most have been swallowed up. Even the Airdrie Savings Bank is gone. But there is one pure Scottish building society left, with headquarters in Edinburgh, and a handful of branches in the main cities – none outside Scotland. We will bring in the Chief Exec on IDay, and if he does not want to be Scotland's leading banker, we'll work our way down their senior management list until we find a patriot who does. There is no reason we can't set up accounts on day one, and then we will release the numbers to the public.'

'Wait, all that sounds good on paper, but won't the currency just go into freefall as soon as you separate it from the English pound?' said Simon.

'Nope,' said James. 'We will peg it to the English pound and force the English government into supporting that while we still have their nuclear weapons in our hands as ransom.'

'It actually sounds as though it may work,' said Simon. 'But what about the rest of the world? They won't just accept a Scottish pound as payment for trade.'

'They will, if it's linked to Sterling,' said James, who stood up and started pacing up and down in front of them. 'Stevie has a good point about the cost of paying for major changes, but we will have other income streams. If all goes well, we aim to have in our possession at least one, and possibly two, of the UK's nuclear deterrent submarine fleet, not to mention any of the smaller nuclear subs that may be in dock on the day. We will own three of the Navy's newest frigates – one is almost complete, and two more are in construction on the Clyde. We will control two major naval bases, an airbase and, last but not least, most of the UK's nuclear arsenal that they so conveniently stored on Scottish soil. What do you think the resale value of a bomber sub would be? Or a ballistic nuclear warhead? A brand-new frigate? Or what would England pay to rent the base or to prevent us selling anything to the Russians or the Chinese?'

'NATO may get a little upset if we start threatening to sell to Russia or China,' said Stevie.

'Yes, probably. That's maybe not such a good idea! But the point is we will hold huge leverage over the English government. Of course, we would try to negotiate reasonable terms so that England would not lose face and give them time to build storage facilities to rehome and move the stuff. There is back rent to be considered as well, and reparations for the squandering of Scottish oil. In any event, they will be paying us billions and billions of pounds. That should see us through the first few years before our currency is recognised and we have an improved tax system that will be acceptable to the international monetary funds. And on top of that, we will invest billions like the Norwegians and the Gulf States. A Scottish Sovereign Wealth fund.'

Karen laughed, and the others joined in. 'So, Scotland will become one massive shareholder while we legislate against shareholders in general!'

James joined in. 'Yep, beat them and join them, I guess! The difference is that the people benefit from the wealth.' He stopped pacing and came back to the table, topped up everyone's drink from the jug, then took his seat again. 'Back to the manifesto, I think, Isobel.'

'In summary, the manifesto will state the return to public ownership of the gas, electricity, telephone, and energy infrastructure, railways and bus services, the landline telephone system, and the postal service. All social care services will be brought under local authority control. There will be separation between the private and national health services.

'The third and final item is the new Ministry of Labour. OK, OK! We don't know what to call it yet – Work, Employment, Opportunity, Citizenship. I favour the Ministry of Civic Contribution. This is still in the development stage, and there is work to do yet. The basic tenet is that everyone contributes in the best way they can. Everyone contributes to society, to making it a better place, the best country in the world.

'Unemployed, disabled – obviously there are limits there – prisoners. We envisage it as an umbrella organisation that incorporates the benefits system, the voluntary sector, and the prison system – at least for low-risk offenders. It will supply workers, and people where work is needed on a voluntary basis. Work that does not take away jobs from others – non-productive work, for example. Jobs like the separation of recycled material, which is really hard to do by anything other than hand. Litter picking, street cleaning, and even companionship for old people, or help with their gardens, their shopping. Yes, it will intersect with some charities, but we will work with them, and charities will become part of that umbrella.

'If there is a shortage of fruit or vegetable pickers, we will bus people there for the day to avoid waste. We will improve child care arrangements to make it possible, even if that means using willing pensioners in safe, open group sessions. Volunteers will work alongside benefit claimants working for extra cash, and prisoners working for days deducted from their sentences, students to reduce their student loans, but importantly, all doing the same work. Work valuable to the community. Community service, if you like. Hopefully, it will come to be seen as a positive. We don't see it as compulsory at present, but a privilege to improve quality of life if on benefits, not only by additional money but mental wellbeing and being with other people. Advantages to prisoners and students are obvious. Disabled or the disadvantaged are more difficult, but suiting work to them wherever possible.

'This also dovetails with the housing policy. Housing has also become dominated by capitalist structures, so that it is harder and harder for people lower down the ladder to own their own homes. It has also become a victim of profit over people. Housing should not be about creating an income stream for the wealthy. There is a place for rented accommodation for holidaymakers, or for students and temporary workers, but not as permanent homes or for profit. Housing is a crucial factor in wellbeing, mental and physical health, and community security.

'We will build good quality, well insulated, efficient local authority housing, or renovate existing stock. We will make rent-for-profit housing a losing strategy by high taxes. We will prevent housebuilders limiting numbers or holding back land to keep prices up. We will prevent local councils selling land to private housebuilders. We will reclaim or compulsory purchase private land to build houses if it is suitable, and wherever it is in Scotland. Housebuilding will come under the Ministry. It will train and employ core experts and construction workers but will also use prisoners aiming to reduce their sentences and the unemployed, if they wish to work for extra money. They can be trained to do the less skilled jobs like decorating or landscaping, or if they prefer, to undergo full training as builders, electricians, joiners, and plumbers, with a view to a job on completion of their sentence. A further incentive will be that if you work on government housebuilding programmes, whether as employee, volunteer, prisoner, or student, you earn points to owning one yourself or for your parents or for your children.'

Isobel paused for a moment. 'Obviously we won't put all that in the Manifesto. It will be billed as improved benefits, reformed prison system, and solving the housing crisis. There is a lot of work still to do on that, and getting it up and running will be a major task for the government.'

'I think it's way over the top – it seems to be all taking away. Is there not anything that will make the punters think we are a good bet?' said Simon. 'Perhaps some more specific items that are more personal, that people can identify with, and preferably something that we can afford.'

'I disagree,' said Isobel. 'It's time to start treating the electorate as grownups. I have a few suggestions here.'

She opened a brightly coloured folder and took out a sheet of paper. 'These smaller items are still open to debate, so feel free to comment; they have all been discussed previously. We should discontinue the giveaway freebies that were largely brought in to bribe the electorate to vote for the SNP. It's crazy to have well-off people getting stuff like free prescriptions and eye tests for free. They should only apply to people on benefits. We should also remove free railcards and free bus travel. These do not make sense for well-off pensioners. A much-improved public transport service at low cost and available to all will replace these.'

'Not exactly a giveaway; more taking away,' said Simon.

'Maybe not,' said Isobel, 'but we are going to be a "grown-up" government. Not one that needs to offer bribes for votes.'

'Free contraception should stay,' said Maggie. 'Child benefit should only apply to a mother's first two children. Men fathering more than two children will have a tax liability for the third and subsequent children; the father, not the mother, will be taxed. This will be applied as a reduction in benefits if necessary.'

'Too draconian, surely,' said Simon. 'No one is going to vote for that.'

'It's a sustainability issue. Someone somewhere has to limit the increasing population,' responded Maggie. 'But if we make it "draconian", if I can use your word, it will become self-regulating as far as possible, to put people off the third child and make men more responsible.'

'Ah, I can see the headlines already – rich people can have as many kids as they like, but poor people only get to have two,' said Stevie.

'Anyway, isn't the world population declining?' said Simon.

'Of course, there will always be exceptions, but in general women do not want to be baby-making machines,' said Maggie. 'Worldwide, the population is growing; it is only in developed countries where it is static, or in some cases reducing. Young worker shortages can always be made up by immigration, and that is bound to increase over the coming years as the climate crisis starts to impact more severely on other countries with water and food shortages.'

Karen held up a hand, which she always did when she wanted to speak. The others were used to it and appreciated the fact that she would never speak over anyone or interject into a conversation. Isobel nodded at her to go ahead.

'I'm not sure on this one either,' said Karen. 'It takes away a lot of personal freedom for women.'

James noted that Simon smirked with pleasure at Karen agreeing with him, which to James indicated that he did not know her at all.

'Let's not get bogged down in the argument now,' said James. 'I suggest we forget the tax implications and lead with a campaign to promote and educate that a maximum of two children is enough.'

The others nodded their agreement, and he motioned Maggie to continue.

'Following on from climate problems, we will have a great opportunity to make this country entirely run on renewable power. To be fair, Scotland has done well so far on building wind turbines. At one time we were world leaders in hydro power, and we have a lot of valleys and a lot of water. I'm not talking huge dams here, but small to medium hydro power units. We should also look at small-scale nuclear power as well. If we can put reactors and steam generators into submarines for the last fifty years, surely the technology exists for shore-based plants that we can build quickly.'

'That's not going to inspire people much either,' said Simon. 'Sounds expensive, as opposed to saving people money.

'Not when you consider we will own all production and control energy prices. Prices will be a lot less without an element of profit. Surely we can sell that idea to the public,' said James.

'And,' said Isobel, 'all new houses should be built with good insulation, solar panels, and efficient heating systems. Again, no cutting corners to maximise profits. If we pour as much money into green energy as the oil companies do in extracting oil, we can do a lot more and we can do it quickly.'

'Remember also,' said Stevie, 'that electric cars are completely pointless if the electricity they run on comes from coal, oil, or gas-fired power stations.'

The discussion continued for some time, with Isobel, Maggie, and Karen advocating for the radical social policies as a key part of the project and worth the risk, while Stevie and Simon continued to support a more cautious approach, bearing in mind the need to finance the changes.

Finally, James stood up again, causing the others to look up and cease talking. He took a few paces and then turned back to the table.

'All this is too much and too complex to go in a manifesto, but I'm sure we can distil it into a workable document. It is good to see that we are thinking and talking like a government in waiting. What will be workable in practice may not be what we think now, but we will have the power to make radical changes, and hopefully we will start to change how people see government. We will make mistakes, no doubt about it, but we will also remain flexible and open to change when we need to. Let's not forget that Richard is where he spent his whole career aiming to be, and he and Jack are as ready as they will ever be to mount the revolution, so there is not much time left.

'We have to remember that the public will see this as the manifesto of a somewhat extreme socialist independence party. It will be open to public scrutiny, but importantly it will also be laying the groundwork and perhaps preparing the people for the radical changes we will make.'

Chapter 10

Richard (2022)

Richard pulled the net curtain to one side and waited. He heard the heavy door of the outer hall slam shut even from two floors up and knew she would appear in a few moments. He had often watched her this way after she had left the flat to walk the dog or go to the shops. In the past she would have often turned back and given him a cheery wave, but not today. Samantha soon appeared, heavily laden with a small backpack, a shoulder bag precariously hanging off one shoulder and wheeling a large suitcase. Shadow was on a lead held in her other hand. Shadow looked back once, she did not.

He thought he should feel something. He did feel something – a small loss – but it had always been a lack in him, his inability to commit himself completely; his inability to love. He would not call it a flaw, but he recognised its lack and knew that it made him stronger. There was always some part of him held back, a part that observed, recorded, and analysed everything. He could play the game, and he was good at it; could go through the motions, say the right words at the right time, and had become practised enough that he could hold down a relationship for several years, but he did not believe he was capable of love. His early relationships had always been marred by his fear of rejection and his inability to suppress the urge to control.

As he matured, he recognised this and had found ways to temper it, which allowed for more balanced relationships. Samantha had been with him longer than anyone except Isobel. But of course, Isobel was a special case and had always been casual – well, perhaps not so casual, but definitely on/off over the years. He wished he could have committed more to

Isobel as she had always impressed him. She got things done, not just talked about it, and she was attractive in her own non-ostentatious way. Isobel was the only person he had ever confessed his rather battered childhood to.

That night, the day they had first met, he had walked her home and then decided to skip the late-night bus and walk out to his place as it was not that far and the rain had eased off. He'd reflected on the evening as he walked. It had gone better than he had expected, and it was good to know that so many people shared the same feeling about seeing Scotland free of England. He also decided to have Isobel.

At the second meeting he had been attentive and he consciously, cynically, matched her body movements, allowed her to catch him looking at her, dropping his eyes quickly when she saw him, and using his most well-rehearsed smile and a light touch on her arm when he made a point as they talked. It had probably all been wasted effort, as it appeared that Isobel had had designs of her own, so Richard was surprised how easily that second night brought them together. They saw a lot of each while they were both at university, but he could never bring himself to commit to a full relationship. After they graduated and had both gone their separate ways, they stayed in touch and continued a physical relationship on an intermittent basis until Isobel had put an end to that. He had trusted her enough to tell her about his early years, and she knew as much about him as anyone ever would. He had never regretted telling her about his early school days and some of the trauma that he had endured. In general, he found it best not to tell anyone about his private education, as many viewed it with suspicion or were jealous of the privilege it bestowed.

It was ironic, really, since the whole experience had been a nightmare for him, but he knew that the system had undoubtedly made him strong, resourceful, and self-reliant and had probably done no lasting damage. Those prep school days were some of his strongest childhood memories. He had not been well prepared and had been sold on the new school by his parents, with the talk of sports facilities and a better class of people, so much so that he had bragged about it to his fellow classmates at the council school he attended briefly in London on the family's return from Hong Kong. He was a tanned, slightly plump, seven-year-old who coped with being forced, for a mandatory hour at lunchtime, out into the playground and the cold British winter by hanging around outside the school kitchen, where a blast of warm air from the extraction fans helped create a slightly warmer micro climate. His schoolmates were from all walks of life and many nationalities, and he had no problem fitting in. Even though his tanned skin caused a bit of teasing, he still made new friends and had fun.

He had just turned eight when his world fell apart. He was catapulted from a loving, if somewhat strict, family home into an environment that he was utterly unprepared for. He may as well have had 'Not one of us' tattooed on his forehead. He was an outsider and only there because the Army was paying the fees. His father had gained officer rank during the war but would never rise higher than the rank of major. His parents' return to Hong Kong after their leave did not coincide at all with the start of the school year. So, he started the term at odds with the norm, and because of this there were only three new boys. Of the other two, one was the son of a minor Lord, and the other of a wealthy industrialist. Richard was abandoned as an alien in a strange land, where everyone else seemed to know the rules and no one was prepared to tell him what they were.

The school was a warren of classrooms and dormitories incorporated into a large, rambling mansion, the oldest part of which dated back a couple of centuries. Various extensions and outbuildings had been added over the years, and it accommodated roughly one hundred boys from the age of eight, up until they moved on to public schools at thirteen, after taking an entrance exam. This was the upper-class equivalent of the eleven-plus exam. The headmaster and his family lived in one part of the house, while a few of the masters were scattered in houses near to, and in a couple of cases within, the grounds.

The bullying started within days. His unseasonable tan, his Scottish accent, his plump frame, his so obvious lack of wealth, all worked against him. It was, strangely, initiated by one of the other new boys – the son of the industrialist, Standish. Richard never knew his Christian name, nor ever wanted to. The first thing they did at the school was take away your name – you became your surname and a number. Richard's was 71. Locker 71, coat hook 71, bed 71, seat 71, pupil 71, Ogilvy 71. Standish gave him another name.

Standish turned on him almost immediately, presumably as a good way to deflect any attention away from himself, but why he felt the need to do so was never clear. Standish christened him Brown Boy, soon shortened to Brownie. As it was taken up by his peers and with all the connotations that that era contained, it was not a good nickname. None of the boys ever referred to him by his real surname; it was only used by the teachers and staff. He became Brownie to everyone else, and he hated it. That, together with jibes about his Scottish accent and his chubby build, together with the physical attacks, rapidly turned his life into a nightmare. It was not the severity of the physical abuse that hurt the most, but the incessant nature of it and the isolation that came with it. No one befriends the bullied, for fear of becoming part of it. Once you became a victim, it was hard to undo. Everyone knew, so any boy with the slightest inclination took advantage. In fact, Standish was never the worst offender, just the initiator.

Richard vividly remembered one or two of the worst incidents. A group of boys had surrounded his bed in the middle of a winter night, upturning it and then peeing on the pile of sheets and blankets. It was a mess that he had to clean up and live with for several days. Another time, a group of boys playing cowboys, riding imaginary horses in a make-believe posse, discovered one of his hiding places and chased him down with their imaginary horses, before surrounding him and pummelling him to the ground. His bloodied nose and bruised ribs did not hurt so much as the image of so many hating faces directed solely at him; that was what would always stay with him.

There was no escape, as his parents had returned to Hong Kong. There was no help, no one to turn to. It was a twenty-four-hour, seven-day-a-week nightmare. The evenings and weekends were the worst, because there was less supervision and less structure to the day. Meals, classes, games all protected him. Free time was racked with fear. So, Richard learnt to hide. The grounds had woods and outbuildings that were out of bounds, but they were good places to stay out of the way. The English teacher ran the school library for an hour each day, and this was another safe haven, with the added benefit of warmth. Richard read a lot of books.

Every Sunday the whole school, except of course the day pupils or those who had gone home for the weekend, gathered in the great hall after breakfast to write the obligatory letter home. His first letter home, written in shaky, schoolboy handwriting, was probably the most earnest he ever wrote. It was a cry for help. He did not remember the words; only that no-one ever read it, not even the teacher who supervised the letter writing.

He had not realised that the letters were vetted by the master sitting at the table at the front of the hall. He had seen other boys taking up letters and handing them to the teacher who had put them in envelopes. The master took it from him, gave it a cursory glance, and tore it up. He handed the confetti back to Richard. 'Try again,' was all he said.

Shocked, Richard returned to his seat and rewrote the letter in calmer terms. He promised to be well behaved and help Gran with all the housework if only he could stay with her and go to school in Edinburgh. The master tore it up again. That moment, as he walked back to his desk with another sheet of lightweight airmail paper in hand, was the moment his childhood ended. He finally realised that there would be no escape and that he was truly alone. He would have to find a way to deal with it. Richard learned how to hide, he learned to avoid people, and as an adult he found he liked it that way.

He learnt that the only letters that got through the censorship described the weather, the lessons learned, or whether the school team won or lost against some other school. After a while he stopped writing. He would sit and pretend to write and then slip out using other boys as cover so that no-one noticed. He had hoped that his parents would read this lack of communication as a message and come rescue him. It did not work, and after a month or two his parents must have queried the lack of mail, as from then on, the master took due care to make sure he wrote every week.

He never told them about his little hell, and they died not knowing. They were so proud that they had provided a private education for him, albeit with the financial aid of the Army, so sure they had done the right thing. He spent Christmas and Easter holidays with his grandmother in Edinburgh and flew out to join his parents wherever they were in the world, for six weeks in the long summer break. At least Edinburgh was safe for him, but he knew no one; no school so no schoolfriends; no children of other families, as his grandmother was widowed and lived alone. So, Richard grew up alone. Even during the summer holidays spent with his parents and two younger siblings, he was the outsider, the visitor for only a few weeks. Richard hated the English.

*

He would miss Samantha's companionship, as she mostly did as she was told and took care of many mundane household jobs. There would be someone else when it suited him, but he would avoid any live-in arrangements in the future. It was much better to live alone. He had found that intelligence was a major part of what he found attractive in a woman, but ironically the smart ones were much more likely to see through his façade quicker and realise that he was not worth it. Samantha had been different; she had been smart, submissive, and pliable, and had stayed the course much longer than was the norm. The addition of Shadow to the relationship had not helped, but he was never likely to find another like Samantha.

Bringing a puppy into his ordered life and pristine environment had been a mistake. He had not been able to understand the only thing a puppy could give – unconditional love – nor why it could not be easily trained merely by the delivery of physical punishment. Surely it was the best way to train a puppy. Eventually a balance was reached, but Shadow always regarded him fearfully and became essentially Samantha's dog. He knew that it had changed the way Samantha viewed him and no doubt contributed to her finally leaving.

Perhaps it was better this way. He needed every hour as IDay was coming ever closer; there were immense demands on his time. He had off-loaded as much of his regular Army work as he could to his staff officers without raising suspicion, but there were still significant calls on his time which he could not ignore if everything was to be seen as running as normal. He was in effect running two separate complex organisations, firstly in his legitimate role as Commander of the Army in Scotland, and secondly as head of the clandestine Network.

Maintaining secrecy within the Network had become paramount, as more chances had to be taken now they were actively engaged in organizing the revolt. It was a tribute to the deeply held Scottish national identity and their recruiting process that so far there had been no major breaches. There had been talk that had occasionally reached senior officers, but Richard had managed to bury it or write it off as nationalist talk. He relied heavily on Colonel Hardie, who had been one of his first recruits. He had been with him almost from the beginning and shouldered a significant amount of work in planning the deployment of units for IDay.

The logistics of positioning an army on one particular day across a whole country, at hundreds of locations, was immense.

It was relatively easy to plan the takeover of the bigger objectives, such as the RAF and Naval bases, but what caused the problem was the myriad of other smaller objectives that needed small units of Army or Militia to take and control. Even with the Militia, there was no possible way they could cover everything. So, decisions had to be taken about many individual sites.

He did not think that the engineers would cut off power without good reason, but he had decided to take control of the two nuclear power stations anyway and leave the rest. The road, rail, and ports were relatively straightforward, but wherever a large group of men was situated the logistic support of fuel and food had to be considered. Any airfield with a runway long enough to take a troop transport plane, even if it was just a strip in the highlands, had to be closed and vehicles used to block the runway. The Army units would close the major airports and the smaller ones would be designated to a Militia team. Some teams in the north would be split into sections so that they could target two objectives.

He had been pleased with the way the Militia had progressed, and he appreciated that had a lot to do with Jack and his organisational abilities. Richard had high hopes for Jack, and he had thought at one time that he would bring him into the Governors' circle, but had decided to wait until after IDay. He was sure that he could find Jack a useful place in his administration.

The next meeting of the Governors was due to take place in a few days' time. They were all in place in Scotland, and all eager to get it done. These had been the hardest people to find and to recruit, as they had to know the full plan. These were men who were prepared to take responsibility, to take action and to lead without fear. Some had been dropped along the way, but the five he had finally selected as Governors were the best he could find. They ranged in present rank from Colonel down to Sergeant, but after the takeover they would all be equal.

As the Network had grown, so had the command structure within it, so he had appointed regional commanders who would handle the logistics and deployment of the troops on the day of the revolution and manage security during the changeover period. It was Colonel Hardie who had begun to hint that surely they could do a better job of running the country. This had fitted in with Richard's own thinking, and he had long considered taking control of the country himself, but he let the idea mature among the commanders to see how it would take and was not surprised that it was readily accepted.

They had decided to reposition their objective to take a longer-term view of how they would control their regions, and he had suggested that they change their designation from commander to Governor – more in keeping with their expected role. Each commander had built up their own networks consistent with the Army units that they commanded or had been involved with in past positions. After the shift in thinking and as the day became nearer, each Governor, again at Colonel Hardie's suggestion, had formed special Army units within their own networks. These were comprised of soldiers who were fully committed to the cause and were aware of the action plan and ready to fight for it from day one. It was thought that the main bulk of the regular Army would take some time to adjust to the new regime and could not be deployed on the first day in full combatant roles. These units were smaller in number than the Militia, but they would serve to act as shock troops which could be deployed in support of the civilian Militia, or to replace them if they fell short in some of their objectives. The Governors referred to them as hard-core units.

They had agreed the system of government that they would put in place and the measures to ensure compliance. They would manage their own regions, with only minimal oversight from him. The borders of the six regions had been carefully marked out and agreed upon. The Edinburgh area and Fife he had kept for himself. Highland, Argyll, Central, Glasgow and

Ayrshire, and finally the South border region, would make up the other five autonomously governed areas.

He had always recognised that he was inherently superior to the civilians, but in truth he had intended to allow the Board and their party to govern, leaving him with a sort of overriding control and free to manage defence and security, as he could not be bothered with the mundane aspects of government. But as the years progressed, he had grown tired of listening to them endlessly discuss how to improve this or that, and if they could only nurture and protect everyone and they would all live happily ever after. They wanted some sort of socialist nanny state mixed with a vague form of capitalism and inhabited by perfect citizens who obeyed every rule.

The Board seemed to be under the impression that people were a uniform mass who would quietly fall into line with every hare-brained scheme they concocted. They had no idea how to lead or the complexities of management, and he doubted they could sensibly run a country with the wide range of people types that made up the general population. Neither did they fully understand the power built into the capitalist system of monetary and judicial control, nor how deeply ingrained in the world order it was. Scotland could not stand apart from the world economy. Only by joining it could they hope to be a viable state, independent from England.

The mental switch from regional military commanders to Governors was barely noticeable. The Governors were serious about their new venture, and they spent many meetings discussing the best way forward until they had mutually agreed on how they would rule Scotland. They settled on a Federal state, based on the six regions that were already marked out. They would have autonomy in their areas so that they could raise local taxes and create local laws on whatever they considered beneficial to the local economy. They knew that some people worked best within a strong structure and were happier and harder working when decision making was taken out of their hands, while others were highly motivated to innovate and create wealth, and these would be given free rein to drive industry and commerce.

In the main they would leave things to run as they always had, with a minimum of interference. They saw no need to make huge changes to the existing laws and structure, and would adopt the approach of more stringently enforcing the laws already in place and making the punishment for infringement more of a deterrent by making it faster and harsher. They would give power back to the police and to teachers and parents. Discipline would be required at home and at school, on the basis that unruly children grow into unruly adults. Teachers would have the power to punish, and parents would be held accountable for the actions of their offspring. They intended to create a well-ordered society.

They would meet regularly in Edinburgh as the national government, to decide on nationwide issues and to deal with foreign affairs which would now include England. They would not remove themselves from the world economic order but instead would seek to become the newest member on the world stage. Richard doubted that Lieutenant Cammy would actually be able to hijack the submarine, but either way it would not matter a great deal. They would still have the nuclear arsenal of warheads stored in Scotland. Federal Scotland would be a nuclear power and would be on an even footing with more established countries.

The Board talked more than they ever achieved, and he knew that without him they would still be talking. His vision for Scotland diverged greatly from their prissy socialist experiment. He understood that the only way to run a country effectively was by strong leadership, but he was also aware of the pitfalls that power and hubris would bring. He also appreciated the drawback of being seen to be the controlling hand, and for this reason he intended to allow the Board to be the public face of his government but essentially without any power. He intended to cut the head off it and substitute Simon as the leader, who had already agreed enthusiastically to that honorary position. It seemed like a perfect set-up; a people's parliament to take the flak while he and the Governors ran the country as an independent Federal State.

It would not be all hard work. The Governors had unanimously agreed to purchase a small self-contained Caribbean island – when they had access to the funds – of which there were several on the market. This would be for own their own private use and for their favoured retainers. There should, after all, be some reward for the years of hard work that putting the country into some sort of order and re-building a nation required. In fact, Richard mused, at the last meeting more time had been spent poring over glossy estate agent brochures and internet sites showing white sandy beaches and azure seas than getting down to business.

He knew he was born for this. It needed someone like him to take control. His name would become part of the historical elite, the very few who had done what he was going to do. He was founding a country, perhaps even a dynasty, and his name would be remembered in history.

There were Isobel and Maggie to consider. He knew that he could never completely bring Isobel over to his way of thinking, and he had given up on the hope that he could have brought her into his administration in some form. He had much higher hopes for Maggie. She had a fire that her mother did not have. He had often wondered if Isobel knew that Maggie was his daughter – surely a woman would know? Or had she just kept it from him? He resented her for not telling him. After suspecting for a while and observing Maggie whenever he could, he had become so sure that she was his daughter that he had stolen a glass she had used from James's table to check the DNA. Unfortunately, the testing company had not been able to extract enough from a dried saliva trace to give a result. It was not until he attended a meeting at Isobel's house that he had managed, on a visit to the bathroom, to take hair samples from the women's two hairbrushes. These, the company confirmed, were from mother and daughter, and the DNA indicated that he was the father. Whether Isobel knew it or not, he was not sure, but Maggie was his daughter. She would be his legacy once he had convinced her of her origins.

Chapter 11

Jack (IDay minus 8)

Jack sat in the black Range Rover at the Ayrshire camp and rehearsed his big motivational speech. In his head it sounded crap. Through the rear-view mirror and the tinted back window he could see the four Militia teams across the clearing. They were waiting on the last Ayrshire team to arrive. These would be the last batch to go through the live fire training, and as far as he could determine they were five of the best teams. They would need to be, as they had perhaps the hardest job to do on IDay. He could see that the leaders were still in the process of setting out what was expected from them and what they could expect from the training here.

When the last team turned up, he would go over and give his speech – inspirational or not! From him, the so-called Commander of the Militia. *Jeez, what would old Jake think!* He was sure his dad had not thought the movement would progress so far, let alone envisioned a militia led by his son. Jake would have been proud of him, even if, had he still been alive, he would never have said it.

He had worried at first that building the Militia would be too far outside his experience, but he had started taking over a complex organisation from his father before the cigarettes finally managed to kill him. So, he had been handling most of the family business before he was thirty.

The Militia turned out to be not much different from the organisation which he had ruled, like his father before him, with a few trusted lieutenants, not much paperwork, and a healthy dose of fear. He had respected his father's decision to stay away from the hard drugs, to remain small to avoid coming into conflict with larger organisations, and also to stay below the sightline of any national anti-crime squad. They had much preferred to deal only with the local police. Sure, his father had been a gangster, and the violence he was capable of meting out without a second thought had always been part of that, but there was no denying that he had also been much more than the traditional gang lord. In his own way he had looked after the local community, so if a family was hard up, a food parcel might be delivered, or if a man too long out of work seemed a likely prospect, a job would be offered. Occasionally someone would approach his father to settle a dispute, but this could be a risky endeavour and consequently did not happen often. If Jake had decided the complainant was manipulating the system – for example, someone just taking care of a grudge – the petitioner was likely to end up with a beating himself.

His father had lived in the community with the people he ruled, and the mixture of fear and respect was enough to prevent any assistance to the forces of law and order. Their house stuck out, a beacon of dishonesty in the housing scheme that the community was centred around. It was a post-war council house in a maze of streets of drably grey roughcast semis and blocks of low-level flats, six to a building – the modern tenements.

Jake's own house had been different. It was freshly painted in a pastel shade of salmon – 'Dawn' he remembered his mother calling it, and she was the controlling authority when anything concerning the house was decided. The roof tiles were cleaned every year and were pristine, the windows were white plastic and double glazed, and the driveway which harboured the inevitable BMWs was paved with monobloc bricks in a colour to match the house, and these were pressure washed relentlessly at the first hint of any green taking hold.

Most incongruous of all was the huge cabin cruiser parked on a trailer in front of the house. It was taller than the first storey windows and blocked the light into the living room. The cruiser lived almost permanently on the trailer, and Jack could only remember it being in the water at Loch Lomond a couple of times in his childhood. It was all gone now, and Jack lived in a penthouse flat overlooking the Clyde, while his elderly mother occupied another close by.

The business had changed, too. While it was perhaps not wholly legitimate, he had concentrated on the bouncer angle – although they were now referred to as doormen or security staff. Gradually the business had become more mainstream, and there were a surprising number of clubs, pubs, and band venues in and around Glasgow that were counted among his clientele. The staff had changed as well. Staff! Who would have thought they would be called that? They were no longer the biggest, ugliest bruisers that could be found; his current employees were much more sophisticated. They came from many different sectors of society, factory workers supplementing their pay or the unemployed doing the same, students, fire-fighters, NHS employees topping up their wages. Female bouncers – his dad would have turned in his grave at this.

It was a job for a special kind of person these days, and he had been amazed at the level of skill involved in defusing a situation with a kind word, commiseration, or a firm voice. Of course, that was always the preferred first option, but things could always turn nasty. Jack ran his people through a training course with an unarmed combat expert – an ex-police instructor. He was good and taught them firstly to defuse and then how to restrain, and finally how to do real damage. Jack remembered a story the instructor liked to tell all his students – one he had heard several times, as he had attended the course for a refresher more than once.

An unnamed world class martial artist – perhaps the instructor imagined himself, Jack always thought – is taking a ride on a subway in some US city. The car is crowded with no seats available, and at the next stop a drunken brute of a man gets on the train. He works his way towards our hero, swearing and cursing, and kicking people's legs out of the way. The carriage is tense, awaiting the explosion of violence sure to come; each person hopes it will not explode on them. As the man approaches him, the expert contemplates how best to react. A kick to the knee, perhaps disabling him for life; a series of rapid punches – such good practice; rare is the opportunity to really punch a human not a bag. The expert prepares to show off his skills, reminding himself not to kill the brute. Just before he can act, an old grey-haired lady, scarcely five feet tall and wearing a faded blue fleece and a bum bag, jumps up in front of the drunk and says, 'Here, son, have my seat.' The drunk collapses into it and promptly falls asleep. As the old lady departs a few stops later, he acknowledges her superior skill with the barest of nods as she passes.

A few months before Jake had struggled through his last cigarette – he had steadfastly refused to give up, even after being diagnosed with lung cancer – he had introduced Jack to the group, and with their prior knowledge and approval he had agreed to take his father's seat at the table and continue with the funding. This was when the funding was a mere few thousand a year, not the millions that Simon had poured into the organisation in the last few years. It had come as a complete surprise to learn of his father's secret life, and the fact that his father had not only been funding an independence group but was actively involved in a political movement with people far outside his social sphere, had astonished Jack. His respect for his father had grown, and he recalled that even as child independence had often been discussed in the house. He had just not taken much notice of it at the time.

Richard had taken an interest in Jack and seemed to regard himself as a suitable mentor. He offered advice at every opportunity and let him know that he could speak to him if he needed to. Jack found this patronising; there was something about Richard that made him wary. So, he downplayed his role in running the family business and the number of men who regarded him as the ultimate authority. Jack let Richard think that he was just another attentive subordinate and allowed himself to be 'groomed' so that he could become part of the inner circle. Besides, he thought, there might be something he could learn from a man who was so self-assured, so confident of his right to be obeyed, so in control, and so used to wielding power over people.

He was, however, totally in agreement with the idea of forming the Militia after the 2014 referendum and getting the Board to agree, and he was pleased that Richard wanted him to command it rather than one of his Army buddies. There were plenty of those who had already retired or who had returned to the civilian sector that could easily fill that role. Training the Militia to shoot, to kill their fellow countrymen, was a whole new concept, but deep down he was sure that the only hope of success was through force.

After the agreement to set up the Militia, there were many meetings with Richard alone or with other Army officers as they thrashed out the best way to organise and train. During these meetings, they had set up the concept of 'platoons' recruited and run by leaders who were mostly trusted retired NCOs who had been part of Richard's Network during their time in the Army. Some of the other leaders had been appointed through Jack's own contacts, and others had been selected from party members who had shown a desire to take a more active role, but most were ex-military. The leader of each team would be the only contact with the cause, and the members would not know anyone in the other teams. They would be formed on the basis of the future protests in support of the independence campaign. The leaders would train them and instil a sense of loyalty to the team and the leader, using money, support, games, sport, free drinking nights, and whatever else was needed to make a cohesive team.

It was Jack who suggested paintballing to facilitate a means of bonding the teams and to allow training with firearms and tactics without any suspicion. The Army officers liked this suggestion, and it rapidly became the core around which the teams were built. In the end, most platoons had been formed as paintball teams.

In setting up the Militia, Jack had more meetings with the Army officers and the General than he had with the Board, and he was aware these meetings were often conducted without the direct knowledge of the other members. At first, he assumed that there was nothing wrong with this, as security was such an overriding concern, but later it had bothered him a little that the Board did not seem to have complete awareness of Richard's meetings. He figured that they were content to leave him to get on with the military side of things.

Although all Richard's inner core of Army personnel were of Scottish descent, they retained only the slightest hint of their regional accents, and many spoke with a bland Englishness that would be impossible to associate to any particular region. Jack initially put this down to them having to move around every few years, but after his mum pointed out that he was starting to speak 'posh', he realised that he was unconsciously trying to lose his Glasgow accent and become as blandly spoken as the others. He was aware that, just like his father before him, he was moving in a stratum of society that was foreign to him, but he also realised that he was just as alien to them. None of those privileged Army officers would comprehend either the upbringing Jack had experienced or what he was capable of. They did not know, and had never asked, about the upwards of one hundred men and women under his control and the turnover of several million pounds a year that passed through his organisation. He preferred to keep it that way. So when he was with them, he adopted a persona eager to learn and obey, and he allowed his accent to diminish as well.

These Army meetings, as he thought of them, were conducted at houses owned by the Army – usually in the suburbs – rented out to officers with families who were posted to the area, or at Richard's flat in Edinburgh. It had originally belonged to Richard's parents, but he had kept it on as it would be useful for leave or whenever he was posted to Scotland. On most of these occasions, Richard's wife had been there.

Samantha was younger than Richard by a good few years, Jack reckoned; a tall, slender woman, almost skinny, and very nervous. The first time he met her, he recalled her hands shook a little as she served him a drink, and he noticed her knuckles stood out, covered only by the thinnest of pale skin so that they seemed almost bare-boned. Her hands made her seem vulnerable. She gave him the barest of smiles, leaving the two of them to talk. Richard had not even bothered to introduce her.

She was often at the flat, and although they never exchanged more than a few words, Jack had seen enough relationships to know she was not in the happiest of marriages. The occasional heavy make-up, her nervousness, and her utter deference to Richard told their own story. The household also had a dog – a black Border Collie cross, with a brilliant white flash on her chest and worried eyes. She, too, was not introduced to Jack and was mostly relegated to the kitchen or hallway.

Once on his way to meet Richard at the flat, he had seen Samantha and the dog setting out for a walk. He stopped to chat and pat the dog. The animal shied away from him, but he held his hand still and allowed her time to take in his scent, and when she had moved a little closer, he stroked her head.

'Lovely dog, what's her name?'

'Shadow,' Samantha answered with her ghost of a smile.

'Shadow the sheepdog – suits her.' He smiled back. 'Where are you off to?'

'Just the park. Richard is up there. Just buzz.'

She headed off down the road, Shadow trotting beside her, and Jack watched her go. These were the most words they had spoken together. She was not the type of woman that he usually found attractive, but there was something about her that drew him, possibly because she seemed so vulnerable and so remote. His finger hovered over the door buzzer, but then he abruptly turned and followed her. He had to run a little to catch up, and he startled her when he pulled up beside her.

'Sorry,' he said. 'Do you mind if I walk with you a bit? I feel like some fresh air.' It sounded corny even to him. He was not used to chatting to women in this way or to approaching them in the real world, let alone a married woman. Although, he told himself, he was trying to help rather than score.

He found most of his women online, and if they did not click immediately, he would move on to the next profile without a second thought. He had never had a relationship that lasted more than a couple of years.

She looked nervous and glanced back over her shoulder to check that they could not be seen from the windows of the flat.

'Won't Richard be annoyed if you're late?'

'Fuck Richard, he can wait.'

She gave an odd little chuckle, and he was not sure whether that indicated approval or outright fear for his future wellbeing.

'How long have you been married, er, with him, I mean?'

She bent down to release Shadow, who bounded off, pausing to sniff the grass every few yards without looking back. 'A long time, not actually married,' she said. 'Are you married?'

'No.' He pulled out his phone for something to do with his hands and twisted it around nervously. 'Not found the right one yet; ever hopeful, though.'

She just smiled.

'Shadow seems very friendly.'

'Yes, she's lovely. I've had her since she was a puppy.'

'Yours then, not Richard's?'

'Richard isn't good with animals. The first morning that we had her, Richard came into the kitchen for breakfast, and she was so excited to greet him her whole wee body was wagging with her tail. Bursting with love, she was so excited that she peed on his bare feet. He kicked her across the room. She forgave him, though, and greeted him with max puppy love over and over again until she finally gave up. It is hard to break the love of a puppy. Richard managed it.' Aware that probably sounded disloyal, she shrugged and added, 'It's not that he does not like animals. He just needs absolute control, and anything that falls outside that needs to be corrected.'

'Hmm, yes, I can believe that.'

'Hadn't you better get on to see Richard?'

'Ah yes. Uh... I was going to ask if you wanted my number in case you ever need...' He floundered, suddenly lost for the right words. Knew he sounded stupid.

'Help?' she finished for him, again that odd chuckle. 'I don't have a mobile. Richard prefers it that way.'

He had never felt so awkward or out of his depth. How could he have read the situation so badly? Jack knew that was a dismissal and quickly changed the subject.

'Yes, of course. Well, I better get to the meeting,' he said, taking that opportunity to withdraw. He turned and headed back to the flat.

'Jack, wait!' She called after him. 'Give me your number.'

It stopped him, and he scurried around in his pockets to find a piece of paper and something to write with, but then noticed that she was waiting with a pen already poised. He said the number, and she wrote it down on the palm of her hand.

She briefly touched his arm and held his gaze for a moment. 'Thank you,' she said, and then turned and resumed her walk.

Jack sighed, confused. He was not sure whether he had just wanted to score her, get one over on the General, or just to play the knight in shining armour and rescue her. Crap! She had felt sorry for him and taken his number to make him feel better.

But something had changed between them, and whenever he had been at the flat, she was a little more welcoming and the ghost smile a little stronger. He would often turn up early, hoping to meet her with the dog again, which would have indicated that she wanted to talk to him, but the opportunity never again arose.

Sometimes she would take Shadow out while they were in a meeting. He knew that, because she would stick her head around the door into the living room and ask if the men needed anything before she went out. He resisted the temptation to follow her. Clearly, she did not return his attraction nor need saving. The last time he had visited the General, she was gone and so was the dog. Richard had not mentioned it, and Jack did not ask.

A few weeks later, he had a text from an unknown number which turned out to be Samantha. Jack was surprised but pleased to hear from her, and they agreed to meet up for a coffee the next time he was in Edinburgh. The meeting was a little awkward at first, but they soon both relaxed, helped by their unspoken mutual agreement not to mention Richard. They parted with an agreement to meet up again after IDay.

The noise of van doors slamming announced the arrival of the last team and brought Jack back to the present. He waited until all five teams were lined up and ready for him. He got out of the Range Rover, pulled a black baseball cap down tightly over his head, beamed a mental wink at old Jake, then walked over, adopting the swagger expected of the Commander of the Militia.

Chapter 12

Richard – Afghanistan

Major Richard Ogilvy entered the prefabricated room that doubled as both sleeping quarters and office, and leaned against the wall for a full minute to let the air conditioning unit work its magic. He carefully unwrapped the shemagh from around his neck and used it to wipe the sweat off his face. He had often thought to cut the scarf in half but had never got around to it – they were always too big, but very useful for keeping sand and bugs from getting inside his combat shirt and prevent the sun from burning the back of his neck. He was glad the long, hot, dry summer was coming to an end. The room was sparse – a steel-framed bunk, some fake wood storage units, and a utilitarian metal desk with the top covered in stained fake leather. He flipped the blind in the single window to a steep angle, cutting out some of the too bright sunlight. He pointed the muzzle of his rifle into the sand butt, put there for that purpose, and worked the bolt to ensure that the chamber was clear. He made sure the safety was on and placed the rifle in the rack but left the magazine in place, as even here in Camp Bastion attacks occurred frequently, although rarely did anyone breach the perimeter.

His company had been rotated out of a forward fire base for two weeks of down time, or what passed for that in this god-forsaken country. Ironic, he thought, how through the centuries, religions were the most frequent cause of, or perhaps excuse for, conflicts and often the most vicious.

He sat down at the desk where there was a pile of admin awaiting his attention; he shoved it to one side, leaned back in the chair, and stared at the ceiling and considered. He had just seen someone in the camp that had brought a surge of something like excitement deep down in his gut. It awakened a whole load of memories that mostly he kept securely boxed up in his head. Fucking Standish, he was sure. The camp was so large, almost the size of a small town, that the chances of him spotting the man had been tiny. It was an opportunity he would not let go past.

One of the platoons in the company he commanded had been going through an exercise programme, and Richard had joined in, letting himself come under the control of the instructor. It was a punishing workout in the heat and he did not have to do it, but it was good for morale if the officers trained as hard as the men, and he liked to keep fit. During the session he had noticed the civilian accompanied by a small group of Royal Engineers by the perimeter wall, and thought he looked familiar. Richard was pretty sure he recognised the man. Afterwards, he asked the instructor, who was permanently based at the camp, what the group was doing.

'That's a civilian contractor, a big construction company, they've been involved in some of the infrastructure projects – schools, med centres, that sort of thing. They are also doing a lot of the new buildings in the camp. He's one of the owners, I think; high up, anyway. Comes for a quick visit every few months. Raking it in from government contracts, no doubt.'

Richard headed over to the office admin building for the Army area of the camp and asked the duty corporal to show him the visitor accommodation logs. He quickly found the page for civilians and, running his finger down the list, saw the name Standish. He'd only been here a couple of days and was due out again at the end of the week.

Sitting at his desk, Richard remembered those years of misery and fear, which had been largely down to this man. It was more than just those two years; the after-effects had gone on a lot longer, and as he became older Richard had realised just how much his early school days had affected him as an adult. There was no doubt it had made him stronger, but he knew he had missed out on the ability to make friends or sustain a relationship. He could fake the Army laddish culture when he needed to, but he much preferred his own company. And as for women, well, he'd had to learn how to work that as well.

By the time he was ten years old, the bullies had moved on to fresher game, and Richard had found less reason to hide. He had avoided any more attacks and even taken some small revenge on some of the perpetrators, when he was sure he could not be found out. Although minor, like a stolen shoe or a cockroach in a cup of tea, it had been very satisfying. He had remained so wary of Standish, though, that he had stayed well out of his way.

Now here he is again, he thought, *but this time in my world not his*. Richard did not burn with rage or hatred as he had once pulsed with fear. He remained as cold as always. An opportunity had presented itself for revenge, so he would take it. He merely intended to balance the books and settle a score. Satisfaction assured.

At thirteen, he had left the prep school without ever having made a single connection in those five years and with no fond memories of the establishment. He had been eager to embrace a fresh start at the new school. It had not been easy, as he was a shy and reticent boy used to not drawing attention to himself, and someone who rarely spoke in class.

Almost immediately, a boy in the class started to make fun of him whenever he spoke, even in front of the teachers. The teachers here were much more proactive in asking direct questions that you had to answer. As soon as he started to speak, Bishop – yes, that was his name; surnames were only used there as well – would start a low chant of 'mumblemumblemumble' to the delight and amusement of his classmates. Of course, the teacher would put a stop to it soon enough, but Bishop continued outside the classroom as well.

Richard felt himself being drawn back into the position of the victim. It was all happening again, and the old fears started to resurface. During one class, Bishop was seated behind him and prodding him the whole morning with a pencil or making 'mumblemumble' noises. Suddenly something snapped in Richard, something that would never again reset. He turned and stabbed down with his pen with all his might at one of Bishop's hands. Bishop was lucky he moved his hand just in time, and the pen stabbed deep into the wood of the desk. Bishop did not bother him again that day, and Richard, pleased with himself, thought that was an end to it.

However, the next day Bishop was at it again with his 'mumblemumble' routine, this time from the other side of the classroom. The other boys chuckled loudly. They had heard about yesterday. But this was not the old Richard. When the lunch bell rang, he waited at his desk while the teacher left, and as the boys started to file out of the room he charged at Bishop, bringing him down in a heap on the floor and pummelling him with both fists and all he had. Surprised at his own strength and at how weak the boy beneath him appeared, he sat astride him and battered away. Bishop called for help to his fellow classmates who had all stopped to watch – some now cheered Richard on. They laughed and called out, 'You deserve it!'

Richard revelled in the sense of power he found. He held Bishop trapped on the floor for a little longer and delivered a couple more punches for good measure, making the boy's nose bleed. Bishop never bothered him again.

Richard never made any connections there either, and as soon as his school days were done, they were gone. He made no lasting friendships and would be hard put to remember the names of anyone even if he met them in the street, except of course for those two – Standish and Bishop. There was, however, a third name that stuck with him, albeit for a very different reason: Aubrey.

During the first term, he had enjoyed the exceptional facilities at the school, even though he still remained aloof from the others and was not part of any of the many cliques that rose and fell, flourished briefly, or sometimes lasted a lifetime. There was access to the river with sailing boats, kayaks, and single and double sculls, if you fancied a bit of speed rowing. There were squash and tennis courts, a pool, and a gym with all sorts of activities including fencing and archery. Best of all, Richard did not need to hide from anyone.

At the start of his second term, a new group of boys joined the school, and among them was a boy called Aubrey. Aubrey was to teach him something else about himself and other people. He was small and fat – rotund, really – with a cheerful, freckly face, and a headful of general knowledge and trivia which he freely imparted with excited chatter. Much to his surprise, Richard liked the boy immediately and started to hang out with him; he just found him interesting and liked his cheerful nature.

Aubrey had smuggled a chemistry set into the school and could produce white smoke and green slime on demand, with much fanfare. He liked to show anyone who would look that the palms of his hands folded in a straight line across, unlike everyone else who had two slightly curved ones that did not join. He was proud of his uniqueness. Richard had found a friend, and he was amazed at how good that felt. They were not in the same class, but after lessons and before supper he started to look forward to spending time with Aubrey.

Within weeks Aubrey became a target. A group of boys did not like his fat, freckly face or his monkey hands. The bullying was relentless. Richard knew what it was like, and he backed away immediately. He did not take part, but he did not want to be a target either, so he kept away. Once or twice Aubrey had approached him in distress, but Richard ignored him. Within six weeks of the start of term, Aubrey's parents rescued him and took him out of school. He never returned. This struck Richard hard as well. Aubrey had been saved; loved enough to be saved. What Richard remembered most at the age of fourteen was the greatest act of cowardice he would ever commit in his life.

'I am going to kill that fucker,' he said out loud.

He considered the problem. It was not going to be easy. They were in a war zone and the camp was a self-contained military town and airfield. Leaving it to go out into the wasteland beyond the walls was dangerous, and as the perimeter was closely guarded by sentries, sangars, cameras, and sensors, it would be hard to exit without being observed or even shot. Leaving the camp by any of the gates would also not be possible without drawing attention to oneself and having a good reason. No, it would have to be done inside the camp.

Tomorrow he would scout the area around the airfield. The buildings in that part of the camp were mostly used for storage or workshops, not accommodation, and it was quiet there outwith the working day. It was used for exercise in the cool of the evening by runners and walkers who paced out the miles beside the long straight sections of the runway. The area was illuminated brightly by the arc lights from the airfield and the perimeter which facilitated the runners, but it was not ideal for his purpose. Between the low buildings there were alleys and storage areas that he could use.

At first, he thought he would use an AK assault rifle, but even that would cause problems. Although they had all fired them on the range – you never knew when it may be handy to use an enemy's weapon – they were not just lying around. He could procure one easily from the Afghan Army people, but not without someone knowing. In the end he decided to just use his own Army-issue pistol. The calibre of the pistol round was also used by the Americans, so there were thousands of guns that would need to be checked for a ballistics match. When he considered that, together with the number of troops that passed through the camp on a daily basis and also the large numbers of coalition weapons that had been lost or stolen over the years, it should not be a problem. He just had to be sure there was no connection between him and Standish.

Richard removed all rank insignia and purchased a replacement shemagh in a colour he never normally wore. It would hide half his face if necessary. In his combat clothes there was nothing to distinguish him from a thousand other soldiers.

He waited for three nights outside the main eating hall. This was a huge cafeteria with a wide range of hot and cold food of surprisingly good quality available. Almost all the inmates of Camp Bastion ate there, and although he saw Standish the first evening, he was in the company of some engineers and arrived and left with them. Richard followed at a discreet distance just to make sure he knew where Standish was staying.

The following day Standish did not appear. There were various eating places, and he could have been invited to dine with some of the upper echelons who had access to the private rooms where table service was the norm. Richard was beginning to give up hope, as he could not risk asking anyone for further information, and the days must be limited before his target headed home. He contemplated taking a bigger risk and confronting Standish in the accommodation, but there were too many things that could go wrong with that scenario. He was determined that he would not miss this opportunity, even though he had doubts about actually killing him; perhaps it would be enough to confront him, or even just beat the shit out of him.

On the fourth evening, as dusk was falling, he approached the cafeteria from a different direction. He never stayed in the same place long during his watches or used the same route. He spotted Standish crossing the street and heading towards the take-out window of the Pizza Hut. The Pizza Hut, along with some other fast-food outlets, was an alternate food source intended to give the troops a reminder of home. The pizzas were good but the single storey metal building with its garish signs suggested more *Blade Runner* than high street.

Richard did not hesitate; he hurried across and intercepted Standish halfway across the street. He patted him on the back, and as the man turned, Richard put on his most public schoolboy bonhomie grin.

'Hey, Standish, isn't it?' he said. 'From Saint Leonards? We're old schoolmates. I'd recognise you anywhere. It's been years, how've you been, old boy?'

Standish beamed and held out his hand.

'Oh, St. Leonards, I haven't heard that name for a while.'

Richard could see Standish did not recognise him but was not going to admit that. He ignored the other man's outstretched hand; he did not want any physical contact or any possible traces of his DNA on the man. Instead, he wrapped his arm around Standish's shoulder.

'Listen, I'm just off for a brief walk around the camp and then back here for a pizza – join me, and we can catch up on old times.' He was already steering him by the shoulder, so Standish could hardly refuse as Richard marched them both in the direction of the airfield.

He let his arm drop and mentioned the first teacher that came to mind. Standish relaxed a bit and soon started to reminisce. And with someone to bounce the names off, it was surprisingly easy to recall memories of the school, the masters, and the other boys. It was almost fully dark now, and the heat was fading out of the day. The camp, of course, was never truly dark; in reality the sunlight was merely replaced with the harsh glare of arc lights around the airfield while the residential and working areas were lit by normal street lights that gave a more homely feel to the residential parts of the camp.

They approached the main airfield and the storage area that Richard had identified in his plan. He was relieved to see that there were no runners visible and only a few walkers like themselves, but they were half a mile away down the side of the runway, where a large transport plane was manoeuvring in preparation for take-off. He turned off between two low buildings, where there was a storage area for empty forty-gallon oil drums, most of them painted red with yellow tops. When filled with concrete or sand, they came in useful for roadblocks and the construction of sangers, so they were always kept once their contents had been used.

'Head back now, I think,' he interrupted Standish, who was embarking on a long story about the headmaster.

'Yes, fine, I'm getting hungry.' He looked around. 'Are you sure this is the right way?'

The cargo plane thundered down the runway, halting any conversation. The noise reached a climax and gradually diminished as the jet hauled itself into the sky on the steepest, and thus safest, climb it could manage. When the noise had died down, Standish said. 'I am really sorry, but I don't remember your name.'

'Ogilvy.' Richard hoisted himself up onto one of the barrels that lined both sides of the alley and sat there. He took the pistol from its thigh holster and held it in his lap, just as though it was more comfortable. 'You don't remember me at all, do you?'

'Sorry, no, but are you sure you were the same year as me? What house were you? Er, perhaps we should be getting back now.' Standish looked a little uneasy.

'Same house as you, same year, same start term.'

'But only three of us started that... ah, that was you. I remember now. Well, if that is what this is about, it was all just fun, you know. I hope you're not expecting an apology or anything. We were just kids. Rough and tumble, you know. I think I'll head back now.'

Richard could hear a chopper winding up to take off down the far end of the runway. He raised the pistol and pointed it directly at Standish's face. 'Sit!'

Standish hesitated, looking as though he was about to run. Richard used his command voice. 'NOW! On the fucking ground.'

Standish complied but started to bluster. 'What will the Army do when they hear about this? You'll be finished. I won't say anything. Ok, I'll apologise, I mean it probably did go a bit far at times, but no lasting harm was done. Was it? I'm sorry, OK? Let's go and I'll shout you that pizza.'

The chopper had taken off and headed towards, them getting louder. Richard slipped down from the oil drum, stood over the man on the ground, and shot him in the knee. Standish howled and rolled around over the ground, clutching his leg. As the noise of the departing chopper receded, Richard put his boot on the bully's neck. 'Quiet now.' He increased the pressure until the need to breathe overcame the pain in his leg.

Standish looked up with frightened eyes, pushing against Richard's boot with both hands.

'Can you feel it now? Say my name.'

There was blood on Standish's lip where he had bitten into it, disbelief and fear in his eyes. 'Please, please, stop. I've got money, lots of money. Anything you want. I'm sorry. I am really.'

'Say my name.'

'Ogilvy. Ogilvy. Ogilvy.' It tapered off into a whimper.

Richard just waited, increasing the pressure on the man's neck if he got too noisy. Richard had killed before, of course, but it was different on the battlefield when your own life was part of the game. You rarely got to see that it was a person you killed, or even to be sure you had. An enemy in your rifle sights was just a target, and it was always best not to start thinking of them as people. If you hesitated, it might be you who was just a target, nothing more.

He had not been totally sure he would do this, but now that he was committed it was worth it. A wrong righted, and somehow it made up a little for Aubrey as well.

A few minutes later a helicopter came into land, and Richard quickly stepped back a couple of paces and fired a bullet into Standish's head.

Chapter 13

James (2023)

The clocks had not yet changed over from British Summer Time, so it was still light at six as the group started to gather at James and Nancy's home. It was unseasonably warm, but the last few weeks had seen almost unending rain; today it had eased off, and it was a pleasant evening. The warmth was a good thing, as the war in Ukraine had caused energy prices to spike and the Government had not seemed to be able to do anything about it. To James, the solution was obvious. The people were paying more to feed the wealthy shareholders of the major oil and gas companies. A real government need only reverse that process.

Stevie had turned up wearing only a t-shirt and shorts. James was not sure whether that was due to the unseasonable weather or the fact that he was still young enough not to feel the cold. Richard had arrived with Jack, and he had been pleased to see them both, as they were not frequent attenders at their meetings. It was going to be a full house of Board members tonight, and Nancy was already laying out some sandwiches and soft drinks on the large dining room table.

When they had all taken their seats around the table, James opened the meeting.

'As you all know, IDay is not that far away, and Richard's plan is complete – more or less – with only details to be ironed out and briefings to be finalised. The training and recruitment of the Militia is going well. In short, there is not much else to discuss for the takeover, but what comes after is now much more important. There cannot be a vacuum after we take power. There must be a provisional government and a plan ready to be announced so that the people know what to expect and how they will benefit.'

'There has to be strong leadership, and I suggest a single leader for the first few years. That is the way to get things done,' said Richard. 'Strong government is the only way.'

'Whoa,' said Karen, 'this is not a military coup. It's a new country, a new way, a new system, not military dictatorship.'

'But we are taking the country with a military force,' said Jack.

'True,' said James, 'and it is hard to know how it will develop on the day, as the military will be in control but the switch to civilian power must be seen to happen almost immediately. As co-leaders, Isobel and myself will be the face of the provisional government, and we will be visible on social media and TV, and we will also announce the intention to hold elections in the "unspecific" near future, setting out the course to be followed. Hopefully, a good proportion of existing members of parliament will agree to join us in order to continue to represent their local areas, which will bring some stability.'

'It will not be as easy as you think. It's foolish to think that the sitting MSPs will just go along with a new government. All sorts of things will go wrong from day one,' said Richard. 'A single strong leader that people can focus on will help.'

'But we have to present a civilian side early on, clearly distinct from the military. The military takeover will be the most visible on the day, but then we have to switch quickly to government – using the current MSPs is a good way to have a smoother transition of power,' said Isobel.

'I doubt you can get them on board at all,' said Richard.

'Remember, if all goes well, we'll have control of the TV and radio and will be very active on social media. We'll have a huge platform to calm people and explain what is happening and lead them along. No previous revolutions will have had the ability to reach everyone in the first few hours, ensuring that people understand what is happening. We will be able to respond instantly to emerging news as well as to broadcast the statements that we have agreed on,' said Maggie.

'There is that,' conceded Richard. 'It's a tribute to you and Stevie that the Board listened to your input early on, otherwise we would be stuck with broadcasting like dinosaurs only on the BBC.'

'The prepared statements will explain what is happening, what to expect, and that their present MSP will continue to represent them. Most of the MSPs will be forewarned of what is expected of them through the media. People will know that there is nothing to fear, that we are just going through a transition, that their jobs are safe, that the currency is stable, and that all services will still operate. Everything is couched in a "business as usual but Scotland is now independent" tone,' said Maggie.

'I don't believe that the politicians will be able to change so quickly,' said Richard. 'There will be enormous resentment and opposition. Some sort of pressure will be needed other than just politely asking them to join you.'

'We have to believe that Scottish Independence, when it is delivered "fait accompli", so to speak, will be accepted by those who have always believed in it, worked for it, and will now have the opportunity to be involved in its inception,' said Isobel.

'I agree,' said James. 'We will tap into the desire for independence, using the internet to maximum effect, and bringing the people with us. Yes, not all politicians will join us immediately, but I think most will, and others will come on board if we give them a day or two to see how things develop.' He paused, but there was no further argument from Richard.

'We stick to the plan. We outlaw political parties on day one and give the elected representatives the choice to remain as MSPs and represent the people who voted for them. Hopefully, many of them will see it as an opportunity for them to actively work on behalf of their constituents. We all know that most politicians enter politics for good reasons, yet once they are elected, they no longer primarily represent their electorate but are constrained by the party's need to stay in power. They then spend the next four or five years bashing the other parties and dancing with the media in order to convince the electorate to re-elect them. It is not a good system.'

'The media has a lot to answer for,' said Isobel. 'The present government system is an unhealthy triangle between parliament, political party, and press. Politicians rarely move outside the range of public opinion, and that is largely defined by the media, which sets the agenda through the headlines and the main stories of the day and then manages the questions that politicians have to answer. The agenda should not be controlled by the media.'

'That's well put,' said Stevie. 'The media can be haranguing a government for failing to adequately fund the NHS, and the very next day be criticising them for putting up taxes.'

'Agreed,' said James, 'but again it is a hard problem to solve without limiting the freedom of the press. This works both ways – government has to stop manipulating the information it gives to the press, and instead give full disclosure and information in regard to decision making; and the media in turn needs to take a more responsible attitude in publishing all relevant information, not just the juicy bits. Perhaps there is a case to make all media become service industries and therefore run without profit. Then they will have no need to sell salacious stories just to sell more papers or increase shareholder returns.'

'Supposing some MSPs join us early on, how do you envisage them helping the new government initially?' asked Simon. 'Surely, they will take a lot of convincing to suddenly become part of a rebellious provisional government. They may just join to keep their jobs and their position.'

'These are public servants who are already committed to serving the people. That's why they became MSPs,' said James. 'We'll not convince everyone, but as long as a good number come on board, it will give us early legitimacy. Think of the SNP members; we will give them a chance to live their dream, with independence handed to them on a plate. I'm convinced most will come aboard,' he went on.

'I don't think you fully understand human nature,' said Richard.

James ignored him. 'To answer your question, Simon. We intend to set up a system where MSPs not only represent their electorate but actively help manage that area, as well as representing their regions in Edinburgh. They will have more power than ever before. Each area will have a regional council composed of members of parliament, the incumbent council leaders, both officials and elected members, and a citizen Shadow Panel. The panel members will initially be volunteers, but hopefully in the future the members can be selected by sortition on an annual basis or on a short-term secondment.'

'Sortition?' said Simon.

'Selected by lottery is the dictionary definition, uh... think selection for a jury. But it will need to be a little more sophisticated than that, with the criteria for inclusion shaped to widen the range of experience or narrow it down. If the region is contemplating, for example, a new hydroelectric scheme, then the inclusion of environmentalists, hydrologists, wildlife experts, and local residents would be advisable on the panel to balance the views of the power companies, their financial backers, and the construction engineers.'

Karen was nodding. 'Like a Soviet system, I can see that.'

'Yes, but without overriding control,' said James.

'What's the point of that then if they do not have power?' said Simon.

'The remit of the Shadow Panel is to make sure that decisions are taken with the community in mind for the best of reasons, and not because the balance of power is held by the ones who most benefit. They will, if you like, play devil's advocate. They will also try to assess the impact and foresee any unintentional consequences. In short, to try and ensure decisions are made for the best and without bias. We could build in the power to veto to give the panel some power. We're in this to make serious structural changes to the way modern countries and economies work. It will not be easy, but it will be possible. There will be a learning curve, and we'll make changes if and when we need to, to make it work.

'There should also be a Shadow Panel that sits alongside the main parliament with a similar function. They will help ensure new laws or regulations are not only unbiased but thoroughly researched, well-crafted, and fit for purpose from the outset.'

'There needs to be some selection process for these citizen panel members, surely?' said Karen. 'Or at least a way to exclude those with vested interests.'

'Yes, possibly some sort of criteria will be needed, but there is a lot of expertise in all sorts of fields, knowledge and experience that we can use. Government should no longer be left to amateurs,' said James. 'At least with government we can see how to make significant changes, and it will depend a lot on how we put it across to the sitting MSPs and the public. In the case of our other structural changes – the public ownership of networks and service, the redistribution of wealth through tax reform and curtailing the rewards to shareholders and sustainability over growth – these all have tangible levers that we can move or systems that we can change.

'What is much more difficult to change is people's perception of the society and the state. It is not so easy to turn citizenship, which is largely meaningless at the moment, into something substantial that people value. There are no easy tools to use; it is all mixed up with nationalism, mostly around sport, society, culture, and even tax and the judicial system have an effect.'

'Stevie and I have been giving a lot of thought to prisons,' said Maggie. 'One measure that reflects the healthy state of a society is by the number of people imprisoned, and taking that to a logical conclusion a perfect society would have no prisons. So perhaps the less prisons one has, the better the society. No prisoners is obviously never going to be entirely achievable but is something to be aimed for. The only way to significantly reduce prison population is to remove poverty, injustice, and to ensure that no one feels left out.'

'Another, better way to cut the prison population is the death penalty,' cut in Richard. 'The state should have the courage and the unquestionable authority to dispense the death penalty. It is strange how we baulk at executing a serial rapist/killer in our own country, yet at the same time consider it perfectly OK to kill unarmed civilians in other places that do little more than get in the way.'

'The state should be morally above killing people,' said Karen.

'Presumably you mean its own citizens, as opposed to those of other countries,' said Richard.

'I agree with Richard. I don't see why the death penalty should not be mandatory,' said Simon. 'Those who commit crimes that are clearly unforgivable, and where it is unlikely that they'll ever be rehabilitated. Murder, crimes against children, violent rapes, violent serial assaults, that sort of thing.'

'No. The death penalty signifies state failure, not a successful justice system,' said Karen. Besides, there will always be innocent people who are wrongly convicted.'

'Modern DNA testing makes that less likely,' said Simon. 'I also think prisoners handed down life or very long sentences should be offered euthanasia, with a financial incentive of a cash payment to their family.'

'Fucksake, it gets worse,' said Karen. 'Not everything is about money.'

'Well, I suppose the payment could be split between the victims or the victims' surviving family and the family of the criminal,' said Simon.

Karen just looked at him.

'OK, OK,' said James. 'Let's leave the death penalty for now; it's not going to be decided today. Maggie, you were saying about prisons in general?'

'So, for the less serious offences, we should do everything possible to re-educate offenders and give them the opportunity to work, train, and earn alongside voluntary and public sector workers, so that the work is not seen wholly as punishment but in a positive light.

'Each sentence could be part reparation and part punishment, with all inmates having a dedicated mentor to guide them and determine what community service work, training, education, or a mixture of these would suit the offender. For work, he or she will get paid the same wage as other workers, but half of the wages will go to victim reparation until that is paid in full. The debt would be previously set by the court, and once it has been paid then the offender can choose to carry on working to reduce his sentence. Low security prisons should be open and comfortable and will operate on the prisoner's word of good behaviour. Breaking their word would add days or weeks to the sentence. We must do everything possible to turn offenders into useful members of society.'

'Ah, I see how that fits in with Isobel's Ministry of Labour!' James waved away the chuckles.

'We also think,' said Stevie, 'that voluntary national service that offers many options might help channel some of the desire for adventure and appeal to the risk-taking nature of the young that sometimes manifests as aggression. The service can be a choice between all arms of the military, fire service and rescue, or Service Corps that assist other countries. So, for example, instead of giving financial aid to poorer countries, Service Corps can supply work teams to help build hospitals or schools or supply emergency assistance to forest fires, flood, earthquakes, and other natural disasters.

'What we need is a complete overhaul of the existing system,' continued Stevie, 'so it's a long-term project. To get the prison population to near zero means fundamentally changing society, and we must start with the children. By eliminating poverty, ensuring that from birth every child is wanted and cared for, and that every person has the opportunity to fulfil their potential and find what suits them best.'

'Reforming the school system is also crucial,' said Maggie. 'All education establishments should be of equal merit – no child should be disadvantaged by attending a substandard school. All will be secular; there should be no segregation of children, no Catholic, no Muslim, no Jewish schools, no home schooling, and absolutely no private schools. The best teachers should not be siphoned off to private schools with higher salaries. Religious studies must only happen outside the public school system.

'When new buildings are required, then preference should be given to community hubs that host education, retirement accommodation, and community services, like libraries and swimming pools, all on the same campus. Interaction between them should be promoted so that children visit pensioners, and they share their experiences through talks or active participation. Secondary pupils give extra tuition to those who need it in the primary school. The idea is again to foster a sense of community.'

'Thanks, Maggie, Stevie,' said James. 'I can see that it would take a whole generation to even start to achieve these goals. But I promise that we will start the process.

'Improving the feeling of citizenship may also help to improve the perception of paying taxes,' he went on. 'Somehow, we need to get across that taxation is not inherently bad, and if you want to live in a society with first class health and public services then they have to be paid for. A large part of our present infrastructure problems is due to governments being too weak to raise sufficient taxes to cover the cost of what is actually needed.

'So, a complete overhaul of the tax system will be part of our manifesto, with the aim of redistributing wealth. That ties in with our Fair Economy strategy. The message has to be that no matter how rich you are, you can't buy everything. Yes, at present, you can buy private health or private education for your kids, but you still want the police, the fire service, or an ambulance to turn up when you really need one, and to deliver you to an emergency unit where you will get instant attention. And it's not just the emergency services you can't buy; you also want the streets that you live on to be clean and the rubbish taken away, and you want your kids to be safe.'

'But won't all the rich people fuck off somewhere else if we make it too demanding?' said Simon, defensively.

'Some will, but most people will begin to see that high quality public services are only possible with a high tax regime. We must gradually change the perception of the wealthy paying more tax to make them feel good about it, just like they do when they give to charity. Additional voluntary taxation for the super-rich, with a say in where their money goes, may be a possibility. Fund a hospital, or a ferry, or a school, or a library and have it named after you. Even if it is a general gift, then a street name or square can be your legacy. Choose to pay an amount well above your tax liability, then you won't even need to fill out a tax return or pay an accountant.'

'There is a certain truth in that,' said Simon. 'Sometimes I have had accountants working for me who have saved me x amount in tax by some clever dodge and then charged me fifty per cent of the saving as their fee. A sort of win, win, I suppose.'

'Trickledown economics just does not work,' said Karen, 'and it quickly becomes "flows up and sticks" economics. I mean as in hoarded. OK, maybe the wealthy employ a few people and spend into the economy, but much more wealth becomes locked up. It is used to make them feel good, to generate more wealth, or to pass down to future generations of already rich families, or merely to have a bigger number next to their name on the world's rich list.

'It is what our four main strategies are designed to do – redistribute wealth, eliminate poverty and hopelessness, so that everyone has a job and feels part of the country. Citizenship is the most important, but also the most difficult to change. We'll make it a great country, a place where everyone will want to live and work, such a great country that we will be turning the super-rich away.'

The room was quiet for a while. For those brought up in the ways of democratic capitalism, it seemed an insurmountable challenge to change so much.

'On a brighter note,' said Maggie, 'with climate change on the way, we're likely to have a Mediterranean climate soon. We may well become the foremost European holiday destination in a few years. Just think of all those lovely beaches we have, but with sun instead of rain. That's another reason why people will want to stay or come and live here.'

Chapter 14

HMS Ambuscade

As soon as Lieutenant Campbell MacDonald's hand closed on his rolled-up dirty socks and felt the weight was wrong – much heavier than it should be – his pulse rate and breathing quickened. He suddenly became conscious of the low background drone of machinery, the murmur of voices from cabins further down the passageway, the hum of the air circulating system, the smell of many bodies packed into an enclosed space, and the slightly woolly metallic taste of the air itself. This was his world, and he was proud to be part of it. He was normally so attuned to the sounds and smells of the submarine that they did not impact on him at all, except now it was different. Now it felt suddenly alien. It was as if the sub knew he was really not part of the team anymore and had already marked him as an intruder.

There were four bullets – he pulled one out and ran his fingertips over the smooth metal. The copper that jacketed the lead was brighter than the brass case. So small, so neat and clean. He had eight of them all together; four more hidden in other dirty clothes. They were military calibre, so at least could be explained away as having come from the practice range that all officers completed regularly, although it would still be a serious offence to have removed live rounds from the range. This could not be said of the pistol, the mere thought of which had his heart pounding again. He had not looked at it since MacQuoid had come to his cabin door a day after they sailed. Without ceremony, the man had handed it to him in a fast-food container, with no other comment other than a loud, 'Leftovers as you requested, sir!' As he marched off, Cammy had watched him duck his large head as he cleared the hatchway at the end of the passage.

Cammy had hidden the pistol under his bunk, taped to the underside of the metal support. He was angry at first that he had to be the one to hide it, but he understood that his cubby hole of what passed for a cabin was far more secure than the limited private space of a crew member. Although a modern pistol, it had long been superseded in the military, and he was not familiar with it. The cabin was not safe enough to take it out and check he knew how to use it, so he would have to smuggle it to the head soon. It was the only place you could sit without being disturbed. He would do that tonight, and even though he knew the pistol could carry twice that number of rounds, he would load it with the eight bullets. Eight bullets. Eight bullets to take down a bomber, the most powerful weapon in the world.

He looked at his watch: one more day now and a few hours. The time was fast approaching, and he had to decide to keep to the plan or do nothing. He was more and more tempted just to let it slip past. There was no way to communicate with the others. If they had decided against going ahead with the revolution ashore, or even delayed it, he was going to be out on a limb – a long, lonely limb. If they failed or it did not go ahead, he would lose everything and no doubt spend the rest of his days in a military prison. Would his part make a difference? Militarily no, but as a bargaining chip it was a major factor in Scotland's future. It had to be at that time on that day.

Then there was MacQuoid to consider. Cammy was a little afraid of him, he admitted to himself, and was not sure how the man would react if he failed to go through with the plan. MacQuoid could have been a poster model for the Royal Navy, unlike some of the other weedy youths that looked too young to be crew members. He was big and burly, filled out the uniform, and looked like a matelot should, with his closely cropped beard and hair. He was also likeable, Cammy acknowledged, although he would not want to be on the wrong side of him.

MacQuoid had very carefully, over many months, recruited ten members of the crew willing to join them and take the risk for Scotland, or for money, or both. There were several more he was less sure of and were not included in the plan, but who might be useful after they had taken control. Cammy worried about this, as although a good proportion of the crew were Scottish, he was not sure that their loyalty to their country would override the Navy's programming and influence, or for that matter the status quo. To combat this, each of the ten, and MacQuoid, had been paid five thousand pounds up front, with another fifty to follow on successful completion. He hoped this would be enough insurance, but it had to be assumed that all crew members who had not already committed wholeheartedly to the cause would need to be treated the same as the English on board.

It was not the same for the officers. Except for him, they were all English. In the submarine service, by far the majority of officers were English. Cammy had wondered about this for a long time – could they actually have imagined this scenario? No Scotsman had ever captained a bomber, although one or two had reached second-in-command. If the plan succeeded, he would become the first ever Scottish Commander of a Royal Navy ballistic missile nuclear submarine, and shortly afterwards the first ever Captain in Scotland's new navy.

There was a sharp rap on the bulkhead beside his doorway, and he hurriedly pocketed the rounds, stood, and pulled the curtain aside. 'Captain wants to see you in his cabin, straightaway, sir.' A seaman delivered the message and then hurried away.

Cammy closed the curtain and put the bullets and dirty socks back into his laundry bag. He quickly checked his appearance in the mirror, straightened the epaulette of rank which was attached to the front of his uniform shirt, ran his fingers through his hair to neaten it, and swept it back from his forehead. The Captain had a bug about his hair. It was very dark and naturally greasy and was just getting long enough to be described as 'unregulation'. No doubt he would be advised to have it cut again if he did not take care of it soon.

The Captain's cabin included an outer section that served as an office and was located just beside the main control room. Cammy knocked, and looked into the control centre as he waited. It always reminded him of a starship from a movie, although somewhat more compact. Along the sides, rows of screens ran at head height and lower down at each of the operator's stations, where men, most wearing headphones, concentrated on them and their keyboards. At either end, hatchways joined to the central passageway that ran the full length of the submarine. To one side of this and facing forward, a smaller section held two sailors who sat in high-backed swivel chairs. This was the manoeuvring station, and the two pilots controlled the movement of the sub; although most of their job involved monitoring the automatic systems rather than actually steering the vessel. They were, however, always ready to take manual control in case of an emergency. The submarine moved in three dimensions like a slow-moving aircraft rather than a surface ship, and the controls reflected this.

There was little talking, only a quiet murmur and an occasional call out as a crew member drew the attention of a supervisor for a double check. In the centre of the room was a chart table, and standing leaning against it was the officer of the watch. At this time it was the First Officer, Lieutenant Commander Ray Nichols, second-in-command of the submarine. He looked up and gave a friendly wave, and Cammy nodded back in return.

He had been on submarines for most of his career and knew every station, every system, every control, as well as and probably better than all this boat's officers and most that he had sailed with before. *Why had he been overlooked again and again for promotion?* There was always some minor negative report held him back.

He heard a grunt from the cabin and assumed that was his cue to enter.

'Hello, Campbell, take a seat.' The Captain liked to use Christian names instead of ranks when they were in private areas or the officers' wardroom.

'Commander,' replied Cammy. He knew this would not be lost on the Captain, as although his actual rank was Commander, all Navy men expected to be addressed as Captain when in command of a ship. The Captain always insisted on calling him Campbell, even though he had repeatedly expressed his dislike of it. He resented his hippy parents, who in some weird way had thought that combining the clan names of Campbell and MacDonald was their gift of love and peace to the world. They did not have to live with it, and he adopted Cammy as soon as school made it an imperative to survival in the playground. The fucking Englishman probably did not understand the significance anyway.

Cammy sat. The Captain leaned back in his chair behind the desk and eyed him for a moment.

'You're a good officer, and you know the boat better than anyone.'

'Thank you, sir.' He recognised an incoming praise sandwich.

'But I feel that I have to pull you up on a couple of things, for the sake of your future career.'

Cammy just waited.

'I think you need to look at your behaviour with the crew. You are tending on the too friendly side, if you get my meaning. I know that in the service we have a much more relaxed atmosphere because of the close living in the confines of the boat, but all the same, that must not be taken too far. I notice in the control room that you are very relaxed with the crew, so a little more firmness would, I think, generate a bit more respect. Do you agree?'

Cammy knew from past experience that there was no point in disagreeing with the Captain or defending a position that to all intents and purposes had already been decided on.

'Well, now you mention it, sir, I probably should take more care.' Cammy could not think what he was getting at. He was sure he was no different to the other officers in this respect.

'Also, you seem very friendly with one of the cooks. Just make sure it does not cross any boundaries.'

Fuck, thought Cammy, *now it makes sense.* Although most of the framework of the plan had been discussed and finalised ashore and off base, far from prying eyes and ears, he had recently had several lengthy conversations with MacQuoid to finalise the details and set the times. They had chosen public areas at quiet times where they could have come across each other, but it would have been hard to think of a reason for a long chat that was not on a personal basis. He wondered who had reported that back.

Then a horrible thought occurred to him. *Did the Captain actually think I was propositioning him? Fuck, no!* Surely not; it was unthinkable, but it still made Cammy squirm inside and his hatred for the Captain notched up another degree. The Navy would view that sort of relationship between officer and crew as bad as stealing one of their submarines. That thought made him feel better.

'So, Campbell, are we on the same page?'

'Yes, sir, I understand. Thank you for the chat. I will be much more aware in future.' He got up to leave and turned smiled pleasantly at the Captain. 'My name is Cammy, remember?'

The Captain did not return his smile. 'Thank you, Lieutenant, that will be all.'

The idea had come to him long ago as an oft repeated favourite daydream and even before he had become disillusioned with his career. He was probably one of the most experienced and knowledgeable submarine officers in the service, but there was something in his character, something that was evident to his superiors, some streak of awkwardness, individualism, or perhaps disrespect that his seniors often picked up on and disliked him for. He knew that many times he would have been much wiser to have bitten his lip rather than utter some smart-assed comment that often bordered on insubordination.

As his career progressed, the eagerness to learn and be the best was gradually replaced by more and more resentment. This was made worse by knowing that some of his peer group who had been promoted ahead of him were nowhere near as knowledgeable but had the advantage of being English. Ironically, even though the upper echelons were not keen on promoting him, they had no hesitation in exploiting his expertise when it came to selecting the best possible men to be assigned to the build and commissioning of the new fleet of submarines that would replace the existing V class. So here he was, still a Lieutenant, but with a prestigious posting to serve on the Navy's newest ship – the *Ambuscade* – the first of the new class.

Sometimes, lying in his bunk, he had dreamed of giving it all up and retiring to a Caribbean island with a shedload of money. As winning the lottery seemed statistically near impossible, his favoured alternate plan was to hijack one of these very expensive submarines and hold it for ransom. Each sub was worth billions, and especially this one as the first of its class and on its maiden voyage. What would the government pay to get it back? Millions, surely? The plan he dreamed about was straightforward. Put together a small team of like-minded crew members, hijack the sub, dump the rest of the crew somewhere, demand a ransom, and then go hide until the money was paid into bank accounts already set up. The submarine was designed to hide, so it would be almost undiscoverable. And when the time was right, he could surface at some tropical island paradise – preferably one without a criminal extradition treaty with the UK – and live happily ever after.

But now, in this real world, he was actually going to do it, put his plan into action. And although he grew ever more anxious each passing day as it got nearer to implementation, it was somewhat tempered by the fact he was no longer in it for personal gain but for a much higher and nobler purpose. His plan had been hijacked, so to speak. It was Karen who had turned his idle daydream into something much more substantial, and his aim from personal gain to something far more honourable. One night, lying in bed, he had sought to amuse her with his get-rich-quick-scheme, much embellished and padded out for the story telling. She'd laughed along with him and agreed to join him on his island paradise.

It was only in retrospect that he realised that she had become overly interested that night and probed him with many questions.

*

Often he did not bother returning to his flat in Glasgow for weekends or short leave periods, as the Navy had supplied him with satisfactory accommodation in Barrow where he had been based for a number of years, watching over, learning the systems, advising and improving where he could, as the construction of the submarine progressed. But this time he had decided to take the two-week break and catch up with his parents and siblings and visit his old Glasgow haunts. He was glad that he had.

Walking home one day along his street, he noticed that a shop front that had previously always seemed closed was open on this occasion, the door invitingly ajar, and had the rather intriguing sign of the Caledonian Independence Party printed on it. The windows were covered over up to shoulder height with some sort of fabric, with the only embellishment being a repeat of the sign. The whole effect was austere and obviously designed to signal its office status rather than a mere shop. He had not heard of it before, but then spending half your life underwater was not good for keeping up with the news.

If anyone had asked Cammy what he thought about independence, he would have responded positively, and he had voted 'YES' in the referendum, but that was about the limit of his interest. He had certainly never considered joining a campaign or a political party for that purpose, so what piqued his curiosity that day he was never sure.

It was a single, open space, and there was not much in the room except a table with a few left-wing newspapers and magazines scattered on its surface, whilst a number of mismatched chairs did empty duty around the table or against the wall. There were a couple of racks with leaflets containing a wide array of subjects, from littering to local care homes. At one side was an office-type desk with stacks of paper and a computer monitor, at which sat a woman, speaking on the phone, her head turned away from him.

He noticed in passing that she had great hair in a deep shade of shiny black, but there was little of interest in the room, so he was about to leave when the woman turned towards him, smiled, and gave him a 'be with you in a minute' wave. She had blue eyes and a nice smile, and he was mildly surprised that she seemed so friendly. He paused, thinking that it would be rude to leave now after her wave, but also because she was the most attractive woman he had seen in a long time. He took a seat at the table and pretended to read one of the magazines.

After a few minutes, she put the phone down, got up, and came over to him. This surprised him, as he had expected her to call him over to the desk to conduct any business, and there was an empty chair there for that purpose. He could not help noticing that she fulfilled all his favourite criteria – bright smile, dark hair, nice eyes, and a good figure. Unexpectedly, he felt that unconscious tiny visceral tremor deep down in his abdomen, somewhere between stomach and balls, which signalled that her attractiveness was not solely in his head. He hoped that the animal chemistry was going to be mutual.

When she pulled up a chair and sat, he realised that she was a good deal older than him, but his gut immediately discounted that as irrelevant. He just knew he wanted to know her better. No wedding ring either.

It had been a while since he had had a girlfriend other than a short-term hook-up. Being away at sea was not conducive to sustaining any sort of relationship, and finding a woman suited to him and life as a Navy wife had not been one of his priorities. She was probably too old to have children, anyway – not that he was even sure he wanted them.

She had asked him something. He reran the question quickly in his head. She'd asked if he supported the independence movement, and jeez, here he was contemplating marriage.

'Yes, strongly support,' he said, feeling vaguely embarrassed.

'Good to hear. You came to the right place.'

'I've not heard of you before. Are you new?'

'Yes, fairly new on the scene. We are just starting to build a base of members. The aim of the party is primarily independence, but we also believe that there should be a better and fairer form of government, and we are working towards that.'

'But hasn't the SNP more or less captured the independence vote?'

'Ah yes, probably.' She did not seem offended by this question. 'But their big disadvantage, and also why they are half hearted in their pursuit of it, is that as soon as they achieve independence then their reason-to-be no longer exists. So, Scotland would almost inevitably revert to Labour. Hard to be committed when success means the end for them.'

'Interesting thought. I'm not sure they think that way,' said Cammy, 'but doesn't the same apply to you?'

'NO! Because we are focused on what comes after. The important bit, if you like.'

They talked on for a while, and without too much resistance she signed him up as a member of the party. Only after he had paid his first membership did he summon up enough courage to ask her out for a drink. She looked at him long and hard before answering.

'You're too young for me,' she said. 'No offence.'

'I'm pretty sure we are in the same decade, so you're not too old for me.'

'Smooth talker!' She laughed. 'And I'm sure we are not.'

Chapter 15

Karen (IDay minus 1)

Karen sat at a table in the café where she had been several times with Cammy. He had first brought her here soon after they met as, although he spent most of his time at the shipyard in Barrow, he knew the area around the Clyde Naval Base well. Helensburgh was the nearest town to the base, so it was not surprising that all the Navy personnel knew it well. One of the attractions of the town was the Hill House mansion, which was one of the few private houses designed by the renowned architect Charles Rennie Mackintosh.

Cammy had taken her for lunch at the café at the Hill House visitor centre early on in their relationship, and she had thought then that he was probably trying to impress her with his cultural knowledge. After lunch they had done the tour of the house, and she had been impressed with its feel of a timeless family home, even though it had been built over a century before.

Karen ordered a coffee and an empire biscuit. Apparently, according to the waitress, the biscuit had won awards, but she barely tasted it. She was waiting for Maggie and Rena to join her. Maggie had recruited the housekeeper after the billionaire had joined the Board. She had come to the office one day to sign up as a party member, and Maggie had remembered her from her initial visit to Simon's estate. They got to chatting, and Rena had offered to work in the office on her day off from housekeeping duties. She had been a regular ever since. Karen and Maggie, who mostly ran the office, had come to know her well.

Karen thought that Rena did not have many friends stuck out there in the Ayrshire estate, so several times they had invited her along with them for a coffee or lunch. Today they were all skiving off, as they had closed the office for a few days. They would open it again on IDay, and Karen and Rena would staff it. Karen was happy with this arrangement, preferring to be on the side-lines on the actual day. She suspected that the Party office might become a focus for people seeking reassurance or more information once IDay commenced.

She could see the Firth of Clyde from here, where a few weeks ago Cammy and his submarine had headed down to the open sea. By now it would be somewhere deep in the Atlantic.

How do you dump a sailor? Before he leaves, so he is miserable the whole time at sea with no opportunity to meet someone else to soften the blow? In the middle of the voyage by a letter or a text? Although apparently, apart from family emergencies, communication is restricted while the vessel is submerged. When he got back? So, he's been missing you for months and looking forward to the reunion, and then you dump him? No easy answer, she thought.

She knew she should not have let it go on so long. She tried to avoid making herself feel bad, but in truth she had stayed with him much longer than she had intended or really wanted to. Initially it had been fun, but then the hijack plan came up and it had seemed too good an opportunity to miss. She had stayed at first to persuade him, which took time because he was continually getting cold feet about the whole idea. And then she had stayed to stiffen his resolve, as he frequently waned on the project. It had been made easier once Cammy had mustered the courage to approach a crew member – a Navy chef (apparently the Navy no longer had cooks) he had sailed with several times. The chef was a stout member of the SNP and was a loudly vocal supporter of independence, so Cammy had been as sure as he could be that he would not report him.

In the event, the chef took immediately to the plan, and with his deeper knowledge of the other crew members with similar leanings he recruited the rest of the team that would try to take the submarine. Cammy was certainly more comfortable once there was someone else to carry the load.

That did not stop him becoming increasingly nervous about someone letting slip the plan as the chef recruited more crew members to the cause. She had worried at times that he would give up on the scheme.

To help steady him, she had come up with the incentive that she hoped would cement his resolve, by reinforcing the loyalty of his co-conspirators with a financial inducement. She had taken the idea to the Board, and they had agreed to an initial five thousand pounds payment to each member of the team, with the promise of a further fifty thousand to each mutineer on successful completion. They had not been too hard to convince, as the thought of taking the newest nuclear submarine was too good an opportunity to miss, even if the chances of success were not good. Even Simon had not put up too much of a fight, as he knew – if successful – the larger sums would come out of the new government's coffers, not his own pocket.

The die was cast, the ship had sailed; she chuckled to herself at that. Whether he would go through with it or was even capable of it, she was still not sure. Had she abused his trust? Coerced him with her sex? Cajoled him, more like. He had not been easy to convince, and overcoming his fear had been easier than overcoming his reluctance to go against the Navy. She had given him two years, and she knew that was enough.

Karen had never told him that her preference was for her own sex, although he was not the first man she'd had brief affairs with. She found him attractive and enjoyed herself with him, but it had gone on just a little too long. Her long-term relationship had ended a few years ago, and it seemed hard to find another suitable partner at her age. Hook-ups were easy enough, but anything more permanent was more difficult. She had become wary of overly enthusiastic women promising the earth, after a couple of bad experiences with women who had been straight and were taking advantage of her to satisfy their curiosity.

She admired Isobel immensely, and they had been friends almost their whole adult lives. Karen knew she did not have what Isobel had, and whatever it was, she would make a great leader or co-leader. She liked the idea of both a joint male and female lead, and wondered if that could be part of a new system. Two leaders of equal power – no patriarchal crap. Two leaders who could both listen; that would be hard to find, and harder to repeat.

It was remarkable that both James and Isobel did not consider their own ideas to be the best or immutable. They listened, they compromised, they changed, they backtracked, they u-turned if it made sense. Nothing was set in stone that could not be improved or altered. For all her socialist genes, Karen believed that James was right. Flexibility had to be better than dogged adherence to outdated ideologies.

She knew that she was not a forceful character, but was content to know that she had had a significant input in tempering James's right wing and too authoritarian tendencies with her much more socialist viewpoint. She was aware and greatly appreciated that he had been willing to listen and learn and temper his own ideas. He often said that the best way might be just to take the best bits of everything and combine them together.

Karen looked up to see Maggie and Rena making their way through the tables. She raised her hand to get their attention, and they both waved back. Rena smiled broadly at her, and she stood out amongst the other more sober diners, with her cropped spiky hair, so blonde it was almost white. She had a pierced nose and many ear piercings that seemed all the rage these days. Karen did not wholly approve of piercings and thought they got in the way – there were some very sensitive parts of the body. She had wondered if Rena had them anywhere else, but quickly stamped on that thought. She adored Rena for her youthful enthusiasm and positive character, and the way she slotted in well with the two other women.

They chatted amiably for a while and Rena, who had been very reticent at first, joined in. She had become much more open and confident about speaking to them as she got to know them better. Karen had wanted to ask her more about Simon, but had refrained up until now.

The waitress came to take their lunch order, and once she had gone, Karen asked, 'What's it like working for Simon? He always struck me as a bit if a misogynist.'

Rena looked confused.

'Hates women,' said Maggie quickly. 'Like, you know, not exactly supportive of feminist principles.'

'Oh, yes, I know what you mean,' said Rena. 'But actually, he is not too bad. It's his wife Louise that is the bitch. He tried it on when I first started working for him, but only once, and to be fair when I told him that wasn't going to happen, he accepted it and never approached me again.'

'Sounds like a story there,' said Karen.

'Yes, do tell,' said Maggie.

'It's almost funny really. I was working in the kitchen, chopping veg.'

'Wait!' said Karen. 'You cook as well? I thought you just cleaned for them.'

'No, I do everything, really, but remember I live there free. They pay me ok, and they even bought me an old banger because the place is so isolated. Of course, that meant they did not have to drive me around anymore.'

'Figures,' said Karen. 'Tell us the story.'

'So, I'm there chopping veg. Louise is out. Mr O'Sullivan comes up behind me and pats my bum, puts an arm around my shoulders, and says something like, "I could pay you more for some extra service if you'd like." I just froze at first – didn't know what to say or do – but after a few seconds, I thought, *Fuck, I'm not having that.* I shrugged him off and turned round but I still had the knife in my hand. I didn't mean to frighten him, but he backed away pretty quick and looked worried. It was then I had a flash of inspiration, and I brought the knife down with all my strength onto a carrot that was still on the chopping board. It sliced neatly in half, and both bits went shooting off onto the floor. It was just the right size for a willy. I said calm as you like, "No way, Mr O'Sullivan."

The laughter from her two companions drew attention from the other diners.

'Loved to have seen his face,' said Maggie.

'To be fair,' said Rena, 'he was not too pushy, apologised, and he never tried again. I probably overreacted.'

'Oh no, you didn't,' said Karen. 'They always apologise afterwards, as if that makes it alright. You did good.'

'He's OK now. It's Louise who is bitchy.'

'I've met Louise once, only briefly,' said Maggie. 'She's like a cut-out from a glossy fashion magazine.'

Rena laughed. 'I never thought of that, but you're right. She thinks she's the queen of Glasgow. She reads those magazines all the time, and everything she buys or uses comes from them. She spends hundreds of pounds on her hair stylist every two weeks. You know, she has hand cream that costs a hundred pounds for a tiny pot! Sometimes I dip a finger in to steal a smidgeon just so I know what five pounds of hand cream feels like!'

Maggie laughed and recalled how immaculately Louise had been dressed and her hair perfectly styled.

'She may be rich, but she's clatty, though,' said Rena. 'She'll give me row for not cleaning the bath, but I know full well that she hasn't been in it since I last cleaned it three or four days ago.'

They were interrupted by the waitress bringing their lunch orders. The women ate in silence for a while, and Karen was not sure what had changed the mood, but after a while Rena said, 'Do you think it will all go off ok, tomorrow? IDay, I mean.'

'Well, they are committed and have planned and planned,' said Karen. 'Tomorrow is Richard and Jack's day, and if all goes well, we can really get to the real work after that.'

'Yes, to that,' said Maggie. 'My big worry is that people who want to stay in the Union come out onto the streets against us. And if that happens, I worry that Richard may go over the top and send the Army against them. We have not planned for that at all. We don't have enough people to deal with public disorder against us, and it would be hard to control. Richard says it just will not happen, but I still worry about it.'

'We haven't got a plan for that, it's true,' said Karen, 'but remember, there is a difference. People are passionate about independence and will fight for it. Unionists do not have that same passion, and it's much harder to be enthusiastic about the status quo. It's passion that brings people onto the streets.'

'Hope you're right,' said Maggie, but she did not look convinced.

'Some folk just don't care either way,' said Rena. 'Mr O'Sullivan is totally committed to independence, but Louise wouldn't bother as long as there are plenty of fancy fashion shops, a spa, and an expensive hairdresser. She couldn't care less who runs the country.' That brought a smile to their faces. 'So many men have gone through the training camp, mostly boys, really. I worry for them more,' said Rena.

'Someone in particular,' said Maggie, who had picked up on Rena's concern.

'Oh no,' said Rena. She giggled nervously. 'Well, there is maybe one lad.'

'I knew it,' said Maggie.

'Do tell,' said Karen, hoping the conversation would be lighter again.

'It's not really happened yet, just he helps me take the food down to the teams.'

'Wait,' said Maggie. 'You're feeding the teams – all those men – for weeks?'

'No, no,' said Rena. 'I do the tea and coffee. Simon got some big electric urns in, so it's not too much trouble. All the meals are brought in by a catering firm that he hired. I just keep it warm in the kitchen and take it down to the camp. It's so the firm does not find out there's a wee army hidden in the woods!' She smiled. 'So, my new friend helped me this last week, and it made a big difference.'

'Good for you,' said Karen. But she was thinking about what tomorrow might bring.

Richard, although she despised him, seemed so powerful, so sure of himself, that he appeared almost infallible. It was hard to imagine that anything could go wrong. She was sure everything would work as they had planned.

PART TWO

Chapter 16

Jack (IDay minus 1)

On the day before IDay, Jack headed back to the Ayrshire estate from Aberdeen. His Army colleagues had started calling it 'I minus' a few days ago, so it was now 'I minus one'. IDay was tomorrow. It had always seemed an age away, and the last weeks had really started to drag, but now suddenly today it was rushing up on him. The last month had been intense, and he had been surprised at how much work had been done by the Army Network and Richard in particular.

The logistics of depositing so many units at so many sites at the right time was immense, but he guessed it was what the Army did. It was not just the fighting units, of course, but the support systems as well, such as fuel tankers and field kitchens for the larger units that would seal and guard the border. A nationwide major Army exercise was in full swing, and the media had been informed so that the public would not be alarmed by the movement of large convoys of Army vehicles. Organising a revolution was immensely complex; especially when you considered that the majority of the men making up the Army units did not know what was going to happen.

Jack had started to feel the weight and responsibility of it all as he drove. There were a lot of lives that would depend on their careful planning, and not only that but he was directly responsible for the lives of the men in the Militia. He knew the Board wanted to make life better for everyone, but he worried that if it all went wrong it could turn into a catastrophe for Scotland as a whole. It was all very well to bandy about the fact that half the population were committed to independence, but it made them sometimes forget that the other half did not want separation from England.

Now, when he had nothing to do but drive, he felt the doubt wash over him; there was too much time to think of what could go wrong. He was not as confident as the General, who seemed completely in control and portrayed not a shadow of doubt. He could not bring himself to like the man, but he could forgive his idiosyncrasies as there was no doubt he was a great leader, and his men seemed to hold him in high regard.

He had been north with Richard for a couple of days, as they wanted to show their direct support to the teams that would take Lossiemouth and Arbroath by being at the final meeting. The Regional Army Commander had led the briefings, and the General had given an inspiring speech to the men afterwards. Richard had remained behind to finalise some details with the Regional Commander, and so Jack drove back alone.

The major bases which were garrisoned with combat troops were the most difficult targets and also posed the biggest threat should things go wrong, and for this reason they had been assigned the largest number of Militia teams. No matter the size or function of a military base, the remit of the Militia was the same, and this was primarily to contain the men, prevent access to their weapons, and prevent them putting together any organised resistance should they receive instructions from London. Perhaps just as important was to inform them of the new Independent Scotland in which they were now located. Each team had a script that could be read out if for any reason the broadcast statements had not been heard, and, of course, hundreds of the statement leaflets.

Lossiemouth was the home of an RAF Regiment Squadron, a unit of at least two hundred men and a unit of RAF Police. It was a large base, as not only was it home to Typhoon jets but also the much bigger aircraft that fulfilled the coastal protection and anti-submarine roles. In addition, the base was a major storage facility for conventional weapons and missiles, located in a bunker system within the perimeter. The General had admitted that this would be almost as difficult an objective as Faslane, but as long as the assault was fast and a complete surprise, it should not be a problem. The men were barracked there, and there would be armed patrols around the perimeter, but they would not be expecting or have trained for a full assault on the base. In normal times, a good proportion of the regiment would be on overseas duty protecting bases abroad, or on leave between postings.

They had assigned five Militia teams to Lossiemouth. One would take and hold the main gate and prevent anyone entering or leaving. Two teams would be deposited at the barracks to capture and hold the men and to secure the armoury. As soon as they had established control, they would broadcast the media announcements and hand out the statement leaflets so that the men would quickly understand the reason for the assault and would hopefully be less likely to be aggressive.

The remaining two Militia teams would deal with any patrols by each driving in opposing directions around the perimeter road to sweep up any guards. They would then secure any planes on the ground and disable the runways by positioning as many vehicles as could be found to block them. Their orders were to use overwhelming force, and to shoot to kill when necessary, but capture if possible. When the base had been secured, they would explain the situation to the captives as soon as possible, then offer the English safe return home and Scots the opportunity to stay and eventually join the new Scottish armed forces, or go with their comrades to England.

A similar procedure was planned for the Royal Marine base at Arbroath, but because it was not so large, only four teams had been assigned to it. The former airbase at Leuchars was not a problem, as it had been transferred to the Army several years before, and Richard had a unit based there which would secure it, so no Militia involvement was required.

These large establishments required much more complex plans than the other smaller bases in and around Edinburgh and the Central belt that did not fall directly within the control of Richard's network. Mostly these were Engineer or Admin units. They could not in any way be described as difficult targets. A team, or sometimes a squad, had been assigned to each base. Most of these minor bases were guarded by barriers, with unarmed personnel checking IDs, and armed guards in the guardhouse.

Richard had arranged the supply of heavy Army trucks for each team. The Army trucks had reinforced run-flat tyres and the capacity to operate a heavy machine gun from the top of the cab. And even if somewhat limited, this would give each team a little heavy firepower should they need it. The trucks were robust enough to break through any closed gates or survive any tyre-breakers, but this was considered unlikely as there were only simple barriers and unarmed security in normal alert status.

Jack had made an additional stop on the way back, and it turned out that it had been a good thing that Richard was not with him. Of the many team leaders, there were only a few that were not ex-Army and these Jack had appointed himself. Alistair had been in his organisation before moving north to Oban to be nearer elderly parents. He had always maintained good relations with Jack and had still been useful for business when a coastal collection of merchandise was needed. Gordon was younger and had been appointed early on, after he stood out as a leader in the paintball crowd. He had been ambitious and made a big effort to get himself noticed. And his appointment was helped by him being based in Perth, because finding people outside the central belt had not been easy.

Jack had arranged to meet these two team leaders on his way back south. Another non-Army leader was in control of the Inverness team, and Richard and Jack had seen him at the Aberdeen meeting. These teams had relatively easy jobs: their main function was to secure the airports, power stations, ferry ports, and railway stations, at their respective locations.

Gordon had chosen a large, wooded layby just outside Perth, where a mobile café dispensed drinks and snacks to truckers who regularly stopped there for a break. It was too close to IDay to risk a pub or somewhere public. Both men were there when Jack arrived. They clambered into the Range Rover, carrying takeaway coffees from the café.

'Black, no sugar,' said Alistair, handing a capped disposable cup to Jack.

'Thanks, good to see you guys. It's been a while,' said Jack. 'You all ready for the big day?'

'Yes, no problems,' said Alistair, and Gordon confirmed the same.

Jack went through their local plans with them and was pleased that they both seemed as ready as they could be. He felt comfortable with the two of them, as he was always more wary of appearing to lack experience with the ex-Army team leaders.

'Er, there is one thing,' said Gordon, after they had finished the briefing. 'Not sure how important it is or not, so just passing on the info, really. Alistair said I should.'

'It's a bit weird,' said Alistair. 'See what you think.'

'Ok, tell me,' said Jack.

'My team was down at the camp a few weeks ago,' said Gordon, 'for their live fire training. You know how there are Army instructors that carry out the training.'

'Yes,' said Jack. 'The General arranged them.'

'One of my guys overheard two instructors talking. He hadn't been feeling well and was taking a snooze in the upper part of the barn during the day. Several of the Army instructors came in, and they obviously didn't know he was there. and something made him keep quiet. They weren't there long, but they were talking about how useless most of the Militia guys were and one said it didn't matter much because the hard core squads would clean up after them.'

'Probably understandable from a soldier's point of view,' said Jack. 'I've no idea what "hard core squad" refers to.'

'That was mentioned several times,' said Gordon. 'But this is the weird bit. As they were leaving, one soldier said that he wished they would hurry up and get on with it as he had a megabuck job lined up on the staff of the Borders' Governor.'

'Hmm, yes, strange,' said Jack, 'and I've no idea what that means either.'

He had stopped off at his flat in Glasgow for fresh clothes and something to eat, and had considered trying to rest for a couple of hours, but he knew he would not sleep. In the end, he decided to head out to Ayrshire. He had the plans for Faslane to run through one last time with the five teams assigned to it.

He was halfway there when he had the idea to call Samantha. They had been in only sporadic contact since they had got together for a coffee a few weeks after she had left Richard. She had been hesitant to take things any further until more time had elapsed, and they had agreed to wait until after IDay. Jack was content with that, but he still hoped that it might develop into something more. He was still unsure whether she was just being tactful, and he was just not her type, which was probably a compliment if you considered that Richard was perhaps the standard. He was never sure why Samantha had taken up with Richard, but he knew she was a lot stronger beneath her vulnerable exterior than he had at first thought.

He used his personal mobile for a hands-free call, as the satellite phone could not be connected to the car. It had been a long time since he'd had cause to use it. He was single at the moment, and the lieutenants that were running the family business had rarely any need to contact him.

There was a long pause, and he almost hung up. 'Hello,' she said eventually.

'Is that you Samantha? It's Jack.'

'Yes. How have you been?'

'All good with me, and you?'

'Fine, thanks.'

He wasn't sure how to broach the subject without appearing to be interrogating her.

'Have you seen Richard recently?'

'No. Definitely not,' she said.

'Listen. I've heard some strange talk about the military commanders. Have you heard anything, or heard Richard mention "hard core squads"? I mean, obviously, when you were still there.'

'No, I don't think I've heard that before. There were a lot of meetings with the Governors, and a few that you weren't invited to. At least, I never saw you there.'

'Governors?' repeated Jack.

'Well, they started calling themselves Governors instead of Commanders a while back. I thought you knew. They have a President as well.'

'What! You mean James? He doesn't believe in presidents.' Jack was struggling to make sense of what she was saying.

'No, I don't know his name; he's a short, plump guy with expensive clothes. He had a few meetings with Richard but never when you were there. What do you think that means, Jack?'

'I think our political leaders will be sidelined, or maybe worse.'

'I can't imagine Richard taking orders from anyone, can you?' she said.

'No,' said Jack, 'not even a President.'

They talked on for a short while, but Jack could not glean any further information from her. He offered to catch up with her after the takeover, but she did not take him up on that and he ended the call. For a few minutes he drove on, not really concentrating. A layby came up quickly and he braked hard, intending to pull in. But a blaring horn behind him changed his mind, and he gave an apologetic wave as the other driver pulled out to overtake him. He slowed down so that when the next turning came up, he was able to move off the carriageway and park up. He needed to give himself time to think.

He was beginning to suspect what all this meant and mentally berated himself for not having seen it before. He had always felt uneasy with Richard, and in fact, looking back, he was pleased that he had held something back and not fallen completely under Richard's influence. The man was possibly as great an actor as he was a leader, as Jack and all the others had believed without question most of what he told them. He could see why they had so easily played into his hands, because he held the means to do what they all wanted so much but were powerless to achieve without his network.

If it was true, it would explain why Richard had maintained the separation of his Army Network and his so-called 'military' leaders. Even Jack, who had attended numerous meetings with them, had not suspected that they were anything other than the Army Commanders for each region, and of course, the Board had all assumed they would just return to their Army roles when control was passed to the politicians. The Board had been naïve in the extreme.

He could see now why the Militia would take on the hardest and likely most violent targets. They would be in the most danger, while the Army force would remain intact. Worse, if – as he now suspected – Richard took full control of the country for himself, he would be a dictator in control of nuclear weapons, sharing a border with a powerful, very angry enemy. Scotland could become an isolated pariah state, and it could well initiate a full-on civil war. And there was no doubt England would win that.

It might be a false alarm. Perhaps he was making a lot out of his own long-standing unease with Richard and a few scraps of information. There was a choice, and he knew it would be easy to put an end to it all now. All he needed to do was start phoning the papers, the Police, and the Ministry of Defence. But supposing he was wrong? Could he risk the whole project, everything they had all worked for and Scotland's independence, on such flimsy evidence? If he raised the alarm now, it would be the end of any hope of independence. After a while, he drove on.

By the time he arrived at the Ayrshire estate, Jack had decided that he would do nothing, for now. Knowing, or at least suspecting, meant he was at least forewarned, and that might be enough to forestall Richard's plan. So, he would be alert and ready to act if it was required. He could not be the one to stop Scotland becoming independent. The revolution must go ahead.

He had phoned Alistair and Gordon and shared his concerns with them, telling them to carry on as planned but to be aware that he may need them in Edinburgh if things started to go wrong. In some ways he wished they had not warned him, as now he had the added responsibility that the knowledge gave him. He considered telling James and Isobel but decided against it. *What would they do?* He was sure they would come to the same conclusion as him, so it would only share the problem and they could probably do without the added stress. He would talk to them tomorrow, after the takeover, and then they could decide together what was to be done if the General looked as though he would not pass control back to them.

He arrived at the estate to find the five teams already assembled in the barn, ready for the final briefing. They were all armed; they had been carrying their weapons for the last week to become totally familiar with them. He was pleased to see that they looked much more like soldiers than the last time he had seen them, even though they were dressed in a motley collection of combats and civilian clothes. They looked comfortable with their weapons and gave the impression of a formidable force. These were the teams that had had the most live fire exercises.

Compared to all the other sites designated to be taken, Faslane was a fortress. And even though the element of surprise would be in their favour, they were still likely to meet armed resistance. Malcolm, who led team G3, would be in overall charge as he had the most combat experience from his time in the Army. The teams had been through the plan many times. They had studied the layout and the Google satellite images until they could have found their way in the dark. Jack stood to the side and let the team leaders run through their respective team plans.

The first three teams would just drive through the main gate without stopping; the gate was always open during the day, from the early morning, as there was a near constant stream of traffic from civilian workers, contractors, and Navy families who lived on the base. Being in military trucks, it was unlikely that any anti-vehicle traps would be deployed in time to stop them. And if there were, they would continue on run-flat tyres. Or if the trucks were disabled, they would dismount and move on foot to their objectives.

The base was not that big. Team one would take and hold the two jetty complexes that accommodated the hunter killer submarines and the nuclear-armed subs. This complex was protected by an inner fence that completely surrounded the area. The gate on this access road was normally closed and of solid steel construction, which even the heavy trucks would have difficulty breeching. The plan was to drive through the fence at a suitable point to gain access to the road on the far side of the gate. There would definitely be a small number of armed guards within the inner fence, and they would need to be dealt with.

The men had been primed, like all the Militia men, to assume that most of the armed guards at the base were English. Their instructions were the same as all the other teams, which was to open fire immediately there was any sign of resistance, and to shoot to kill. Surprise and firepower would only be to their advantage for a short time. Once the objective was secured, any guards that surrendered should be well treated, and the independence cause explained to them.

The second and third trucks would carry their teams deeper into the base. One would cordon off the large housing section, while the other would take the Marine unit barracks and secure the armoury. The fourth truck would take and hold the main gate. The truck-mounted machine gun would cover the access road. One section of this team would deploy and conceal themselves in ambush positions along the access road and the perimeter road further in from the main gate. This was to deal with any armed Marine patrol that was active and which would in all likelihood react to the sound of shooting by heading for the source at the main gate from wherever they were.

The fifth team would take and hold the nuclear weapons storage facility up in the hills of the adjacent peninsular, only a few miles away. There were armed guards there, but the team only had to take the main gate and hold it. It was more of an insurance card really, rather than a necessity, and to ensure that any personnel here could not go to the assistance of Faslane. Once the nuclear weapons site was secured, and if all was quiet, one section of the team would return to Faslane to reinforce the teams there.

The UK government would have lost almost all their nuclear weapons.

The Board had decided against capturing the strategic fuel storage depot which was also in the area; they saw no real need, as it would essentially be on Scottish soil after independence, and there would only be a few personnel at the site.

Jack was pleased that the leaders knew their stuff and, judging by the faces of the men, he was confident that they understood what was being asked of them and were committed to carrying it out. He was encouraged to see that they were all wearing their 'Free Scotland' armbands and looking determined. He was proud of the way the Militia had developed and proud of himself for bringing it together. He moved to the front of the room after the last leader had outlined his team's plan.

'Men,' he said. 'Stand.' He waved them to their feet. They did so instantly, with a rumble of chairs on the rough wooden floor and the clink of weapons.

'Tomorrow. You are going to make Scotland a free independent nation. This will not be easy and will not be achieved without cost. You will have to fight for what I know you all believe in. You may have to kill. Do not hesitate. Your life, and the lives of your comrades, will depend on it. But remember, although most of the guards will be English, there will be some who will be Scottish people. So once your objectives are secure, act with restraint and mercy. I know every one of you is up for it and will do your best. Tomorrow we will make history. Good luck!'

The men cheered loudly, stamped their feet, and slapped their comrades on the back, while some waved their rifles in the air. Jack shook hands with the team leaders and left them to it.

Chapter 17

Kenny (IDay minus 7)

Kenny awoke early and lay in his sleeping bag, enjoying the quiet. He had elected to sleep outside, as it was a relatively warm night and was at least dry. He had always found it strangely comfortable to sleep on the ground; as long as you took the time to dig out a wee hollow for your hip and shoulder, it was fine. He had had trouble taking in all that he had learned yesterday. He had heard of the Caledonian Independence Party, and it was reassuring to know that it was part of the project and that there was a plan to form a government after the takeover. The news about that, and the involvement of the regular Army, gave the whole thing substance; it was all much bigger than he could have imagined. He was certainly relieved to know it was not just a few teams with guns. He was really starting to believe it was possible.

Breakfast was held in the barn, and was brought down from the main house in a large metal container by a young woman with spiky hair, who looked almost too slight to be carrying it. She made a second trip for two urns of tea and coffee, but at least these were piping hot. The eggs and bacon tended to be barely warm, but were passable when loaded into rolls or between slices of toast. The men helped themselves and then sat around on crates or old rusting farm machinery, left over from when it had been a working farm.

There was a hubbub of excited chatter, partly due to the enormity of the news they had been given, and partly anticipation at the live firing that was scheduled for after breakfast. Kenny sat and ate with Craig. When Craig noticed the woman returning with a stainless-steel urn in each hand, and obviously struggling with the weight of them, he jumped up to help. She gratefully released one to him, and he helped her set them up on the table with the other breakfast food. They chatted briefly, and Kenny could see them both laughing at some shared joke. Later, Craig helped her carry the empty containers back to the house.

As it transpired, it was nearer midday by the time G3 was called to the range. This turned out to be a small quarry which was cut into the side of a small hill and had previously been used to quarry stone, presumably originally for the house and farm buildings, and then later for farm tracks and boundary walls. The open space in front of the quarry was taken up by a large shipping container with its doors wedged open. Two long trestle tables, with rifles laid out in a line across them, stood in front of it, and off to the side was a smaller table which held two large car batteries and a red lamp in a vertical holder. A cable ran from the table down the length of the quarry, and Kenny could see two other red lamps on posts to either side.

A man, dressed in Army combats and with the look of a soldier, sat at this table with a satellite phone held in one hand. He was rocking the chair backwards and forwards on its back legs and looked bored. Several more soldiers were relaxed in chairs or on the ground. As Kenny, Craig, and the other members of their team approached the tables, they could see through the open doors into the container. There was an assortment of weapons on show: assault rifles, rocket-propelled grenade launchers, and pistols. There were many wooden crates, some opened and empty, while others had not been touched. Cases of ammunition lay open at the entrance, with many more stacked behind. Some makeshift racks had been cobbled together out of empty packing crates and held dozens of weapons.

Two other soldiers stood behind the tables. One, who had prominent Sergeant stripes on each arm, introduced himself as the lead instructor for the day.

'Welcome, gentlemen,' said the instructor. 'Listen carefully. If the red lights go on, you stop firing instantly – and I mean instantly. We have several scouts out touring the roads around the estate. They make sure there are no walkers, parked cars, or inquisitive people wandering round. If they spot anyone, they phone into the lookout table, and he operates the red lights. Everyone got that?' There were murmurs of assent.

'OK. We do not have a lot of space here, so the range is not very long, and all these weapons will sting out to half a mile at least. But you will be using them for close-in fighting, so that's not a problem. Just remember they will hit faraway targets if you need to, and you should also bear in mind that you can kill innocents who may just be in your line of fire but a way off. Understand?

'Your choice is between the US M4,' he pointed to one of the tables, 'and the AK 47,' he indicated the other table. 'They both hold magazines of thirty rounds. The American is slightly lighter, fires smaller calibre rounds, and is more accurate. The AK is robust and rarely jams; it's simple to operate and the easiest to use.'

'How fast do they fire?' someone asked.

'It doesn't really matter. The AK six hundred rounds a minute, the M4 seven hundred and then some. Both fire as fast as you can pull the trigger. Both have full auto but... anyone want to work that out for me? No. Watch.' He loaded a magazine into an AK and checked with the soldier with the sat phone at the lookout table. The man nodded and mouthed 'all clear'.

The instructor clasped the rifle firmly in both hands and pointed it into the air. He pulled the trigger and held it down. The shock of the sustained noise so close blasted into their ears, and they all stepped back instinctively, some covering their ears. Empty brass cartridge cases clattered onto the table.

Into the silence, the Sergeant spoke. 'Empty. Ten rounds a second. Thirty are gone in three seconds. Even for experts, full auto is difficult to control; each round forces the muzzle up a little higher. So, if you are not careful, you end up shooting sky. Much better to shoot single rounds; fast as you can pull the trigger, it will shoot. We will show you how to use full auto in short bursts, but it takes some practice, and you don't have enough time to be good at it. However, auto can be useful if only to frighten your enemy or to make them keep their heads down.

'Ok. Split into two at the tables, and my colleague will give you the dry lecture on the AK while I'll do the M4, then we'll swap over.

'But listen up. When we get to live fire, there are three rules. Do not point the rifle anywhere but down-range. Two, obey immediately any instructions from your trainer. Three, if the red light goes on, stop immediately. One more thing. With a weapon like this in your hands, you need to stay focused. Untrained troops regularly shoot their own people. Sure, it's fine if you are in a trench or holding a position, but when you are moving other than in a straight line – and lines disappear real fast in a firefight – it's easy to shoot anything that moves.'

After they had all fired a magazine or two from each type, Kenny and Craig had a brief chat, but there was no competition really. They both preferred the American-made gun, and so both their squads were issued with their own personal M4 rifle and went back to the range to become more familiar with it.

Kenny enjoyed the hours at the range. They practised over and over again, changing magazines, clearing a jam, sighting targets quickly, and how to shoot short bursts. The paintball training did come in handy in some respects, but really there was no comparison. The feel of so much power in their hands was intoxicating. The instructors allowed each of them to fire a magazine on full auto, and it was easy to see from the clouds of dust climbing up the wall of the quarry that controlling the gun was not easy.

When the next team arrived for their training, G3 was escorted back to the barn with their weapons, and they were shown how to take down and clean them ready for use. Malcolm took Kenny and Craig aside afterwards and repeated that training again, then he tasked them with ensuring that both their squads stripped and cleaned their rifles at the end of every day.

Every day they were allowed an hour on the range to perfect their weapon skills, and this was more enjoyable than some other parts of the training. Almost all hours of the waking day were spent on some sort of exercise, which included watching Army videos – not only of technical assaults, but also ones that were a composition of graphic images in full colour and intimate detail of what modern weapons do to bodies. A deadpan voice on the soundtrack only gave the name of the weapon causing the injury and nothing else. The bodies remained unidentified, unimportant, just images on a training video. It made for very uncomfortable viewing and even though Kenny knew that these were designed to inoculate them to anything they might see in the coming days, he would rather have not witnessed them. The teams maintained a stunned silence through these films, their usual macho banter silenced for once. When a couple of the lads got up to leave, the instructors insisted they stay, even after one of them was sick. Afterwards, some of the men made jokes and there was some nervous laughter, but Kenny knew it was just their way of reasserting their manliness to themselves.

Every day, with empty rifles, they practised *not* shooting each other while moving through the woods in various formations. Every day they studied plans and Google map images of the naval base at Faslane and Coulport, rehearsing the plan. Every day brought them nearer to IDay.

Malcolm was constantly with them every day, encouraging, pushing, and inevitably swearing at them. In the downtime, they did not see so much of him, as he spent time finalising the plan with the other team leaders and instructors. They had all been told he would be the senior leader and in overall charge of the assault. Kenny and Craig were tasked with more duties as section leaders. They were to ensure attendance at the range or the other exercises for the squads. They also had to make sure the men cleaned their weapons, ate their meals, and generally kept the place neat and tidy. This was relatively easy for them, as all the men were too deep in anticipation of the coming event to be any trouble, and they all meekly followed their squad leader's instructions.

A consequence of the extra responsibilities was that they felt further isolated from their men, so they began to hang out together in the down time. Craig took to sleeping outdoors with Kenny instead of in the barn where most of the men slept. The barn tended to be very crowded anyway, as the men from all five teams shared it.

Everyone tended to turn in early, as the days were exhausting, and without their phones to engage with, there was very little else to do. On the third night, the weather turned wet, and Kenny had moved both their sleeping bags under the overhang of the barn roof to keep out of the rain. Craig had disappeared again, and Kenny wondered if he was off seeing the girl from the house. He had become a regular helper, going up to the house in the morning and evening to help her carry down the food, and returning the empties with her. Kenny had thought he might get into trouble because of the ban on approaching the house, but the team leaders seemed to recognise that the girl needed help and did not challenge him.

He liked Craig and had found out a lot more about him over the last few nights. Compared to his own close family, Craig had endured a terrible childhood. Born to a mother who had a drug problem, mostly paid for by an unending succession of male companions, he had been taken into care while young, and had become a regular attendee at the Children's Panel at an age no child should need that help. He had been a cute wee boy and had found a foster home before long, then been abused by an older sibling in the family, both physically and sexually. He never told anyone, and at nine he absconded and spent the rest of his childhood in children's homes. He never again accepted a placing in a family home, even though there were offers. At seventeen, the system abandoned him as he abandoned the system. Malcolm had found him living on the streets and had helped him get set up in a bedsit. Kenny had been surprised at just how much Malcolm had done for Craig, and he realised now why he had tried so hard to impress the older man.

Kenny saw torchlight bobbing through the trees, and soon after Craig turned up. He sounded in a good mood. He struggled into his sleeping bag but did not switch off the torch, and Kenny could tell he wanted to tell someone about his evening.

'You shagging that bird already?' said Kenny.

'Naw, it's not like that. She's nice. We're just talking... know what I mean?' Craig sounded happy.

'Bit old for you, no?'

'Her name is Rena, short for Catherine. She's only a few years older. Has a hard life. The woman treats her like shite, but she likes the job and it's a roof over her head. We get on... know what I mean?'

'Sounds good, if it makes you happy.'

There was silence for a short time, then Craig said, 'These guns are better than the paintballs, no?'

'Yeh, they feel good; maybe too good. Sometimes I think they make us invincible, which is probably not so good.'

'Know what you mean,' said Craig, and then after a pause, 'What you thinking about the plan, the attack thing? Think it will go alright?'

'I think so, it seems well planned. It should be a walkover with all these guns.'

'I'm scared I don't do it right. Don't want to let Malcolm down.'

'You'll be fine. He'll keep us right. Our team has the easy bit, I think, just to hold the gate.'

'Exciting as well... know what I mean?' Craig switched the torch off.

'Yea, I do. Night, Craig.'

'Night, man.' And then, after a long pause, Craig said quietly into the dark, 'I've had hook-ups, you know, but I've never had a girlfriend before.'

*

On the night before IDay, Kenny turned in early. The rain had cleared up and it was a lovely spring evening, so he had moved his and Craig's sleeping bags back out into the open, as he found sleeping under the eaves of the ramshackle building much more prone to spiders and bugs. He found the hollows that he had previously made for his hip and shoulder still there and strangely comforting as he settled into them.

This last day had been fairly quiet. Every few hours a huge Army truck would arrive, until there were five taking up almost all the space in the clearing. The trucks had a circular hatch mounted in the roof on the passenger side of the cab, and the team leaders had been busy fitting a mounting on the opening of each truck to hold a heavy machine gun. Kenny and Craig watched them for a while and felt reassured by the addition of some heavier weaponry to their transport.

The instructors and team leaders had eased up on the exercises, and they had gone over the plans with the Militia Commander in attendance, but after that they more or less had the evening to themselves. The house had ordered in a mixture of Chinese, Thai, and Indian takeaways, as a bit of a treat. But it did engender a lot of 'last meal' jokes.

Kenny was just resting and reading one of the daily papers brought into the camp when Craig came by, smiled shyly at Kenny, bundled up his sleeping bag, and headed into the woods. Kenny decided not to say anything and pretended not to notice, but he was pleased for his friend. Craig did not return until the early hours, moving quietly so as not to disturb Kenny.

Early in the morning, as they were loading up onto the trucks, the mood was sombre and the men were silent, with only the occasional muffled curse or the clink of a weapon as they clambered aboard the five trucks. When they were nearly all aboard, Rena came into the clearing and called for Craig. His face red and a little unsure of himself, Craig swung down from his truck. She went into his arms and kissed him hard. The men roared their approval, and when she finally broke away from him and skipped back to the edge of the woods, the men cheered again. Craig climbed back onto the truck, his face almost split with the huge grin he carried.

Rena stood at the exit of the clearing and waved and blew kisses at each of the trucks as they drove past, so that all the men felt she was a proxy for their wives, lovers, or mothers who shared that wave.

Chapter 18

Jack IDay

They had considered taking both the independent television studio – Scottish Television (STV) – and the BBC at the same time, as they were situated within spitting distance of each other, but Maggie and Stevie had consistently pointed out that their social media posts would reach far more people much more quickly than traditional TV. So, they had decided to stick to the BBC, as it not only produced television but also several well-known radio stations.

They had initially planned to breach the delivery gate behind the building, which gave access to a secure storage area and the rear of the studios. This, they thought, would put them in quicker overall control of the building, but Jack and Stevie had both reconnoitred at different times, and they both considered that walking through the front door was all that was needed. There was tight security but no armed guards. They reckoned they could take control of the people and the building by force with no problem. They hoped to be able to find and rely on sympathisers to the cause to operate the systems, and if not, they would use whatever force necessary to ensure compliance.

Jack drove as close as he could to the main entrance, ignoring parking restrictions. He, Maggie and Stevie carried only concealed handguns to avoid any initial panic. They entered the building quickly, and Maggie engaged the security guard by handing him a statement leaflet which she advised him to read. He tried to protest as Jack and Stevie jumped over the rotating people barrier and walked to the reception desk, but Maggie let the guard see her handgun, which stopped him. She did not threaten him with it, but motioned for him to stay where he was and read.

Jack hung back and watched the area while Stevie handed over leaflets to the two receptionists. They both read it and one nodded, as if in agreement, but they both looked unsure and worried. The leaflet had been carefully prepared and printed in the thousands and would be carried by all soldiers and the Militia men, and handed out to civilians whenever they could.

It was short enough to read quickly, and they hoped it conveyed enough information to calm people while it was also weighted with a veiled threat:

Please do not be alarmed.
Today Scotland has announced its independence from England.
The people who have handed you this leaflet are acting on the orders of the Provisional Government.
Please obey their instructions and assist them wherever possible.
Please comply and you will not be harmed.

Meanwhile, the military truck carrying Team G1 had deposited two Militia men at the goods entrance. Their job was merely to take over the security guard's job and prevent any access to the rear of the building by preventing anyone opening the gate. The gates were substantial and operated by one guard in a cabin outside the gates.

The truck then pulled up at the main entrance exactly two minutes after Jack's car, and Team G1 dismounted, looking like a bunch of heavily-armed bandits. As had already been planned, the team leader left two men to guard the entrance. Stevie took three Militia men and went off to secure the control centre, guided by a compliant receptionist.

Maggie politely asked the still shocked guard if he would mind escorting her and a couple of the Militia to Studio C – the news studio. He remained speechless but rose and led the way at gunpoint. Maggie's job was to hold the studio ready and prepare to read the statement as soon as they were sure about the tech needed.

Jack asked the remaining receptionist to announce a national emergency on the PA system and instruct all staff to assemble in the open central area. 'This excludes all staff operating transmission for all radio stations and Studio C,' he told her. 'Warn staff operating these to prepare to make an emergency announcement. Tell them to keep normal broadcasts for now.'

The team leader and his remaining men took up station around the open central area. As people started to arrive, the men removed phones and handed a leaflet to each person. They herded them all into one part of the area and gave the instruction, 'Take a seat, sit quiet, stay silent and stay safe' to everyone. It was still early in the day, so the number of staff on duty was limited to a couple of dozen, and Jack was sure that the team had enough men to cope. They had monitored the mornings and knew there was a big influx of staff from around 8am onwards, but by that time it would not matter, as the announcements would have gone out and they could prevent entry from outside.

Stevie returned to the reception area, accompanied by an excited looking man with a shock of curly brown hair, matched with a curly beard. 'One of the engineers. He knows the system and is willing to cooperate fully. He has already told us something we had not allowed for... a remote master... uh—'

'Yes,' interrupted the engineer, 'the Master Transmission Cut-out – MTC we call it – can be operated from here, or remotely from London or Birmingham, or several places within this building.'

'Shit,' said Jack. 'That's not good.'

'Is it really true we've declared independence? I never thought I'd live to see the day. I have been a lifelong supporter. Let me help. I used to be a member of the SNP but gave it up as they were so useless. I've read the leaflet. I'm really happy... hap—'

It was turning into a rant, so Jack broke in. 'That's good. Thank you,' he said. 'We want to transmit on TV and radio to Scotland – I don't much care about the rest of the world, as long as it goes out to Scotland. Can we bypass the cut-out?'

'Yes, I can. I can disable it, but I need to get to the transmission room. That shouldn't be a problem.'

'Great. Stevie will go with you. What else do we need to broadcast from Studio C? Do we need cameramen or what?'

'Oh no, it's all automated from the control room. I could probably do that, but it would be better with a producer to work the system. I know one or two who will do it. No problem.'

'Right, take us to the control room first, and then you can disable the cut-out. We want to transmit at 8am if we possibly can.'

'No problem.' The man was shaking with excitement.

The engineer led Jack and Stevie down to Studio C. They explained to Maggie, who was in the control room with one of the Militia men, what the engineer had said. There were several worried-looking BBC staff members, and the engineer went to speak to them.

After a while he waved Maggie over, and following a brief chat the staff went back to their consoles and started setting up for broadcasting under the watchful eye of the Militia guard. Another took Maggie into the studio, fitted her with a microphone, and started explaining about where to stand for each camera angle. Jack saw her shake her head and, holding up one finger, could tell she just wanted to keep it simple – one seat facing one camera.

He turned to Stevie. 'Maggie has got it covered here. Take Curly here to the transmission room and make sure he disables the cut-out. After that, let the staff go home if we don't need them. Make sure Curly runs an eye over them first to make sure we don't need someone later.'

'No worries.'

'I'm going to head up to Faslane now, see how it's going. I'll listen in to the broadcast on Radio Scotland. I'm on Sat phone if you need me – remember to keep yours on in case James or Isobel need any other announcements.'

Jack decided to use the motorway and cross the river at the Erskine Bridge. The road out of the city was still quiet, but the normal rush hour traffic was building up on the other side. He wound the car up and was almost at the bridge before the statement came on. Maggie's voice sounded a bit shaky at first but then firmed up, and she delivered the message like an old hand.

GOOD MORNING, ladies and gentlemen.

This morning at eight o'clock, Scotland announced its independence from England. You are waking up to an historic day – do not be alarmed, but please listen carefully. This broadcast will be repeated at regular intervals throughout the day.

At eight am this morning a Unilateral Declaration of Independence was announced by the provisional government of the newly-formed independent state of Scotland. Your new government will work in close collaboration with the SNP to ensure the smooth transfer of power away from England.

You are all now citizens of an independent Scotland. Go about your business as normal. Schools, shops, hospitals, places of work will open as normal.

All government staff are still employed. Only your employer has changed. Please report for duty as normal. This includes all civil servants, NHS staff, Fire and Police services.

However, please note that all borders are closed; that is by land, rail, and road, and all sea ports are closed except internal ferry services. All airports are closed. Please do not travel today, at all, except to carry out your normal work. There will be major disruption on transport networks for the next few days as all international borders are closed.

We expect this to be temporary and only for a brief period. Things will rapidly return to full function within a couple of days.

Please stay connected, as there will be further announcements throughout the day.

There will be specific instructions broadcast here soon for MSPs and Police – stay connected.

Jack thought that sounded good and he knew that Maggie would now be busy sending out the same message on all the social media accounts that she and Stevie had set up. The older members had worried that one TV station and a couple of radio stations would not get the message out quickly enough, but Maggie and Stevie had assured them that the whole of Scotland would know within an hour, and the whole world by lunchtime. They had even argued that control of the BBC was a waste of time, and that social media would do the job on its own, but they had decided that the authority of a TV station would be worth the manpower.

What follows is a special message for Members of the Scottish Parliament:

All MSPs, no matter what party you are associated with, should report to parliament today at 2pm. You have been elected by the people of your constituency and that has not changed. You will still retain your seats if you wish. We expect everyone to attend unless you are too ill, in which case a nominated deputy will be accepted. There is much work to do to build a better Scotland.

The following is a special message for members of the Police service:

All Police Scotland members should continue to carry out their duties as normal, but please be aware that there are large scale movements of the military as they seal the borders, and there are some minor military operations taking place. Police should not interfere with any personnel carrying out the orders of the provisional government.

The Chief Constable and the three Depute Chief Constables will report to Bute House for discussion with the First Minister and the Provisional Government at 10am this morning.

Jack was just coming off the north side of the bridge when he noticed the flashing blue lights in the rear-view mirror. He glanced down at the speedo. It showed eighty, but he had slowed down a lot on the bridge. *Fuck! Do they not listen to the radio?* He carried on for a while, but the cruiser was starting to get annoyed and was tailgating him enthusiastically. He slowed to a stop then got out of the Range Rover quickly, while the policemen were still taking their time to get organised.

He tapped on the window – they both looked angry at this unexpected assault on their authority. The driver wound down the window.

'In a hurry, are we? Please return to your car, sir. We will be there when we're ready.'

'I'm on Government business,' Jack replied. 'You heard the radio? Get in front of me and blue light me to Faslane – now!'

The driver looked at his colleague and they both laughed.

'Have you been drinking, sir?' said the driver. 'You're not going anywhere today.'

Jack lost patience; he took out the handgun, tapped it on the windscreen. 'This is my authority. I don't have time to waste.' He enjoyed their transition from officiousness to alarm.

Giving up any idea of an escort, he shot the front tyre out then stuck his head in the window and told them to tune into Radio Scotland. They pulled away from him. Halfway back to the car, he turned and went back. The officers were now seriously worried and started to get out of the patrol car. He shouted at them to stop – he still had the gun in his hand. He handed the driver a leaflet.

'Get on to your control. Get a new car. Meet me here in an hour or so. I will need an escort to Edinburgh.' He returned to his car and drove off, strangely pleased with himself.

As he drove along the coast road, he could see a thin column of grey-brown smoke rising ominously in the distance. It got bigger and thicker as he approached Faslane.

He drove slowly up to the main gate and stopped behind one of the Army trucks that was partly blocking the entrance; it looked as though it had been pushed to one side, but he did not want to risk driving around it into the unknown. He got out cautiously, with the pistol in his hand, and edged his way around the truck. The ground was covered in spent shell casings and the heavy machine gun on top of the cab was pointing aimlessly into the sky. He could hear sporadic gunfire in the distance.

The blackened skeleton of another Army truck was still smouldering a couple of hundred metres in from the gate. It was giving off more smoke than flames, and Jack could taste the acrid smell of it even from this distance. There was more smoke rising from deeper in the base. All the windows were shattered in the guard house at the main gate, and the walls were pockmarked with bullet hits. Debris and brass casings were scattered all around, and there were bodies. A lot of bodies.

His brain had trouble processing the scattered humps as human, dead humans, and mostly Militia by their clothing. They seemed strangely deflated, limp, and bloodied. He did not want to look too closely. He wanted to turn and drive away, but he gripped the pistol tighter and went on.

He called out, 'Any Militia here?'

'Identify yourself!' someone cried from the shattered remains of the guardhouse. 'Or we'll shoot.' But this was immediately followed by the crack of an assault rifle, and a round whistled high over his head.

Jack ducked and screamed. 'Stop, stop! I'm Jack. Militia Commander. No one else here but me.'

Two men came slowly out of the building, their assault rifles at the ready. They were wide-eyed and shuffled forward nervously as though ready to dive back inside at any moment. Jack worried that they would shoot him by accident.

'Rifles down! Report to me what happened here,' he instructed.

They lowered their weapons, but neither spoke.

'Name?' said Jack. He pointed at the older of the two.

'Kenny.' The man seemed to have recovered some composure, but he was a mess. His face was ashen under the streaks of grime, and his jacket was ripped; there was a patch of dark red/black on his jeans.

He saw Jack looking at the stain. 'Not mine,' he said. 'One of ours. Tried to help him…' His voice tapered off.

His companion had collapsed onto his knees on the road with his head in his hands, as though he thought it was all over. He did not speak even when Jack prodded him for a name.

'That's Ryan,' said Kenny. 'It's been too much for him.'

They lifted Ryan, one to each arm, and pulled him to his feet. They dragged him into the guardhouse, where he returned to the floor. There were bodies here as well. Not Militia but armed police. Someone had covered their faces. It smelled strongly of gun powder in the confined space.

'Kenny, why are there only two of you guarding the gate? Where is your team?'

'Too many killed. Malcolm took the rest with the Army to take the jetties.'

'Army?' said Jack, not completely surprised. 'Maybe you better start from the beginning. Ryan! Keep a lookout.'

The boy did not stir until Kenny nudged him in the ribs with a boot and then heaved him to his feet and shoved him in front of one of the shattered windows.

'Something for him to do,' Jack mouthed at Kenny.

Kenny nodded. 'All went according to plan at first. We took the gate no problem, no shooting. All this,' he waved his arm around at the destruction, 'was done by them attacking us later. The other trucks went through, sealed off the residential area and the Marine barracks. One truck broke through the fence into the inner compound, but once back on the road again, something blew all the wheels off. Malcolm thought there had been some other protective device on the inner road that we did not know about. He was still here then, co-ordinating on the Sat phones.

'The other team set up positions on the perimeter road to take out the Marine patrols, like in the plan, but they did not come that way. They came in vehicles straight here, and they were fucking vicious. They killed everyone out in the open, mostly before our guys could fire back. Some just turned and ran, and the Marines shot them down anyway. We were OK in here, and Malcolm got us all shooting back. There were also some of us at the other truck, and they shot back as well, but they hit it with something that blew it up... and there was no more firing then. The men guarding the perimeter road came back to help us, but they were in the open and most were killed as well.

'After a while the shooting died down a bit. Malcolm said that because they were just on routine patrol, they would not have much ammo with them. He made a run for the truck and used the machine gun on top of the cab. He blasted their position and vehicles and killed some, and they started to withdraw. That's when we got a few of them. We were angry by that time. At first, I did not want to shoot, but they were fucking animals. Even when our guys were wounded, they shot them again and again.'

Jack was still struggling with a sense of impending disaster and had trouble staying focused on what Kenny was saying.

There was so much killing; the easy takeover at the BBC had led him to believe this would just be a walkover as well. He needed to get to Edinburgh.

'Where's Malcolm now?'

'He's with the Army. I think he knew they were coming.' Kenny was shaking again, this time with anger not shock. 'Why the fuck were they not here at the beginning? The Army came. They had fucking tanks; no, well, uh, armoured cars, I guess. Why did we not use them in the first place? We made it easy for them. We didn't need to get killed!'

Jack could not answer. He shook his head.

'The Army took out the rest of the Marines – I think they had no ammo anyway, and then Malcolm led them down to the inner compound. There are still a few guards fighting around the subs.'

'Fuck,' said Jack.

'I'm going over to the truck. I want to see if there are any of our lads alive there,' said Kenny.

'OK, I'll go with you.' Jack was glad to get out of the stench of the confined space.

'Ryan! Stay here, keep watch.' Ryan stared out the window but did not respond, other than a brief nod of his head.

They approached cautiously, but behind the burnt out remains of the truck was only carnage. Shattered bodies, raw, opened, and bloodied flesh. Nothing moved. The smell had been better in the guardhouse; here there was a stench of burnt oil, scorched steel, and the rich greasy smell of what must be burnt bodies within the remains of the truck.

Jack saw Kenny looking at a badly disfigured body with the face mostly shot away, along with part of a leg. One arm lay uselessly protective across the man's chest. The arm had an eagle wing tattooed high up near the shoulder. It was clear and untouched. Kenny dropped to a knee beside the body but seemed unsure what to do. He put a hand on the tattoo and the other on the dead man's hand. He gave it a little shake as though to wake him. Whether this was recognition or farewell, Jack was not sure.

Jack pulled on his shoulder. 'Nothing we can do here.'

The sound of a heavy vehicle approaching made them hurry back to the guardhouse. One of the trucks drove up and several Militia men dismounted, along with Malcolm.

'Everything OK, Kenny? I brought some men back to help guard the fucking gate. Hi Jack.' Kenny ignored him.

Jack pulled Malcolm to one side. 'What's going on?'

'We did it. The base is secure – there are a couple of guards still holding out, but they're isolated, and it won't be long. Two subs were at the jetty, and we have men on both. Big fucking success, I'd say.'

Kenny shook his head. He did not look at Malcom directly, but he was uneasily flicking the safety on and off on his rifle. Jack decided to keep talking.

'Did you know about the Army?'

'Wasn't sure, but I knew that the boss had a reserve plan. I guess that was it. They seem to be the General's shock troops, all from different units. Good fucking men. The Army will guard the base now there are anti-aircraft weapons and radar systems on their way. I'm going to clear the gate for them now.'

'England won't bomb here, surely?'

'Oh no. It's in case they try to retake the base with paratroopers or some sort of airborne assault. Helicopters, maybe. They want the Militia to hold the main gate for now, and to help guard the residents.'

Jack looked at him. He could not believe Malcolm was so unconcerned by the loss of so many of his men. Men that he had recruited and trained.

He took a long shot. 'Well done, Malcolm – to get the base and two subs means a lot. Which one of the Governors have you got a job with, when this is done?'

'Oh, I'm with the Glasgow and West Region. Fucking ace job for life,' said Malcolm without hesitation.

'I need to go to Edinburgh. I'm going to take Kenny with me.' He shouted at Kenny. 'Get me a rifle, and make sure you have plenty of ammunition for both.'

'No problem. Tell the boss we were grateful for the Army support,' said Malcolm.

Jack led Kenny out to the Range Rover. Malcolm had just confirmed his worst fears. And the fact that he considered Richard as the boss and had had contact with him that he, the Militia Commander, was not privy to, only added to his conviction.

Chapter 19

Dumbarton Castle, IDay

It was 0400 hours, and the last watch change had been at 0100 hours, so the boat was as quiet as it ever got. Although they could be several time zones away from the UK, the boat always stayed on British time. There was not much point in changing when it was always dark outside, and she would only ever surface in the direst emergency. This, however, was Lieutenant Campbell MacDonald's earnest intention. Take the ship, surface, and send a message at precisely 0800 hours, and then head home. The sub could communicate from just below the surface without giving away its position. But surfacing sent another stronger message, not only to the British government but to the rest of the world.

Cammy was wide awake and dressed. His hands shaking slightly, he was double checking the bullets in the magazine – even though it was only yesterday that he had loaded it in the washroom – when MacQuoid came into his cabin without knocking. He carried a large carving knife. This and the gun were the only two weapons they had. They had planned it as best they could, but there was little room for error.

There were two separate locks to access the small arms locker, and the keys were held by the senior Warrant Officer and the First Officer. They would take the senior officer first, using the gun to control him and get his keys. But they needed to keep him with them and quiet as they went to the Warrant Officer's accommodation, which not only served as his sleeping quarters but also as the ship's office. This was the tricky part, as escorting a gagged and bound man down half the length of the central passageway was risky. The watchkeepers would all be at their posts in the various operational centres, but one could not discount someone being sent on an errand or a visit to the heads. To counter this, MacQuoid had placed two of the conspirators at either end of the route, with instruction to head off anyone appearing on the path. The others would wait at the arms locker and stay out of sight.

They had carefully rehearsed exactly what they would say and do, but they both knew they could not account for the actions of the targets themselves. If one of them put up too much resistance or even made too much noise, all could be lost from the start. They had resolved to follow a rapidly escalating sequence from subterfuge to severe violence if the officers did not comply. Cammy hoped that the latter would not be needed, but he also was aware that once they had started on their path, time became limited. And the longer the process lasted, the greater the chance they had of being discovered before they had a chance to arm the group.

Cammy knew the First Officer's keys were in a key safe on the bulkhead in his cabin, and the same at the Warrant Officer's accommodation. They needed access to both these safes, with the additional problem of them both being protected by combination locks.

'Ready?'

'Ready,' MacQuoid said. Cammy noted the lack of the 'sir'.

It was only a dozen paces to the First Officer's door. Cammy glanced at MacQuoid, who looked absolutely determined. He passed the pistol to him and entered the cabin. MacQuoid was a chef, so it would look out of place if he went in with him while he tried the soft approach.

Cammy switched on the bulkhead light over the bunk and shook the sleeping man awake.

'Sorry to wake you, sir, but the Captain's having an anti-terrorist drill, unannounced, at 0600 hours. He needs the key to the arms locker. Sent me for them. Where are they?'

The First Officer struggled to a sitting position, still groggy, and rubbing the sleep out of his eyes. He pointed at the key safe on the opposite bulkhead.

'Combination?'

'2361.' The officer did not hesitate. *Too easy,* thought Cammy. *Oh so easy.*

He rapped twice on the doorway, and MacQuoid entered quickly and shoved the barrel of the pistol into the officer's mouth. The man's eyes opened wide, and he gagged on the gun. He did not struggle, however, and Cammy wondered if his still sleep-addled brain now considered this a part of the exercise. *All the better*, he thought.

MacQuoid replaced the gun with a balled-up rag and ordered the man to turn over.

'Hands behind your back.' He roughly locked the officer's wrists together with a cable tie and did the same around his jaw, to hold the gag in place. When that was all done, MacQuoid hoisted him to his feet. The second-in-command looked much smaller out of uniform, even pathetic in a t-shirt, stripy shorts, and bony knees, which were all a far cry from his normal impeccable uniformed appearance.

Meanwhile, Cammy had opened the safe and found the keys. Step one was complete. He caught MacQuoid's eye. There was no going back now. Suddenly he felt confident and in control.

'Ready? Let's go,' he said, and MacQuoid pushed the officer out the door, and they moved quickly down the passageway. They passed the first lookout without a word, and he slotted in behind them. They reached the Warrant Officer's cabin a minute later, now with both of the lookouts in tow.

They paused outside. Leaving the three of them with the bound officer, Cammy took a deep breath, entered the cabin, and switched on the light. The room was small, but as it incorporated the ship's office, it was larger than most. A built-in desk ran along one wall opposite the bunk, and above it was a noticeboard mostly covered in paper notices. A much larger key safe was positioned to one side.

Cammy shook the Warrant Officer awake and repeated the line about the terrorist exercise. But immediately he realised this was not going to be so easy. The Petty Officer took his time before he replied.

He sat up slowly, exposing a hairy chest and belly running to fat. 'Can't do that, sir, not with the firearms. Mind if I call the Captain for confirmation? I've never heard of an exercise like that before.'

'Just do it, sailor. I need the combination now.'

The man looked suspicious and stuck to his guns. 'I can't do that, sir.'

Cammy knew there was no time to waste. He called MacQuoid in with the pistol. One of the lookouts came inside, holding the big knife to the throat of the First Officer, while the other remained on guard in the passageway. When he saw the bound man, the Warrant Officer started to scramble out of his bunk, but MacQuoid quickly shoved him back down.

'Stay where you are, cunt.' He handed the gun to Cammy, while keeping one hand on the man's chest. 'The combination. Now!'

The man shook his head, and MacQuoid punched him full in the mouth. His lip split and a few drops of blood formed and dropped onto the sheet. MacQuoid hit him again. The Warrant Officer shook his head and sprayed a bit more blood around.

'I always hated this bastard. Give the gun to Stewart there and hold him down. I'll cut a finger off every fucking time he shakes his head.'

Cammy could feel it all slipping away. The chance of discovery grew more likely with every passing minute. He pulled MacQuoid aside and shoved the pistol in the man's face. 'Combination?' He saw the resistance in the man's eyes, and it surprised him; he had always thought of the man as lazy. He only ever did the bare minimum and was not only the oldest man on the ship, but also the fattest. Lazy. Lazy men take shortcuts.

'MacQuoid, don't touch the lock, but read out the numbers.'

'4736.'

'OK. Listen carefully. Make sure you do not touch the other three, but try moving the last dial to seven and try it.

'Nothing.'

'Again, eight.'

'No, nothing.'

'Ok, move the last wheel one digit at a time, and try to open the safe each time.'

'Back at six,' MacQuoid said eventually.

'OK. Leave it on six. Now do it with the first dial; try it at five.'

MacQuoid shook his head but complied. At eight, the door unlocked and swung open.

'Shit!' MacQuoid said. 'Good one, Lieutenant, how's that work?'

'Lazy bugger only moved one dial, so he did not have to reset the whole thing every time he opened the safe. Instead of ten thousand combinations, that only leaves ten.'

They left him and the First Officer gagged and bound on the floor, guarded by Stewart and his fellow lookout, both armed with knives.

He and MacQuoid made their way to the arms locker on the deck below the control room. Cammy's heart sank as he approached and saw no-one at the locker. But as they got nearer, a seaman with the insignia that identified him as an engineer artificer appeared. Seven others silently followed him from a store across the passageway where they had stayed out of sight. Cammy remembered his name as Granger, and it was his job to take the engine and reactor control rooms. The two control rooms were adjacent to each other back aft in the submarine.

Cammy unlocked the arms locker using both sets of keys. There were 15 assault rifles and 15 pistols. The key rings also allowed access to the ammunition safe, which was a heavy steel box welded to the deck beneath the gun racks. Magazines for both rifles and pistols were held in racks above the box. While Cammy and MacQuoid armed themselves with pistols, each man took a rifle, a pistol, and two magazines for each. MacQuoid and one of the others broke open the cartons and passed out handfuls of ammunition, and each man started loading his magazines. Cammy handed two extra rifles and pistols to a wiry little Highlander who had been given the job of carrying them to the two men still guarding the First Officer and the Warrant Officer in the ship's office. He then carefully locked everything up again, leaving all the remaining weapons in the locker, and pocketed both sets of keys. The Highlander was still kneeling on the deck snicking rifle rounds into magazines as Cammy gathered the rest of the men around him.

'Well done, guys. Everyone Ok?' Some were still strapping on the sidearm holsters for the pistols, but they all nodded or gave the thumbs up. 'We go in five. That ok for you, Granger?'

'No problem, we'll be ready.' Granger checked his watch. He looked absolutely calm and in complete control. 'We'll head aft now.' He and his team of three, all engineers, started off heading aft down the central passageway.

Cammy knew that Granger and his team could operate all the mechanical systems of the boat, providing there were no unforeseen breakdowns. Most systems would run automatically anyway. Granger knew exactly what to do. Overpower the six-man watch in the engine and boiler control rooms and the two who monitored the reactor. Once he had taken over the control rooms, there would be little for him and his men to do other than guard the deposed crew and make sure nothing could interfere with the smooth running of the engineering plant. There was no need to gag the captured control room crew, just bind their hands and guard them until Cammy and his men had full control of the ship.

Cammy led the remainder of the group to the bottom of the ladderway which led to the mid deck, the main control centre, and the officer's accommodation. He waved MacLeod, the Highlander, on up the steps. He went up carefully to ensure that the extra rifles he carried did not clang on the handrails.

He would deliver them to Stewart and his comrade, and the three of them would sweep up the rest of the officers and herd them into the officers' wardroom. They would then bind their wrists, and Stewart would guard them while the other two returned to the main group.

Although Cammy knew all the men by sight, he checked the name badges of those remaining: Thompson, Smith, Brady. They would take the main control room with him while MacQuoid captured the captain.

Cammy slammed into the back of the duty officer, knocking him off his feet, while the three others took up positions covering the room with rifles raised.

'HEADS UP!' Cammy screamed, 'STAND UP. STEP AWAY FROM YOUR STATION. NOW!' Most of the men complied. The officer of the watch, still on his knees, stared at the gun in Cammy's hand, struggling to comprehend. One or two with headphones on were still seated. Brady quickly nudged them with a rifle barrel until they complied.

'Helmsman, are we on autopilot?'

The helmsman part turned towards Cammy, 'Yes, sir.'

'Good, eyes front.'

'Listen up. These are live weapons. If you do not obey our instructions immediately, you will be shot. Now, hands behind your backs and stay facing your stations. You, too, helmsman.'

Everyone in the room jumped, even Cammy, as a shot rang out – too loud in the confined space. A split second later its echo bounced back at them from the hull. It had come from the Captain's cabin.

Shit, thought Cammy. 'Everyone stay still or the next is for you.'

MacQuoid came into the control room, hauling the Captain after him. There was a large bruise developing on the older man's cheek, and he was dishevelled and partly dressed in uniform trousers and a t-shirt. He looked very small and frightened.

'He didn't seem to think I was serious,' MacQuoid said. 'Put a bullet in his bunk.'

Brady held a rifle on each man while Smith secured their hands with plastic cable ties. MacLeod and the other lookout entered the control room then nodded at Cammy.

'All officers secure and under guard with Stewart in the Wardroom, sir!'

'Thank you, MacLeod,' said Cammy. 'Take the helm now. Bring her up to full speed and set the course as planned. Check everything is ok with Granger in the engine room first.'

'Yes, sir,' said MacLeod, taking a seat at the helm and lifting the intercom handset.

They knew that with so few people they could not hold and man the submarine for more than a few days, so the plan was to head for the coast of Ireland at top speed, then put the English crew ashore using the inflatable lifeboats. They would then make their way up the coast to Scotland and the Clyde Naval Base. That was, of course, providing that everything had all gone to plan ashore.

Cammy would not know for sure until he could pick up news bulletins when they were on the surface. They were several hundred miles to the west of Ireland, which meant at least a day-and-a-half at full speed, so they needed to start as soon as possible. He would fine-tune the course when he had a more up-to-date position.

'All secure back aft, and good to go from Granger, sir,' said MacLeod. 'I'll start the course correction.'

Cammy saw that MacQuoid had the Captain sitting on the deck and bound back-to-back with the Watch Officer. They were also gagged with rags and bound with cable ties. They had decided to keep the Captain separate from the other officers to prevent him being a focus for any comeback, and also as a hostage in the control room in case of any unforeseen events. They could always use his life as a bargaining chip.

All was going to plan. He felt the sub start to pick up speed, and the deck tilted slightly as she curved onto her new course. Those still standing adjusted their bodies without thinking to take account of the slope.

Cammy unhooked the microphone from the communicator panel above the central chart table and pressed the 'General Alarm' button for five long seconds.

'Attention, all hands. Attention, all hands. All those off duty report to the crew messroom immediately to await further instructions. I repeat, all hands report to the crew messroom. No exceptions.'

'Ok, MacQuoid, time to go. Herd this lot down there, and then secure the rest. Bring the First Officer here to go with these two.' He indicated the Captain and the Watch Officer. 'The three code holders will be staying on board. Leave Thompson here with me and MacLeod. Ping me when you're secure, and I'll make the announcement that will hopefully keep everyone calm.'

'Yes, sir.' Cammy noted a new tone of respect in MacQuoid's voice.

He and the three other conspirators, using their rifles as prods, herded the control room crew through the hatchway in the direction of the crew's mess.

Cammy took a deep breath and leaned against the chart table. He noted the latest estimated position on the navigation console and punched in the co-ordinates for a spot two miles off the Irish coast. He had previously selected this as suitable place to drop off the crew in the inflatables. The computer almost immediately produced a new course.

Cammy looked over at the helmsman. 'You got that, MacLeod?'

'Yes, sir, no problem. It's only a minor correction; the autopilot will adjust.'

All was quiet. The control room seemed strangely empty and undermanned. Thompson walked up and down, keeping an eye on all the other monitoring stations. MacLeod leaned back in his pilot's seat, looking relaxed, and let the computer control the boat.

Time slowed, and Cammy took a breath. It had all gone to plan. There was a chance, he knew, that things could yet go wrong; a problem with the boat, or worse, a major breakdown that his miniscule team could not deal with, or even losing control of the captive crew. But for now, all was well, and he was in control. No, he was in command.

He had not realised how good it would feel to be in command. To be the Captain, finally, of a ship; his ship. The first Scottish naval ship in centuries, and it was his to command. The first time a nuclear submarine had ever been hijacked, and not just the first but also the Royal Navy's newest. It all felt good.

The intercom pinged, and MacQuoid reported that all the crew were now secure in the mess room while the officers remained contained in the wardroom. Cammy thanked him and switched the intercom to 'All Stations Broadcast'.

'Attention, all personnel! This is Captain MacDonald speaking. I am now in command of this submarine, and she has been commandeered into the Free Navy of Scotland. As of 0800 hours this morning, Scotland will announce its independence and will be a free and independent country.

'Please remain calm. You are hereby relieved of your duties, so no one can blame you for any of these events. We are currently heading at full speed towards the coast of Ireland, where you will be disembarked and may return to your families. If your families live in Scotland, they will have free passage to England. If you are a Scottish national and wish to remain on board and be returned to Scotland, this will also be acceptable. If you also want to join the Free Scottish Navy, you will be welcome, on completion of vetting and taking an oath of allegiance to the new state. We will need submariners to fully crew this vessel in the future. If this is the case, make yourself known to one of the guards.

'We will not hesitate to shoot if there is any attempt to escape or sabotage this vessel, so please stay calm and safe. You will be repatriated in approximately thirty hours. Please be assured that in no circumstances will we be making any attack on England from this submarine. Our only mission is to defend Scotland.

'For your information, this submarine has been renamed *Dumbarton Castle*, which was the name of the last ship in the Royal Scottish Navy several hundred years ago and before the union. It is fitting that the name now passes to the first ship in Scotland's new navy.' Cammy hung up the microphone.

Only one thing left to do, and that was the most important one. He looked at his watch. Not long now.

With all the crew secure, MacQuoid and Stewart moved the Captain, the First Officer, and the Watch Officer, who was also the third code-holder, to the Captain's cabin. When Cammy came to address them, he found them seated on the floor with their hands bound with plastic cable ties but with the gags removed.

As soon as he entered the room, the Captain spat at him, 'Campbell! I always knew you were a shit officer. You'll never get away with this; you think the government will allow this? Your career is finished, your life is finished.'

'Paul, isn't it? Perhaps you should address me as "Captain" now.' Cammy did not try to stop the pleasure from showing on his face. 'Well, Paul, you've just lost the Navy's most expensive ship. What do you think your next command will be?' The ex-Captain scowled but fell silent.

'I suggest you listen carefully. You heard my announcement. We will put the crew ashore in Ireland tomorrow, but I'm afraid that will not be possible for the three of you. You are the three code-holders so you will remain with us.'

'You'll never get the codes out of us, not in a million years! No matter what you do,' said the ex-Captain, and the other two murmured their agreement.

'Thing is,' said Cammy, 'we don't actually need the codes; we are never going to launch these missiles. We only need your government to believe we have them. And if we have you and your families – all of whom, I believe, are resident in Faslane or nearby – and could be used to break you, the government can never be sure that we have not broken you for the codes. So, I'm afraid you and your families are hostages of the Scottish Government for the long term.' He paused, enjoying the look on the ex-Captain's face.

'Of course, if you decide to give up the codes, that will secure your release and that of your families. But bear in mind you are all in it together, so we cannot release one of you until we have all three codes. It may only be for a few years. We might sell this boat back to the English in a couple of years, or perhaps it will be replaced by another newer US one in a decade or so. In the meantime, you will remain prisoners of the Free State of Scotland.'

Cammy looked at his watch – nearly time. He left them to mull over his words and returned to the control room.

'MacLeod, take us up to periscope depth so we can signal. Thompson, ready the comms to send the message. Plain text, not code. At 0800 hours precisely.'

'Yes, Captain.'

'Message begins:

To the Government of England

This message informs you that *HMS Ambuscade* and all her weapons are now under the control of the Independent State of Scotland.

From Captain MacDonald of the Free Navy of Scotland, Commander of the *Dumbarton Castle,* formerly *HMS Ambuscade.*

Message ends.'

Chapter 20

Bute House IDay

The black, highly polished Army staff car pulled up outside Bute House in Charlotte Square at precisely 0700 hours. Three men got out. Major General Richard Ogilvy was dressed in full military parade uniform, while his two companions – Colonel Hardie and a Lieutenant acting as their aide – both wore combat gear. He led the way to the door which was opened almost immediately by the security guard.

'General Ogilvy to see the First Minister immediately.'

'Morning, General. The FM is still having breakfast in the private quarters. You can wait here while I phone up, if you like.'

'This is a national emergency. Phone to warn the FM by all means, but get someone to take me there now. Meanwhile, you will muster everyone in the building in the drawing room immediately. Colonel Hardie here will address them. I mean everyone, and those in the adjoining buildings that are connected internally.'

'Yes, sir. I'll get the housekeeper to show you the way.' He lifted the phone.

'One other thing, do you have close protection officers on site?'

'Yes, sir, two.' He indicated a door off the hall. 'In there.'

'I'll need their help. Get them out here.'

'They monitor the area, so they would have heard that.' Sure enough, a few moments later two police officers appeared. They wore side-arms only, having left their larger firepower in the room.

'Can we be of assistance, sir?' said the more senior of the two.

'Yes, thank you. Guard the main doors for now, and wedge them open. My men are delivering some communication equipment. Assist if you can. Only allow entry to Army personnel.'

Outside, a communications vehicle in full camouflage pulled up, and immediately a large satellite disk unfolded and raised itself into position above the vehicle's roof. It looked ungainly and out of place in the genteel Edinburgh street. It was accompanied by two military trucks and an armoured personnel carrier. The trucks blocked off both ends of the street, and men started carrying communications equipment into the building. Armed soldiers took up positions in the street and at the attached buildings on either side of Bute House.

A few people had arrived in the hall, and the Colonel directed them into the drawing room where his aide removed their phones and asked them what role they carried out. There were very few staff in Bute House at this hour – cleaners, a cook and a couple of housekeepers, the security guard, and one assistant to the FM. The aide sent the FM's assistant back out to report to the Colonel, who pointed to the phone on the security guard's desk and told him to contact the Chief Constable for Police Scotland and all three deputies, ordering them to Bute House for 1000 hours. He was ordered to then start phoning MSPs and advise them to attend parliament at 1400 hours. After a few minutes, the man returned and said all the phone lines were jammed with incoming calls so he could not get a line out. The Colonel handed him his Sat phone and told him to use it.

The General followed the housekeeper up to the private quarters and knocked once. The door opened immediately, and the FM let him in with a brief nod.

'General Ogilvy. We've met, I'm sure. State your business at this hour and with no appointment. I'll finish my breakfast, if you don't mind.' The FM sat down and did not offer the General a seat. He took one anyway.

'At 0800 hours this morning,' he looked at his watch, 'that is in about forty minutes, Scotland will secede from the union. My organisation will close all airports, ports, and borders on that hour. We will have secured most of the government bases in Scotland by then. The BBC will announce Scottish Independence.'

The FM stopped chewing. The General held up his hand. 'Best not to talk until I'm finished.'

Richard poured himself a coffee and drank slowly, watching the emotions sweeping across the FM's face. He was not sure what would settle there: disbelief, outrage, fear perhaps. He wondered if there was a panic button under the table – not that it would do any good, but he would prefer no additional noise. 'Your close protection officers are at present helping my men unload some communications equipment, so best leave them to it. We are avoiding as much violence as we can.'

A phone started to ring in another room. The tone was unfamiliar.

'Unh… the phone.' The FM made a great effort to swallow the mouthful of unchewed toast, finally getting it down. 'That's the emergency sound. I should get it.'

'You'll understand there is a lot going on today right across the country. You don't need to answer it. I know what is going on.' He paused. The First Minister struggled for something else to say.

'I'm going to leave you now to digest what I have told you. Listen to the BBC at eight. You have two options: help us, or not. A broadcast from you in a few hours will help to calm fears and help the transition. But make no mistake, as from today Scotland is a free and independent country with all that entails. Isn't it what you wanted?'

The General got up, opened the door, and let two soldiers in. 'This is your thinking time. These men will ensure you cause no trouble.' And to the soldiers, he added, 'No phone calls in or out.'

The First Minister called to him as he was leaving. 'Wait! Are you saying I can stay on as First Minister?'

The General smiled thinly. 'Oh, good god, no. I was thinking a minor advisory role, just until the Provisional Government has its head around everything.' He went out.

In the cabinet room, the big table had been pushed against one wall and was covered in communications equipment and rugged-looking laptops. Five communication specialists sat at the table, busy taking reports and relaying commands.

The General sat to one side while the Colonel gave him an update. 'No major problems with the border plan so far. Civilian airports, main railway stations, ports all closed. Roads are closed, long tailbacks on the two major routes. The units are turning them around on our side. All looks good. Much more congested south of the border.'

'Good, that will hold up any move north.'

'We have oversight monitoring at Faslane, Lossiemouth, and the Marine base, as you know. The Militia are still fighting at Faslane, but it does not look good. Will I send in our reserve force?'

'Yes. Do that. The Militia should have taken the edge off by now. Lossiemouth?'

'Yes, the Militia did well there, and the airfield is closed. They have the armoury, but they are having trouble controlling the men of the RAF regiment. They are rioting without weapons, and the Militia are trying to contain them in barracks.'

'OK, send in the reserve there as well, and tell them to use lethal if they need to. The RAF is made up of a lot more English people.'

'Otherwise, the Militia seems to have done well. All the other bases are secure or contained. The Militia has the BBC broadcasting to plan, and Commander Jack phoned in and is now on his way to Faslane.'

'Any response from London?'

'Several phone calls from the Prime Minister's office, trying to reach the FM, but we've not responded as yet. Do you want to take the next call?'

'Yes, let me know when it comes in. I heard the hotline phone upstairs.'

'The latest one came from the situation room. No official public announcements, except a "situation" requiring a Cobra meeting. The media is going crazy, as of course BBC Scotland is picked up in Northern Ireland and the north of England. They seem to think it's a hoax at the moment.'

The General decided to meet the police contingent in the FM's private office. He sat at the desk while the four most senior police officers stood before him. He had been pleased to see that they had arrived on time and were wearing formal uniforms.

'Thank you for coming,' he said.

'Where is the First Minister?' asked the Chief Constable. 'I want to hear this from the First Minister, not the Army.'

'I suggest you hear me out. You are all aware of the situation, but you probably have not yet realised the full impact. Scotland is now independent. The air, sea and land borders are closed; all military bases are under our control. The government has been replaced.' He let that sink in for a moment. The police chief did not respond, and the others looked bemused.

'There is no going back. Scotland is under the control of the Provisional Government, and for the purpose of this meeting you can assume that I speak with the full authority of that government. The FM is irrelevant. As yet, I have had no reports of the police service interfering with the process, which is good, and it is too early yet for any reaction from the public. What I most need from you all is a commitment to continue to police Scotland as before, and to calm any fears among your ranks and the civilian population.'

'Sir,' said the Chief Constable, 'the force's duty is to serve and protect the people, not the government, whether that is the legitimate government or a self-styled one.'

The General ignored him. 'It is extremely important that the police force is seen to support the Provisional Government. It will go a long way to ensure stability and a smooth transition to independence if the police continue in their role to maintain order. Should any civil unrest develop, it may save a considerable amount of unpleasantness if is controlled with the minimum of delay. The force will have a very important role, not only at this time but in the coming months.' He paused. 'Ladies and gentlemen, the world has changed, and this is an historic moment for Scotland. All I am asking is that you continue to serve.'

'I have reservations, as I am sure my colleagues do as well.'

'I understand,' said the General. 'I will allow some time for you to discuss it between yourselves.'

He left them to it, with two guards on the door, and returned to the cabinet room for an update. When he returned fifteen minutes later, he could hear raised voices from inside the room. He listened for a bit and smiled to himself. *Civilians! They'd be forming a committee soon to arrange the next meeting.* He pushed the door open. The voices subsided as he entered, and he looked expectantly at the senior policeman.

'We are not all in agreement,' said the Chief Constable, 'but it seems to me that for the sake of the people that we serve, we should support the new government for the time being. This may change if we see that it is illegitimate or lacks substance.'

'Excellent,' said the General. 'Thank you. I don't need a consensus, so I'll ask you all individually. If you are with us, you can take the oath and return to work immediately.'

'Oath?'

'Your allegiance to Scotland.' He handed the Chief Constable a slip of paper. 'Read it out loud, and obviously insert your full name.'

The Chief Constable read it through slowly to himself: 'I *(name here)* swear my allegiance to a Free and Independent Scotland, and I renounce my citizenship to any foreign government. I swear to serve and protect the people of Scotland in good faith and with all my strength.'

He then hesitated for a full minute before reading it aloud, and this time included his name. He handed the slip of paper back to the General, but before it could be given to the next officer, that Deputy stepped forward aggressively.

'I decline to take this oath. I serve His Majesty's Government, not some jumped-up general,' said the Deputy.

'Fair enough,' said the General.

The next Deputy read the oath in a loud clear voice. She had not hesitated and seemed to relish it. The last Deputy also refused to take the oath. The General stood and shook hands with the Chief Constable and the loyal Deputy.

'Thank you, and welcome aboard. We are going to build a better Scotland. Your first job will be to make a general broadcast, reassuring the public and your officers that normal service continues and that the police are doing what they always do. I will get an aide to take you to Colonel Hardie, who will arrange a broadcast. I understand you can do it here with a direct link to the BBC.'

He ushered them out of the room, and one of the soldiers escorted them away. The General motioned the other guard into the room.

'You're English, aren't you?' he said to the first Deputy who had refused to take the oath. 'Your last position was in... ah, Birmingham, is that correct?'

'Yes.'

'And you.' He turned to the other Deputy who had refused. 'You've come up through the ranks in Scotland, but you don't believe in independence.'

'That's correct.'

'You are relieved of all your duties for now. You will understand that we can only have patriots at your command level. Go home, for now on leave, and then you and the Chief Constable can decide later what to do with you.'

He turned to the Englishman. 'The same applies to you. You are relieved of your duties.'

'I won't work for this crap, anyway,' replied the man. 'You'll know that I'm due six months' salary if my contract is terminated early. I shall enjoy the holiday.'

'Oh… I'm sure the King, that you serve, will take care of any payment issues. This man will escort you out.' The General addressed the soldier. 'Drive this man home, allow him one hour inside to collect belongings and family, and then deposit him at the border and leave him on the other side of it. Use force if necessary.'

The General returned to the operations centre in the cabinet room. James and Isobel had arrived and, as agreed, would then go on to the parliament to address the MSPs in the afternoon. They both greeted him enthusiastically, and he shook hands with them both. Isobel gave him the briefest of hugs. They listened in as the Colonel brought him up to date. Everything was going well so far, with even Faslane almost fully under Army control, while the other problem at Lossiemouth airbase had been resolved with the additional Army support. They had been lucky with Arbroath, as there was only a small contingent of Royal Marines in residence, most being on duty elsewhere or training in Norway, the Colonel told them. They were now just mopping up a few pockets of remaining resistance. They had captured one V class bomber submarine at the jetty, another undergoing refit within the giant hanger, and one of the smaller hunter submarines.

The General looked pleased; practically the whole English nuclear fleet. 'Any word on Lieutenant MacDonald's sub?'

'No word yet, but we can't access the Admiralty's communication system, so we don't know for sure either way. But there is no talk about it on anything we are monitoring,' said the Colonel.

'We should have given him a Sat phone,' said James.

'Karen said that he was worried enough smuggling the gun, so I don't think he would have risked the phone as well. He'll stick to the plan, I'm sure. And as soon as he is close enough to drop the crew ashore in Ireland, he'll have a signal for a standard mobile,' said Isobel.

'One other thing,' said the Colonel. 'We have had a call from the White House – yes, the Washington White House. They want to speak to the First Minister. We have a secure line and an arrangement to call within the next thirty minutes. I thought it best to go with it.'

The General looked surprised. 'Interesting. I did not foresee that. At least, not this early, anyway,' he said. He looked at his watch. 'It's very early over there. They would have heard the broadcast. You did right,' he said to the Colonel and then turned to Isobel and James. 'Perhaps that falls under the political wing. Would you like to deal with it? Colonel, will you take them up to the First Minister's office and arrange the call from up there. Probably a good idea to know what they think.'

'Yes. Time we did our bit, I think,' said Isobel.

One of the soldiers manning the communications gear called out for the Colonel.

'Sir, the forward scout on the M6 reports an Army convoy heading north. 'Seven LSVs, one Land Rover.'

The Colonel turned to the General. 'That's a quick response. Too small to be an assault, and too big to be recon.'

'Yes. The M6 team is strong enough to deal with them. Put the border reserve on alert, but leave them centrally placed for now. Get the scout to track them and report. Oh, and confirm definitely no armoured vehicles.'

'LSV?' asked James.

'Logistics Support Vehicle.' The Colonel smiled. 'We like our acronyms in the Army. Trucks to you, or should I say HGVs.' As he led Isobel and James out of the room, the phone which was a direct connection to the Cobra Office, started to ring.

The General let it ring eight times before answering. 'General Ogilvy.'

'Home Secretary here. We will not put up with these delays any longer. Get the First Minister on the line now.'

'The post of First Minister no longer exists. I speak for the Provisional Government of Scotland, and I'll only speak to the Prime Minister.' And he hung up.

He waited a full five minutes before the phone rang again. He again let it ring eight times. 'General Ogilvy.'

'This is the Prime Minister of the United Kingdom, and I demand an explanation. This situation has already resulted in the deaths of numerous British citizens, and we will not stand for it.'

'That's a bad start, Prime Minister. You need to rethink what the terms United Kingdom and British mean.'

'Bullshit. I have a rapid response force forming to retake Faslane as we speak. I have fully armed aircraft ready to fly. In two hours I'll have ships close enough to hit your forces with cruise missiles anywhere in Scotland. I have your own location, General. I can hit it any time. I can kill you at any time.'

'I repeat, you need to rethink your position in the world. England is no longer the only nuclear power on this island. If one English soldier steps onto Scottish soil, or if one aircraft or missile or drone violates our airspace, or if one ship enters our territorial waters... I will nuke London. I'll repeat that. I *will* nuke London. True, I'm a few hours away from getting full access to the codes, but I'm happy to start the evacuation for you by broadcasting my intention on the BBC any time. I imagine that may cause you some problems.'

'You'll never get the codes!' the Prime Minister snapped. 'We will have Faslane retaken long before you can get them.'

'I have a folder here with a lot of personal information on Navy people. Ah, let me see. Here's one: a Lieutenant Commander Nichols, serving on submarines. He has a lovely family living near Helensburgh; thirteen-year-old twins, a boy and a girl. We'll offer the children a long weekend holiday, an all-expenses paid stay in Barlinnie jail – the sex offenders' wing. Are you beginning to understand your position, Prime Minister?'

The line went dead.

James and Isobel settled into chairs at the desk. The First Minister's office was surprisingly compact but with good views over the city. After a short time, the phone rang, and Isobel picked it up.

A voice said, 'Connecting you now.' The line clicked and twanged for a few moments, and it made Isobel think of the line stretching all that way under the weight of the ocean.

An American voice announced in an officious tone, 'Please hold for the President of the United States of America.'

'Oops,' said Isobel, 'I was thinking it would be some official.' She quickly handed the phone to James. 'I'd rather not talk to him, if you don't mind. Anyway, I think he's the type who would prefer to talk to a man.' She shrugged. 'God knows how he ever got elected.' She put on a headset so she could listen in.

James waited, and after a minute or so, the President came on the line. 'Who am I talking to?' he asked brusquely.

'James Sinclair, and this is my co-leader, Isobel Anderson.'

Isobel leaned in and said, 'Good morning, Mr President.'

'So, you've got yourself a little revolution there, I hear. How's it going?'

'Pretty well so far. In fact, I can tell you that the last directly governed British colony is now an independent state. Just like the US.'

'Well, I reckon that's two hundred and fifty years after we did it, so you've a way to go,' laughed the President.

'Better late than never,' said James.

'My military people tell me a nuclear sub has surfaced in the Atlantic and has broadcast that it is part of the Free Navy of Scotland.'

James and Isobel exchanged thumbs up and smiles. 'Good for Lieutenant Cammy,' mouthed Isobel, silently.

'That is correct, sir.'

'I remind you that the sub carries hardware that belongs to the US. That is not just any hardware; it's American hardware. You understand me? You have just broken a whole load of agreements that we had with the Brits.'

'I can assure you, Mr President, that any agreements that you have concerning that submarine and the others in our possession can be rewritten between an Independent Scotland and the US. Further, we intend to become independently part of the Western Alliance as soon as that is feasible. Scotland is now a nuclear power. I hope you can personally support us to facilitate that with NATO and the UN.'

The phone went dead.

Isobel looked worried. 'Is that a no?'

James shrugged. 'He's probably talking to advisors or something.'

The phone beeped back on. 'You have other subs?'

'Yes, most of the missile capable nuclear submarine fleet – a couple of bombers and one Astute Class hunter killer, and not to mention a significant number of the warheads which for many years and rather foolishly have been stored on Scottish soil.'

'You seem to have dealt yourself a strong hand.' The President laughed. 'I have always loved Scotland. I guess you know I have real estate there. I don't just mean real estate, but major real estate, if you know what I mean.'

'Of course, and I'm sure the new government will respect that in a mutually good way for our friends.'

'Good to know. Good to know.'

'Can we know when you will formally recognise Scotland as an Independent country?'

'You need to give me a day or two on that one. See how it pans out. Yes, give me a day or two.' The line went dead.

'Amazing,' said Isobel. 'You were great, by the way. You do realise you just tried to bribe the President of the United States, don't you?'

'Well, we are politicians now so we can say anything! Fuck him anyway. In a couple of years we'll abolish land ownership by foreigners. The golf courses will be for the people to play on.'

'I'm going to phone Karen at the Party office,' said Isobel, grabbing her Sat phone, 'and let her know that Cammy has succeeded. She'll be thrilled.'

James heard Karen's shriek of delight over the phone and waited as Isobel chatted with her. She hung up after a few minutes and turned to James.

'Karen says that, so far, only a few people have turned up at the office and they have all been positive. She is sure that with Rena's help they can handle it even if it gets busier. She wishes us luck this afternoon.'

As they returned to the cabinet room, they heard a loud cheer which was at odds with the calm, professional atmosphere that had prevailed when they were there before.

The Colonel came out, and in answer to their query, he explained that the convoy of vehicles heading north had taken to the hard shoulder when they met the tailback at the border and had unfurled St Andrew's flags from the lead and rear vehicles as they approached the border. They had made contact, and it turned out it was the loyal men of the 4th Scots Battalion based at Catterick, coming to add their support. Richard had ordered them to reinforce the border guard, and sent the trucks north to help decant the English members of the RAF regiment who were going to be transported and dropped at the border.

As he spoke, the Colonel blocked the doorway to prevent them from entering the cabinet room.

'The General wants to have a word with you in private before you head off to Holyrood, so please return to the private office with me and wait for him.'

'Fine,' said Isobel. She guessed that Richard wanted to concentrate on the operation for a while longer.

As they started up the stairs, two soldiers fell in behind the Colonel. He opened the door for them.

'Wait in here till he comes – it may be a while.'

'Why?' asked James. 'I'd rather follow events in the cabinet room, if that's possible.'

'I need your phones – both mobile and satellite,' said the Colonel.

'Why?' said Isobel. She could feel herself tensing up, and a feeling of dread in the pit of her stomach. 'This doesn't make sense.'

James started backing away across the room and pulled out his Sat phone with shaky hands. 'I'm going to phone Jack. You see if you can get Richard. This must be a mistake.'

'No mistake,' said the Colonel. 'Give me your phones.'

'Let me speak to Richard, please,' cried Isobel. 'This must be a mistake. We need to be at Holyrood soon. You can't stop us.'

The Colonel motioned to the two soldiers, who raised their weapons from pointing at the floor to aiming directly at the two leaders. With weapons held at eye level, they closed the space between them. James was, step by step, backed against the wall; all thought of using his phone forgotten. Isobel scrambled back to join him. Although they had become used to the sight of weapons in recent days, they had merely been inanimate objects. Now, staring into the muzzles of the two assault rifles, gave a whole new perspective, and their true reason to be was deadly clear.

The Colonel said nothing, but merely held out his hand. They handed the phones over.

'Thank you,' he said.

The two soldiers went out and took up position either side of the door. 'Stay here. The General has not decided your fate yet, but the more you co-operate, the safer you will be.' The Colonel closed the door behind him.

Isobel stood there, stared after him, and then pounded her balled-up fist on her own thigh. Tears of anger finally found release through her screwed shut eyelids. James tried the phone on the desk where only a short while ago they had spoken to the President. It was dead.

He looked at Isobel, ashen-faced, and shook his head.

Chapter 21

Jack IDay

Jack sped along the coast road, heading back towards Glasgow. Kenny was rigid beside him and not saying anything. He clutched two assault rifles upright between his knees. Jack worried a bump in the road might set them off. He was not sure Kenny was fully with it.

'Safeties on?'

Kenny looked down, checked. 'They fucking killed us; they shot us like we were dogs and the fucking Army was waiting outside in fucking armoured cars. Did you know? Were you part of this?'

Jack was worried that he would crack completely, so he accepted the tirade then answered slowly and calmly, 'I did not know. These were my people, my Militia.' He paused, and at last Kenny turned to look at him.

'Listen, I suspected something was not right, but not this. We are going to sort it now. Someone is going to pay. Are you with me?'

Kenny nodded. 'Fuckers.'

'Put the guns on the back seat and make sure they are safe. I need you to make some calls.'

He handed Kenny the satellite phone and told him to dial James, then Isobel, from the contacts list. There was no answer, but when he tried Maggie, she came on instantly. The Sat phones would not connect to the car, so Kenny put the phone on speaker and held it up so that Jack could speak into it. He told her about what had happened at Faslane and his concerns that Richard had the Army operating to a plan that had not been shared with them. He did not want to mention that Gordon, the Perth team leader, had given him a warning that he had not acted on, especially with Kenny so wound up beside him.

Maggie explained that everything was going fine and that the Army had not turned up at the BBC. All was well. She had not heard from her mother or James.

'Listen,' he said. 'I think Richard has plans of his own, and I think Simon is in it with him. He may have always planned this. It makes sense now. The Militia that he wanted helps keep his Network and the Army intact. The political party gives him credence that it is not a military takeover. We may have done all this for him. I am starting to think that he will not allow James and your mother to lead at the parliament. I'm worried about what Richard may do. I can't reach either of them. Have you spoken to them recently?'

There was a long pause. James thought for a moment that the connection had failed, but finally he heard her. Maggie's voice was strained.

'No, I haven't, but I don't understand. Richard is just as committed as us. It can't be right. Are you worried about what Richard may do? He would not do anything to hurt my mum... would he?'

'I'm heading to Bute House now. Stay with Stevie and be wary of any Army contact. Warn the Militia team there not to trust them.'

'I'll leave Stevie here with the Militia. The broadcasts are taped anyway. I'm going to Edinburgh now.'

'No, Maggie, stay—' But she had hung up already. He tried Isobel again, but still no answer.

Jack was still undecided whether to take the bridge directly onto the motorway, which was a longer route, or pick it up further into the city. The city planners had long ago – for some reason – thought it a good idea to ram a motorway straight through the heart of Glasgow. He had not yet made up his mind, but as they approached the Erskine Bridge slip road, it was made up for him.

'Police,' said Kenny. 'Speed check maybe.'

There was a police car parked up in a layby, and a cop was standing on the verge scanning the cars as they approached. On seeing them, he stepped into the road, causing Jack to brake hard, and signalled for them to pull in behind the patrol car. Jack did not have much choice other than running the man over, and he was preparing for another fight when he realised that they had been waiting for him. *That would surely be amazing*, he thought.

He pressed the switch to lower the window as the cop approached. He was not one of the policemen Jack had warned off earlier.

'Morning, sir, I'm your escort to Edinburgh. Sergeant Greene.' He tapped the edge of the window respectfully. 'This will keep up with us no problem. Keep close enough that no-one can get between us, but not too close. Ready?'

'Uh yes, Sergeant, thank you. Bute House?'

'Yes. No problem, sir.'

Seconds later, they were off, blue lights flashing up ahead. The patrol car took it easy at first but soon realised that Jack was able to keep up no matter what, and they increased the speed. Jack smiled to himself. Mostly he had always expected lights to be coming for him from behind not leading him. *Hope you are seeing this, Jake.*

The street outside Bute House looked like a scene from a war movie. There were several military vehicles, some of which were obviously primarily for communications, with satellite dishes and long, slender antennae on their roofs, all guarded by armed soldiers in full combat gear. The police escort that had whisked them along the motorway at high speed proved a boon here as well, as whatever Sergeant Greene said to the checkpoint guard had him let them through immediately.

Jack drove up to the main entrance and parked. He gave a wave to the patrol car as they turned and left.

He turned to Kenny. 'I don't know what to expect here, but I want to find James and Isobel. Something is seriously wrong if they don't have access to their phones.'

Kenny had called them both several times on the journey but with no response. He had also phoned all the team leaders and held the phone so that Jack could speak to them as their Commander. As most of the leaders were ex-Army, he was careful what he said and did not expect to discover much, but he did get a good overview of how the operation was going and it seemed to be to plan. There were, however, the team leaders who were not ex-Army, and with them Jack was more open and explained the developing situation to them. He knew that Colonel Hardie would be with Richard, and he was the commander for the Central region, so he arranged with the team leaders to send a squad of four militiamen in a private car to the location of each of the commanders for Argyll, Highlands, Glasgow and South, with orders just to travel to the vicinity and await orders.

'I want you ready to shoot if you have to – are you OK with that?' said Jack, as they got out of the car.

Kenny nodded. 'Fucking right I am.' They picked up the rifles from the rear seat. Jack slung his across his shoulder while Kenny held his in front, pointing down but ready for instant use, as he had been taught.

Jack strode purposefully up the short flight of steps and Kenny followed.

'The General?' he said to the soldier guarding the door.

'Identify yourself, please.'

'Militia Commander. Where's the General?' The armbands and Kenny's soiled and blood-spattered non-regulation combats gave weight to the claim, and the guard needed no further convincing.

'Sorry, sir, you missed him. He and the Colonel left a few minutes ago.'

'Shit! I wanted a word before he left. Thanks, soldier. I'm going in to see the leaders before I catch him up. Know where they are?'

The guard looked blank. 'Sorry, sir, who? I don't know.'

'The leaders, the politicians; they should be here.'

'Oh, you mean the civilians? I don't know, sorry, sir. They have not come out this way yet.'

Jack pushed past the guard as though he had every right to be there, and Kenny followed. Inside there were soldiers everywhere, and Jack stopped a passing sergeant with insignia that identified him as a member of the Signal Regiment, asking him where the politicians were being held.

'First floor office, sir.'

'Can you show my man the way and help bring them down? The General wants them over at Holyrood.' He turned to Kenny, caught his eye briefly. 'You go with the Sergeant and bring them down. Tie their hands first.'

'Yes, sir!' Kenny understood, and he followed the man up the grand staircase.

Jack did not want to hang around in the hallway looking lost, so he stuck his head into the cabinet room, identified himself, and asked the nearest operator for an update on Faslane and Lossiemouth. He half listened while keeping an eye on the staircase.

He was starting to think Kenny would never re-appear when he saw the party come down the staircase. Two soldiers were leading, with James and Isobel behind. They both looked angry, and Isobel was twisting her hands against the cable ties that bound her wrists. Kenny and the Signal Sergeant followed at the rear. Jack was wondering how to avoid them treating him as a friendly when Isobel looked up, saw him, and solved the problem for him.

'You fucking arsehole! You were always in it with Richard, weren't you? Bastard! Jake would turn in his fucking grave,' she spat the words at him. James was shaking his head but did not add to the invective.

Jack ignored them and turned to Kenny. 'Get them in the back of the Rover and tie them together. You ride shotgun and keep a gun on them.'

Kenny and the Sergeant ushered them out the front door, while Jack turned to the soldiers who had been guarding the room. 'Thanks, gentlemen, I'll take it from here.' Isobel's outburst had quelled any lingering doubts the two guarding the room had, and they turned and left.

Jack drove off with Isobel trying to convince Kenny to shoot the traitorous bastard. He pulled into a side street a few blocks away and stopped.

He indicated for Kenny to cut the cable ties. The militiaman found a knife in one of his pouches and leaned over from the front seat to free their hands. This at least made Isobel quiet down and allowed Jack to speak. He told them that he had come to get them, and that he and Kenny were not with Richard. He explained briefly what had happened at Faslane and how the Army had used the Militia as cannon fodder. He explained carefully that he had had some prior warning from a team leader that there was some hidden agenda among their military colleagues, and when he had spoken to Samantha yesterday she had told him about the regional commanders renaming themselves governors.

'You knew?' said Isobel. 'Why didn't you do something to stop him? It's a fucking disaster.'

'No!' said Jack. 'I didn't know. I had some snippets of information, but I was not sure what it meant. I couldn't go against him on a guess. On the plus side, it did allow me to put things together quickly today and come rescue you.'

Isobel was not mollified. 'You should have done more, sooner.'

'Think about it,' said Jack. 'What could I have done? Challenged Richard? Take on the Army? Raised the alarm?'

'Perhaps telling us would have been a start,' said James.

'I considered it, but I could not see the benefit. There was nothing you could have done either. I could have gone public, but independence would have been gone for ever. The movement would have all been dismantled, and we would all be in prison awaiting trial on terrorist and treason charges. Scottish Independence would never be possible. They would always have had a remit to squash any hint of freedom on the basis of an armed uprising.' He paused, but Isobel still looked angry.

'I didn't have much time to decide, but I decided to do nothing. What would you have done?' He glanced at Kenny. 'But I did not know that the Militia, my Militia, would be so badly used.'

'So,' said James, 'we are sitting in a car here while Richard is at Holyrood. Do you have a plan?'

'We contacted the team leaders as we travelled. Just to sound them out, but as you know most of them were Army appointees. We were a little more forthcoming with the team leaders who were not ex-Army. Unfortunately, they are in Oban, Perth, or further afield, so not much immediate help, but they are with us. I've arranged for four armed sections to be ready to arrest the regional military commanders, and they are heading for the correct areas but with orders not to do anything yet. Another team is heading to Edinburgh. These teams are in the north, so it will be a few hours before they are all in position.'

'Do you know these commanders?' asked Isobel. She had still not quite accepted that Jack was sincere and on their side.

'Yes, they were there at some of the meetings about the Militia with Richard, but I didn't think they were anything other than that. Samantha says he calls them Regional Governors.'

Isobel was still suspicious. 'And how come you know Samantha so well? So well that you can phone her for information concerning Richard?'

'We, uh, sort of got on. Hard to say, actually.'

'You had a relationship with Samantha?'

'No. No, nothing like that. I thought she needed help as she was completely under his control. I was pleased for her when she left him, but I hadn't heard from her for a while until the phone call yesterday.'

Isobel seemed to accept that. 'Remind me how many of these governors are there?'

'Six. According to the plan, Richard and Colonel Hardie – the governor for the central region – should be in Edinburgh.

Richard retained the capital and Fife for himself. Argyll, Highland, Glasgow, and South, are the other four. The South commander is in Hawick, as he is commanding the Army units that have closed the border, so he will take longest to reach.'

'Yes,' said James, 'there was a Colonel in Bute House with Richard. Good thinking about the teams. Once they are in position, we should hold them back until we know what's to be done. We don't want to start a shooting war with the Army.'

'Richard is against us,' said Isobel flatly.

James thought for a moment. 'Nothing else to do but go to Holyrood, arrest Richard and the Colonel, and try to get the plan back on track.'

'But we have no strength at all now,' said Isobel, her voice rising.

'Yes, but Richard does not yet know that we know... uh, if you see what I mean. We have a window of opportunity,' said James. 'It may not matter; we did not have much strength before anyway. We take over the MSPs as planned, and then give a general order to stand down the Army and return it to barracks. Or get Richard to do that.'

'Richard is totally against us!' shouted Isobel. 'He imprisoned us, for god's sake. He was probably going to have us killed.'

'We don't know that,' said James.

'I fucking do,' said Isobel. 'The man has lost it.'

Jack caught Kenny's disbelieving shake of the head and understood. 'We may have to do a lot more than ask politely. The only thing we can do is push on, keep the momentum going, and see how it pans out.'

'Agreed,' said James. 'Jack, take us to the Parliament – no more delays. We still have some time before two o'clock; that is if the Army has not frightened the MSPs away.'

'Let's go,' said Jack. 'Are you two armed? We have two assault guns and a pistol.'

'No.'

Jack handed his pistol to James. 'Just in case.' James stuck it awkwardly into his waistband.

Chapter 22

IDay

Jack drove cautiously up to the Parliament Building. He had not seen it before other than on the TV, and it was just as bad in real life as on the screen. There were ugly, blocky, pixel-shaped panels mixed with intrusive security fencing, and those terrible, uneven, unordered, poles scattered haphazardly across the façade and windows were surely a joke aimed at the Scottish people and, in particular, every Scottish architect.

At least it had not been turned into an Army camp like Bute House. There were no Army trucks or armed soldiers surrounding the building, only the General's large black staff car with a pennant mounted on one wing showing his commanding general insignia and a St. Andrew's flag on the other. Richard had been smart enough to ensure it looked as little like a military takeover as possible. There was a gathering of what must be MSPs outside, talking nervously to each other in small groups. Two military policemen in red caps and smartly turned-out dress uniforms kept a watchful eye on the crowd. They were armed only with holstered side-arms; no rifles were to be seen.

Jack parked behind the staff car. As they exited, Jack said, 'Walk like we belong, like we own the place. We find Richard and we arrest him. Kenny, you'll act like my driver/bodyguard as we did at Bute House. We'll leave the other rifle in the car. You ready?' Kenny understood what he meant and dipped the barrel of the assault rifle in reply.

'Yes, let's go, first we stop Richard, and then we follow the plan,' said James.

Jack led the way to the main entrance. The security desk was empty, but the space behind it was occupied by a mixed group of worried looking security guards and police who had been relieved of their weapons. Two military policemen guarded them. They, like their comrades outside, were also dressed smartly and were armed only with side-arms. These guards ignored them as they entered. A corporal and another military policeman manned the inner door down the corridor. Jack was again impressed that Richard had decided to keep overt military presence to a minimum. *But what resistance could there be?*

'MSPs?' The Corporal asked. 'Go through with the rest. Be in your seats by two pm.' And he waved Isobel and James through. The Corporal eyed Kenny's battle dirty demeanour as though he was going to tell him no weapons were allowed in the building, but Jack intervened.

'He's with me,' said Jack. 'I'm the Militia Commander. Where's the General?'

The Corporal flapped his arm in the general direction of the main hall. 'That way, uh, Garden Lobby maybe, if he's not in the main hall.'

Kenny and Jack joined up with Isobel and James, and they skirted round the buzz of nervous MSPs gathered in the main hall. They scanned the room for the General, but there was no sign of him so they continued into the Garden Lobby.

James spotted him first, in full parade uniform, walking up the staircase that led to the debating chamber. The Colonel and Simon were with him, and a couple of steps behind was a soldier, the General's driver – also smartly turned out, but not in the military police uniform. Jack thought it wise to hang back a little and let the others do the talking, so he moved Kenny and himself to one side as Isobel shouted at the General.

The shout caused the four to pause on the stairs, and they turned to face Isobel and James. Richard was clearly shocked to see them but quickly regained his composure and turned to the guard. 'Get these people out of here!'

The guard started down the stairs, unclipping the holster of his pistol as he went.

'No!' shouted James. 'You are under arrest for treason against Scotland.'

Richard shrugged his shoulders, drew his pistol, and shouted at the guard. 'Just shoot them.'

The guard hesitated for a second too long, and all in one moment, James struggled to get his pistol out from his belt, lost his grip on it, and stumbled to catch it. Richard opened fire down the staircase, and a split-second later Kenny opened up with the assault rifle in one long thunderous burst that ripped into the guard and threw him backwards into the legs of Richard and the Colonel. But Richard had already fired several times, hitting Isobel and knocking her off her feet. James's stumble had saved him.

The noise of the weapons echoed and re-echoed off the oddly-shaped walls. Empty cartridge cases clattered down the steps, and a section of plaster – dislodged from the wall by the burst of bullets, many of which had passed through the guard – crumbled to the floor in a haze of white dust. The space filled with the faint acrid smell of gunpowder. The quiet after the assault rifle froze everyone for a moment. All noise in the building died with the fading echoes.

James knelt beside Isobel, cradling her in his arms, shielding her from Richard. Richard recovered his feet and raised his pistol again, but Kenny fired a round into the wall. Whether by intention or a simple miss, even he was never sure. But it stopped everyone, and Richard lowered the gun. The hubbub from the main hall was starting up again in a very different tone, but one voice could be heard rising above the others.

'Let me through! GET OUT OF THE WAY!' Maggie sprinted down the hall, took in the tableau in an instant and skidded to a halt beside Isobel. As she knelt beside her, Isobel opened her eyes one last time, smiled, gripped her daughter's hand, whispered her name, and was gone.

Maggie froze for long seconds; inside her head a maelstrom of images flew past so fast that she could not hang on to them. Her mother laughing, dancing with her, playing badminton with her, hugging her so hard, as though she could squeeze ever more love into her daughter. Her mother up there on the stage giving a serious speech, waving her arms to make a point at a meeting. Her mother in the kitchen, somehow making a meal out of a looming culinary disaster, laughing about it. Her mother.

As the images ceased, she vowed she would give each one a lot more time, but later. She slowly looked up at Richard. His gun was still pointing down at them but held in check by the unwavering barrel of Kenny's assault rifle trained on him.

Maggie slowly and deliberately picked up James's pistol from where it had fallen. Stood. Put one foot on the first step.

'Don't,' said James. 'He'll kill you.'

She raised the gun straight-armed at the General and started up the steps. Richard kept his own pistol trained on her. The Colonel was still on the floor and seemed in no hurry to put himself in the line of fire. Simon had retreated to the wall and was crouched there, arms outreached, hands raised, as though that would shield him from the bullets.

'Stop now. We can make this work.' It was the first time anyone had ever seen the General unsure of himself.

Maggie stopped several steps below him, still silent.

'Stop, don't do this.' He was almost pleading now. 'We are made the same. We *are* the same. We can run the country together.' He paused. 'You're my daughter, you know you are... you can feel it, I know. Father and daughter...'

'I am not your daughter. And I never will be.' Maggie fired again and again and again, until the gun was empty. The echoes of the gunshots died away.

Colonel Hardie stood shakily, leaving his gun on the floor and eyeing Kenny, who held the assault rifle still raised. He put his hands up. No one else moved. The spell was broken by the Corporal and another military policeman entering cautiously with guns drawn from the Main Hall. The noise behind them was getting louder.

It was Jack who reacted first. 'Corporal! We've got it covered here. Get back out there and stop anyone leaving. They will be taking their seats soon. This won't stop that.'

'James, Kenny, take Isobel to that committee room over there.'

'What about the Colonel?' said James.

'Shoot the fucker,' said Kenny.

'Not yet. Look after Isobel first. Give me the rifle.'

Jack pointed it at the Colonel. 'You and Simon move the bodies.' He pointed to Richard and the guard who were both leaking blood onto the stairs.

'To the committee room?' asked the Colonel, recovering some of his composure.

'No, on second thoughts, move them to the side there, prop them up against the wall. The Members will walk past them to see what it cost.'

James went up the stairs and gently led Maggie down, and then Kenny helped him lift Isobel and move her into the committee room. Maggie went with them. Simon had not moved from his defensive crouch, but the Colonel had done as he had been asked and even mopped up the worst of the blood using the guard's tunic.

He came down the stairs slowly to Jack.

'What are you going to do about the Army now that you've killed General Ogilvy?' he said. 'How will you control them, stand them down from this? What about the other governors?'

'That's in hand. I have squads on standby ready to take them.'

'Not without a firefight. I suspect. A lot more people will die.' He paused briefly. 'I have a suggestion.'

'Go on.'

'Give me command of the Army. I'm known, respected, part of the Network. I can be a real asset to the new government.'

'And we trust you because...?'

250

'It makes sense. What happens next solidifies into government. It has to. Richard has failed. There is no other option. I'm with you if you'll have me.'

'Fuck,' said Jack. 'Get back up there with Simon.' The Colonel returned up the stairs.

James and Kenny came out of the committee room saying Maggie wanted a moment or two, alone. Jack explained the Colonel's proposal to them, while keeping an eye on the stairs.

James looked at his watch. 'Nearly two o'clock. It would solve a lot of problems, but can we trust him?'

'Not for sure, but there's no time to put anything else in its place. I have an idea that may help.' Jack ran it past them both and they agreed, although Kenny was hesitant.

'OK,' said James. 'Let's go with it. If we don't, we may have an Army revolt at any moment led by any one of the governors.'

Jack motioned the Colonel down. 'We accept your proposal on one condition.'

'That is?'

But Jack turned to Kenny. 'I'm promoting you to Colonel of the Militia, and you will take up a position with the Colonel here, but you will be in overall command. You will shadow him closely. Do you accept?'

'I guess,' said Kenny. 'Uh, yes.' The Colonel did not say anything, but Jack caught the look of surprise flit across his face.

'Ok, you still have my Sat phone. Contact the Militia squad heading to Edinburgh and get them to go direct to Bute House to support you. Watch him closely.'

'Do you accept that condition, Colonel?'

'Yes, no problem.'

'I saw that look. Do you think that promotion is valid?' Jack did not wait for an answer. 'I'll point out that you are commissioned by the King of England, while Kenny is commissioned by the Government of Scotland. I'll let you work out which is more relevant.'

'I understand,' said the Colonel.

'Your first job is to arrange for the arrest of the other four governors and have them handed over to the Militia units that are already on their way. Kenny, Colonel Kenny here, will help arrange that. They will be brought to Edinburgh under arrest.'

Jack handed Kenny the assault rifle. 'You've done a great job today, and I know I'm asking a lot, but I have every confidence in you. I'll catch up with you after we finish up here. Now get back to Bute House with the Colonel and start to get this sorted.'

Turning to the Colonel, Jack said, 'Colonel, I hope you are a man of your word.'

'I believe in Scotland. I hope that's enough.'

'Good. On your way out, tell the men to start sending the MSPs through. It's time to take their seats.'

A few minutes later the politicians started coming through from the main hall. There was a hushed silence as they mounted the stairs. Only a few came singly, most were in pairs or small groups as though they did not want to be alone. Some looked at the bodies, but most turned their heads away, and all fell into a hushed silence as they passed them.

Jack got one of the military policemen to take Simon and hold him under arrest until he could think what to do with him. As the trooper led him away, Jack could already hear Simon starting to offer the man money, but the trooper seemed completely unmoved, so Jack decided to ignore it. He had more vital things to worry about.

James went back into the committee room to be with Maggie. She had found a heat retention blanket from a first aid kit and had wrapped Isobel in it. The body lay on the horseshoe curve of the table, and she sat beside it holding her mother's hand. James sat down beside her.

'It suddenly does not seem worth it,' he said.

Maggie tucked her mother's hand back under the shiny blanket. Wiping the tears from her eyes, she turned to face him.

'Oh yes it is. We are doing this; it's what she would have wanted. James, you and my mother made this happen. Years you worked on this, so betrayed or not, we are still doing this. I'm glad he's dead and glad Jack found him out, otherwise we'd all be in the shit right now.'

'Did you believe the daughter thing?'

'Oh yes, that's true. Mum told me years ago, after she and my real dad split up. The man who brought me up, he's my real dad. My mum and I decided that was the way we both wanted it. I didn't know he knew, though.'

'Perhaps, Isobel, er… your mum told him sometime.'

'No, I don't think so. She was always adamant that she preferred him not knowing. The decision to tell him was always up to me, but I never wanted to.'

'Will you take her place beside me in the chamber?'

Maggie just nodded.

Almost every seat was taken in the debating chamber, and even the Presiding Officer and her two deputies were seated. There were no weapons visible, and Jack and one of the military policemen stood at the door keeping a watchful eye. The members were subdued, quiet, not knowing what to expect after hearing the shooting earlier and having to pass the covered bodies of the General and his guard. A number of the first MSPs to pass were so visibly distressed at seeing the bodies that Jack had relented and had a couple of soldiers cover them with whatever they could find.

When James and Maggie entered the chamber, the hall lapsed into silence. They walked slowly down to the centre of the floor in front of the politicians' desks. James paused a moment and then walked over to the Presiding Officer.

'We are going to address the parliament from the floor. Your services as moderator will not be required today, but they most definitely will be from tomorrow.' The Presiding Officer just nodded. He returned to the centre.

'Ladies and gentlemen, my name is James Sinclair, and this is Margaret Anderson. We are the co-leaders of the provisional government. If you are wondering where the rest of the government is – it is you. You were elected by the people, and that still stands. You have the opportunity to help us build a New Scotland.' There were some murmurings, but James held up his hand.

'Let me finish. There is a lot more.

'We do not intend to merely continue with the old system, which has consistently failed in the past. The old system is now dead. We will forge a new and better system of government. We will govern for the people and in the best interests of the majority. Currently, the potential of political parties to do any good is inevitably overtaken by the need to get re-elected every few years.

'To that end, from noon today all political parties are outlawed. It is an offence to be a member of a political party. Your parties no longer exist. The assets, funds, and property are now the property of the government. This even includes the odd luxury motorhome.'

This last comment raised a weak cheer from the opposition benches, but it quickly died as the import of his announcement sunk in. After a few moments there was a clamorous outcry from all sides of the house, and several members rose to their feet shouting. The Conservative Party leader raised his arms for quiet and motioned for all his squad to get to their feet.

'We are leaving,' he said.

'You're welcome to, of course,' said James, 'as may anyone here. But I urge you to hear me out. What is outside this chamber is no longer the Scotland you knew. You saw the news; you heard the announcements. Scotland is today a sovereign nation, and not only that but a nuclear power. At present the country is under martial law. We hope that will not last long, and we will hold elections as soon as that is feasible.'

He turned his attention fully on the Conservative leader.

'You have just broken the law when you signalled to the other ex-Conservatives as though you all belonged to an illegal party. The penalties for membership have not yet been decided, but they may well involve a prison sentence. In any event, the political party, any political party, no longer has any standing here. The quicker you get used to the idea that this is the New Scotland, the quicker we can get to work. Anyone here is free to leave the building or, if you prefer, the country.' The Conservative leader sat down.

'Thank you,' said James. He stepped back and Maggie took over.

'You do not have to decide now. We will give you twenty-four hours to consider whether you wish to join us or not. If you do, you will continue to represent your constituents and meet here in this parliament to govern at regular intervals.

'What about List members?' someone shouted.

'Good question,' said Maggie, 'and although we hope that all members will join us in this venture, we realise that some may not wish to. List MSPs will be assigned to any seats that become vacant. Excess List MSPs will either act as deputies or be given roving commissions. There is a huge amount of work to be done. Those who join us will continue on their salaries. Those that do not can go home and take up their civilian lives.'

'Won't we need elections to replace those who leave?'

'You can't just use list MSPs to replace sitting members.'

Maggie raised her hands to quieten the shouting and appeal for silence.

'We, and I include yourselves, will rule by decree until the necessary changes are in place, and only then will there be elections. There is no other way to make the huge changes that are needed. Think about the opportunity you have now, it only comes along once in a ... I was going to say lifetime, but that is not enough. It only comes once – a chance to build a country, build a system suitable for the twenty-first century. You can make history. James will tell you more about what is expected of you.'

'I warn you the work will be intense,' said James, 'as not only are you going to continue to be MSPs, but you are also going to help us build the new system. We have a basic framework, but we do not know how it will work in the real world – what looks good on paper, as I'm sure you all know, does not necessarily work in practice. The system will change, modify, and mature, depending on what you decide and what you find works best. On top of that, we intend to start tackling some of the problems immediately.'

There was a murmuring of confusion, and he hoped he sensed a little interest but could not be sure. A few shouted questions were asked, but he ignored them.

'It needs to be seen straight away that an independent Scotland is going to benefit everyone. So, we will get to work immediately to change the things that can be changed easily. The new government, you, will be seen to be acting decisively and for the good of all.

'You will go back to your constituencies and form an oversight group of volunteer citizens, local people, local councillors, businessmen, unemployed, factory workers, whoever. The number and make-up of the group is up to you. You will use this group to gauge what is most needed and most urgent in your area. You will canvas the opinion of the wider community. You will have authority and control of the council or councils in your area, and liaise with the local officials to identify land that can be used for state housing and land with easy access to the grid or to power stations that can be used for solar energy or wind farms. Identify local builders and engineers who are willing and able to build state housing or install solar farms. Start them employing and training the people to do it.'

He paused. 'That will all take time, I know, but we will start the process even if it is only identifying suitable land. More immediately, you will identify and take every care home in your area into public ownership. I will repeat that – you will take all care homes into public ownership by government decree.'

James surveyed the room. He could sense their unease and see the confusion on their faces.

'Yes,' he said. 'You will have immense power to make change. It will take some getting used to.'

The Conservative leader stood. 'Very worthy ideas, I'm sure. But you can't just take away the assets of private companies. Some of the care homes are owned by major companies, with millions of pounds tied up in the properties, and as for the land it may be owned by organisations with immense political power.'

'Why not? We just did. Every care home in Scotland is now the property of the Scottish government and its people. Managers and employees will be offered positions. Shareholders and owners will no longer take massive profits. Is that a problem for you? Think about it – every care home will suddenly benefit from the full rates they charge, and the excess will go back to councils to build more. Everything will be better; carers will be paid more, and facilities will be vastly improved. As for the land, if it does not have a useful purpose or a private house, then it can be requisitioned for the benefit of all. New homes will be built for people, not for rental profit for absent landlords.'

'But the government will be sued; the court cases will be massive.' The ex-conservative leader shook his head. 'It's naive.'

'Not in Scottish courts. We are not constrained by old laws or the financial world, or the courts of any other country. Elsewhere, they can do as they like. Energy security using green production, care homes, and housing, are just three of the problems we intend to resolve immediately. There are a lot more.'

'How will we pay for this?

James paused. 'Our system will be based on four core principles which will form the basis of our economic and political philosophy. They are firstly—'

Maggie stepped forward and touched his arm. 'I'll do this bit.

'The only way it is possible, is by changing the system. We will simply stop the upward flow of money from the many to the few, from people to companies, from the workers to the rich. This happens with every pound you spend. From the bankers investing your savings and taking home million-pound salaries, from the interest rates on your mortgages, from the profit on the rent from your homes, from your food, from your health and care systems, from your electricity and gas and fuel. From everything you buy. The rich manipulate our tax systems and abuse the same system to further maximise their profits. We will simply stop the upward flow of wealth – that is our first policy.

'We will develop a fair economy by the tax system' and by rewarding the workers and producers of the goods for their work. We will eliminate poverty.

'We will build a better place by making citizenship a thing to be proud of and appreciated, so that all feel they belong, are participating, but also contributing.

'We will build a future by putting sustainability over growth. We will prioritise home-grown food and products against imports, and not only for food, but for expertise, goods, infrastructure, and energy. We will make it ourselves, build it ourselves, and grow it ourselves. And be self-sufficient in green energy. We will be a model for how the world has to change.

'We are not just talking sustainability only on climate or the conservation of nature, but sustainability of jobs, of businesses, of culture, of happiness and wellbeing. We intend to make this country something out of the ordinary. Something great. Something special. New Scotland. This is your chance to do something worthwhile that will live on. You can make history.'

She looked around the chamber. 'Are you with us?'

A surprising number of people added volume to the cheers and applause, and James saw that even some of the ex-Conservatives put their hands together. He noted without any dismay how Maggie had managed to capture the crowd much better than he would have.

He did not want to add anything to ruin the mood. He wanted them all to leave on a note of optimism.

'James?' Maggie said.

'Remember, this is not just a New Scotland we are building. It is a better one,' he said. 'You can choose to be part of it or not, but either way you will be living in it. I hope to see every one of you tomorrow. If you decide to join us, to shape the future, to make this vision into reality, then come back here tomorrow. Take the oath of allegiance to the New Scotland and be ready to start work.'

Milton Keynes UK
Ingram Content Group UK Ltd.
UKHW012305120624
443943UK00001B/21